as quietly as t̲ℴ̲ℓ̲𝗅̲𝗅̲.ld allow and, on the way back, noticed the phone's blinking message light.

"Crap." Mae's message taunted from the answering machine. "What to do?" she said to herself. "Check it, or go back to bed?" Years of maternally ingrained guilt won out as she pressed play.

"Hi Lib," Mae's recorded message played. "It's your mother."

"Color me surprised." Libby groaned.

"I just got back from my visit with Dr. Cooper. You remember him, he removed Daddy's planter's wart."

"TMI Mom, TMI."

"Anyhow, he did a splendid job with my colon and said I had none of those dirty pollocks."

"Polyps, unless you've got a ten-foot abstract in your small intestine."

"You can watch now. Did you know that? They have a camera in your bum the whole time, fascinating really. Anyway, a few of my other test results were a bit off, and he wants me to see a neurologist for some silly reason. Nothing to worry about, just a little blip to check out. Anyhow, I need someone to take me for the appointment, and I was hoping you could find the time. If not, don't worry, I'll call your brother Sean. I'm sure he can drop anything less important than his mother."

"Of course. He's Jesus." Libby's eyes rolled.

"Take care, sweetie. Call me when you can, love to all."

Libby replayed the message and returned to bed. Blip speculation haunted her dreams.

Praise for Kathryn Elliott

"*ADDING LIB* is a warm and humorous story of the trials and tribulations faced by every woman who juggles being a mother, a daughter, a wife, a sister, and a friend. I can't wait to read the next book to find out what happens with the McGinns."

~*Andrea O'Day, author of* Goodbye Granny Panties

Adding Lib

by

Kathryn Elliott

The McGinn Series, Book One

Roberta,
Words cannot thank
you enough for all
you and your Mother
have done for Brendan.
We're blessed to
know you!

[handwritten signature]

This is a work of fiction. Names, characters, places, and incidents are either the product of the author's imagination or are used fictitiously, and any resemblance to actual persons living or dead, business establishments, events, or locales, is entirely coincidental.

Adding Lib

COPYRIGHT © 2014 by Kathryn Elliott

All rights reserved. No part of this book may be used or reproduced in any manner whatsoever without written permission of the author or The Wild Rose Press, Inc. except in the case of brief quotations embodied in critical articles or reviews.
Contact Information: info@thewildrosepress.com

Cover Art by *Diana Carlile*

The Wild Rose Press, Inc.
PO Box 708
Adams Basin, NY 14410-0708
Visit us at www.thewildrosepress.com

Publishing History
First Mainstream Women's Fiction Edition, 2014
Print ISBN 978-1-62830-640-8
Digital ISBN 978-1-62830-641-5

The McGinn Series, Book One
Published in the United States of America

Dedication

For Don,
who rescued these pages from confetti fate
more than once.
Your support and encouragement brought Libby
from bucket list to reality.
I love you, now and forever.

Chapter One

Sane women do not plot homicide at Parent Teacher Organization meetings. Libby O'Rourke was the exception.

"Give me one flipping reason not to slap the spray tan right off those self-righteous tramps," Libby screeched, along with the minivan's tires.

"It's not like you didn't see this coming, Lib." Caroline Duffy, Libby's best friend since Immaculate Conception Primary School gripped the overhead chicken bar for dear life. "Oh God," she gasped. "Red light, red light!"

"Of course I saw it coming." Libby breezed through the light and onto the defenseless streets of Rhyme, Connecticut at drag-race speed. "That peroxide-damaged brain trust wouldn't recognize a smart choice if it bit them."

Nestled along the picturesque shoreline, Rhyme consisted of two clearly defined areas: the waterfront—housing elite, old money residents—and the Buy Mart side of town, for all lesser citizens. October was low-tourist season, and as luck would have it, there were few witnesses to Libby's manic traffic skills.

"Jogger!" Caroline screamed.

"Relax," Libby swerved, "he's fast. See how quick he jumped the curb?"

"You didn't give him a choice!"

"Worry wart."

Rounding the corner onto Murray Lane, she slowed. Home to Libby, her husband Bob and their children, Shannon and Charlie, the historically designated neighborhood was perfect for the tool-inexperienced homeowners. Peeling paint, moss covered roofs and structural deterioration all fell into the category of authentic New England charm. Neighborhood associations required meticulous gardens, so as long as you mowed and maintained seasonal plants, drug-den-like exteriors added character.

"I want to live!" Caroline begged, "Slow down, please! I have a date Friday, my first shot at kissing something other than my client's ass in over a year, and I'd rather not show up at Casa Alfredo in sling backs and a body cast. Show some compassion for the repressed and get us home in one piece."

Libby decelerated onto the crumbling asphalt driveway, surveyed the house, and laughed. Fifteen years ago, the chipper realtor described the 1800's Colonial as "a partially restored gem with endless possibilities." Libby described the realtor as "liar, liar, polyester blazer on fire!"

A faded picket fence lined the front lawn, the third post to the right cracked during the unfortunate weed whacker incident of '08. Repair was number eighty-seven on the to-do list, before college educations and after retirement planning.

The property's cedar shingles were a cheery yellow, to be precise, Buy Mart Citrus Blend. The trim was Midnight Black. All colors had been preapproved by the Rhyme Historical Society.

The Society, as they called themselves, was a coven of witches meeting semi-annually for the sole purpose of making Libby's life miserable, and although she did not have any hard evidence, quarterly restoration meetings concluded with a faint smell of brimstone.

In the backyard sat a small, one-time caretaker's cottage. The same delusional realtor had spun a colorful tale in which the building housed members of the Underground Railroad during the Civil War and insisted *a little elbow grease* would spiff the place right up. After a failed recreation room attempt, Libby discovered a dump truck full of vegetable oil wouldn't come close to doing the job.

Calming, Libby jumped two scooters and the remainder of a sandcastle before tearing open the main house's front door.

"Where are the Cheese Bites?" she boomed.

"That good, huh?" Bob answered from his beloved black leather recliner, Old Stink.

"Don't mess with me Bob, where are they?"

"On the table next to the pinot I picked up at Wine Cellar. Call it a hunch."

"I love you."

"I know."

Married twenty years, Bob and Libby had the uncanny knack of anticipating the other's every need. Bob, an easygoing guy, needed solitude for all televised New York sports. This included, but was not limited to, exhibition games and spring training. Libby, a tad more stress eater, required a pantry stocked with wine and Cheese Bites. No couples therapy or separate vacations for Bob and Libby—they maintained their bliss with overpaid athletes and orange snack food.

Caroline entered to witness Libby's first inhalation of orange crackers. "You're so pretty," she teased.

"Bite me," Libby spat. "Wine?"

"Yes."

Libby yanked the fishbowl-size glasses off the top shelf and poured.

Caroline snagged a glass and said hello to Bob. "Hey there, counselor, how's Muggers and Thieves Land?" She loved Bob. His stoicism was the best counter balance for Libby's Irish temper.

A public defender for eighteen years, Bob started his career on the other side of the aisle, but quickly realized he did not like the view. After a brief career with the District Attorney's office left him bogged down in political bull, and out of touch with the flesh and bones of the judicial system, he made the jump to the PD's office and never looked back.

"About the same." Bob answered Caroline. "How's the whole deliberately-misleading-the-public thing going?"

Advertising, in Caroline's opinion, did not mislead the public; it gently guided, with a hint of subliminal manipulation. "Can't complain," she said. "And hey, after tonight's PTO meeting your job may come in handy. Lib needs to put you on retainer."

Libby spun from the kitchen. Cheese Bites spewed. "Me?"

"Yes, you," Caroline scolded. "Or did someone else call Stacy Warner 'an uneducated fundraising whore' and threaten to publish her high school fat pictures online? I'm pretty sure that crosses into defamation of character." She turned to Bob. "What's

4

your opinion lawyer guy?"

He could not help but smile. "Lib, we've talked about this."

"Do not use the Dad Voice with me or I'm wearing the don't-touch-me flannel pjs for a month!" She piled in more crackers, chewed minimally and swallowed. "I know I flew off the handle, but come on! I singlehandedly raised over thirty thousand dollars for that school, and they desperately need a reading teacher. But no. Silicone-Whore and her evil minions have a wicked-great idea!" Chasing down the crackers with an unladylike gulp of wine it was clear tasting the wine was secondary to feeling the effects.

"Do I want to know about the 'wicked-great idea,' or can I safely assume it is crap?" Bob asked.

Libby dripped sarcasm. "Oh no, honey, it's wicked, wicked great!" Hands on her hips, she plastered on a whopping grin. "The Acorn Elementary PTO is going to spend thirty thousand dollars on a new Kiddie Kardio Slide for the playground. Isn't that marvelous?"

Bob frowned. "I'm confused. Didn't you just have some cookie fundraiser deal a couple of years ago for a playground?"

Caroline groaned. "Shit Bob, now you did it."

"What did I say?"

"Two years ago we thoroughly renovated that damned playground!" Libby fumed. "I sold more freaking cookie dough than a chain of bakeries! Half of which I consumed. Cookie dough, for exercise equipment? Does no one see the irony? I had to buy new pants and join Fat Be Gone, but we got the stupid equipment."

Reluctantly Bob asked, "At the risk of losing my

genitals, I'm going to assume you pointed that fact out to the PTO?"

She walked over and planted a quick kiss on the top of his head. "I sometimes make use of your genitals, so I'll let that one go."

Bob continued, "Why's this slide-thing more important than a teacher?"

Libby turned back to Caroline. "I can't go through this without more wine, you fill him in." She tossed the brochure to her and headed back to the kitchen.

In her best ad pitch, Caroline plopped down on the couch and read aloud. "The Kiddie Kardio Slide has two ladders!" She gasped. "This exceptional bonus feature allows more students to experience the cardiovascular benefits of free play sliding while fostering an environment of team building and turn taking, thus successfully combating the growing epidemic of childhood obesity."

"Ladders?" Bob's face pinched in confusion. "That's what thirty grand buys you?"

Libby returned to the couch, wine in hand and said, "Tremendous plan, don't you think? Now we will have a school full of thin, team-oriented, illiterate children. They'll speak without verbs but look fabulous in skinny jeans."

She closed her eyes and laid her head on the back of the couch. "No more, I fold."

"Feel better?" Bob asked.

"Defeated."

"Finish your wine. It heals." Caroline tipped back her final sip as she headed toward the door. "I have to go. Trevor has a book report due tomorrow that I need to proof." Caroline's fourteen-year-old son was the only decent thing to come out of her marriage to Steve-the-Schmuck.

"To be clear," Libby teased, "by 'proof' you mean finish the book, write the report and edit to ensure ninth grade authenticity?"

"No, wise ass." Caroline reached for the knob. "I'll have you know I finished the book yesterday. And enough about my crimes, I'm worried about yours. Remember Lib, homicide is a felony; and no matter how thick the PTO bimbos are, you'd look horrendous in prison orange. Worse...no lattes in the Big House."

"True," Libby said. "Thanks for the moral support tonight."

"Are you kidding? Me miss the show? Never." Waving goodbye, Caroline left.

Libby grabbed a last fistful of Cheese Bites and snuggled into Bob's lap on Old Stink. The ugly recliner was the one item from bachelorhood she had permitted him to move into their marriage. A pool table, air hockey set, and iceberg-sized stereo was sold off to buy baby furniture.

"What did I miss on the home front tonight?" she asked.

"Standard issue O'Rourke night," Bob said.

His late father, General James O'Rourke, had communicated with career military precision. Whether reading a grocery list or delivering a heartfelt eulogy, the General kept it brief. Bob inherited the conversational skill.

"Shannon requests I no longer pick her up in front of the school. Apparently, that was *exceedingly seventh grade* of me to do to her today, but I have been forgiven. Please note: the socially acceptable point of pick up for eighth graders is the side of the building, adjacent to the tennis courts. Also, and this is key new information, we cannot say hello or make eye contact until we have pulled away from said location."

"So noted," Libby snickered. "Anything new with Charlie?"

"Ah yes, Master Charles. You may have noticed the beach in the driveway?"

"I did."

"It's for Cha-Cha."

The toddler-sized tabby cat, Cha-Cha belonged to Libby and Bob's neighbor, Dominic Genovese. "Charlie," Bob explained, "is convinced Stump will eat Cha-Cha if she continues to use the sandbox in the backyard as a playground, and, in an effort to avoid bloodshed, brought sand out front to keep the dueling parties separate."

"Did you explain Cha-Cha is using the sandbox as a toilet?" Libby asked with a grimace.

"Circumstantial evidence." Bob answered.

"Speaking of Attila the Labrador, where is Stump?"

"I had to put him outside for a little gastrointestinal alone time. Charlie shared some coleslaw at dinner. I opened the windows, but it may take a few days to get the smell completely out of the house."

The O'Rourke family had rescued Stump, a three-year-old ball of drool and energy, from the local animal shelter. All they knew at the time was the black dog previously belonged to a single, professional woman who could no longer manage his needs. A month with the family, and Stump's *special needs* became apparent, as did the need for multi-room air fresheners.

"Did you call the vet today for his prescription?" Libby asked.

"I picked it up on my way home. I forgot to throw it in his dinner." He shifted in the recliner, facing her. "Come on Lib, everyone gets gas. Do we really need to drug him?"

"Bob," Libby reasoned, "we all get gas. Stump, however, defies the laws of digestion. May I remind you I am the one trapped in the car with him ninety percent of the time? The smell was so awful on the way to Charlie's soccer practice I almost lost consciousness. He gets the pill or lives in the garage. You pick."

"Fine, we drug him. Nevertheless, you could cut him a break once in a while. We already took the poor guy's balls."

She set her head on his shoulder. "So what else did I miss? Any calls?"

"Mae. Message is on the machine. I was outside talking to Dom after dinner when she called. I started to play it back but had to stop listening after she started talking, in detail, about her colonoscopy." He grimaced. "Really Lib, can you broach the too-much-information factor with your mother?"

"Did she want me to call her back tonight?"

"Again, stopped listening; TMI."

Libby yawned and climbed out of Bob's lap. "All right, I'll check the voice mail before we go to bed."

Bob heaved out of Old Stink and went to the back door to call Stump in for the night. Tail wagging, the loveable dog bounded in and slurped Bob with warm licks. "Hey Stump. Go see Mom. She's had a tough night."

Stump spotted Libby and shot to her side. "Hey

bud, all the coleslaw pass?" Libby scratched his ears. "Not planning any late night surprises for me, are you?" Something about Stump's colossal happy-dog face made Libby's frustration melt away. Then the smell hit. Happy moment gone, she filled his dish with water and double-checked the doors.

Lights out, Libby trudged upstairs with Bob. After a quick peek in on Shannon and Charlie, the couple settled into their bedroom. Stretching, Bob turned to her.

"I've got a deposition in the morning," he said. "Can you get the kids on the bus?"

"What's tomorrow?" She rubbed her forehead.

"Wednesday. Will you make it to Friday?"

"God willing; tomorrow is fine. I don't have to be in until ten."

A part-time librarian, Libby's job was the ideal book-lover/mother combo. The blissfully quiet six-hour days made nighttime family chaos tolerable. There were more lucrative careers an English Literature degree could attract, but none appealed more to her sense of family.

Libby went to the bathroom and got ready for bed while Bob stripped down to his boxers and climbed between the cool sheets. He smiled in anticipation. Two glasses of wine in Libby's system was a green light for sex. Three tipped the scales to the dark side, guaranteeing drool, snores, and in one unfortunate instance, incontinence. For better or worse, she was all his.

Brushed and flossed, Libby exited the bath in Bob's tattered college T-shirt. He wiggled a brow and said, "There is something so hot about a woman in beer-stained cotton." She smiled and he went for gold. "How about it, up for a little lovin'?"

"Um"—her expression said *socks under the Christmas tree*—"sure."

"You're tired," he pouted. "Tomorrow."

Still attracted by Bob's Polish/Irish machismo, Libby weighed her options—romance or sleep. "I'll make you a deal," she said. "I'm up for a quick one, but no kissing. I'm wearing one of those overnight tooth-whitening gimmicks."

"Good oral hygiene is such a turn-on," he said, tossing the sheet aside. "I'll take the deal!"

She slid into bed. "Honey, this isn't a plea bargain."

"I'm pleading. You bargained."

At three o'clock, excess wine and a bladder weakened by two pregnancies woke Libby from a sound sleep. She crept to the bathroom as quietly as two-hundred-year-old floor boards would allow and, on the way back, noticed the phone's blinking message light.

"Crap." Mae's message taunted from the answering machine. "What to do?" she said to herself. "Check it, or go back to bed?" Years of maternally ingrained guilt won out as she pressed play.

"Hi Lib," Mae's recorded message played. "It's your mother."

"Color me surprised." Libby groaned.

"I just got back from my visit with Dr. Cooper. You remember him, he removed Daddy's planter's wart."

"TMI Mom, TMI."

"Anyhow, he did a splendid job with my colon and

said I had none of those dirty pollocks."

"Polyps, unless you've got a ten-foot abstract in your small intestine."

"You can watch now. Did you know that? They have a camera in your bum the whole time, fascinating really. Anyway, a few of my other test results were a bit off, and he wants me to see a neurologist for some silly reason. Nothing to worry about, just a little blip to check out. Anyhow, I need someone to take me for the appointment, and I was hoping you could find the time. If not, don't worry, I'll call your brother Sean. I'm sure he can drop anything less important than his mother."

"Of course. He's Jesus." Libby's eyes rolled.

"Take care, sweetie. Call me when you can, love to all."

Libby replayed the message and returned to bed. Blip speculation haunted her dreams.

Chapter Two

After discovering alcohol her junior year of high school Libby deemed the inventor of the coffee pot timer a humanitarian genius. Feeling her way into the not-quite remodeled kitchen, she began her day with fresh brewed perfection and enjoyed the first cup in silence.

Silence was fleeting.

Bob's squeaky wingtips shuffled up. "Show of fingers, babe," he whispered "how many cups?" He implemented the no-one-talks-to-Libby-before-the-second-cup directive early in their marriage.

"Two," Libby said. "You are safe. Are Cain and Abel up yet?"

"I heard the shower running but didn't knock. Learned that lesson."

Two weeks prior Bob innocently knocked on Shannon's door in an effort to spur her along for school. Unfortunately, the teen's morning personality resembled a hibernating bear and his nudge was a poke from a hot stick. As an only child, Bob often made horrendous errors in hormone swing prediction.

"Did you hear any movement from Charlie?" Libby asked

"I heard the faint rustle of plastic fenders," Bob answered. "We know he's conscious."

Model cars were Charlie's oxygen. If pieces went

missing or someone innocently picked up a single section and applied it wrong, all hell broke loose. Vacuum detail required three days warning, ensuring no critical element sucked into the upright. Stump, a true chewer, ingested a hubcap and Charlie's sobs escalated to projectile vomit level. Bob searched dog feces for days until the plastic auto part resurfaced.

Placing her mug in the microwave for reheating, Libby gave Stump a firm belly rub and headed toward the stairs. "Come on buddy, time to get the troops moving."

On the staircase, she admired family portraits of generations gone by. The last on the left caught her eye. Her parents' wedding photograph was nothing remarkable, a black and white formally posed photo taken by some unnamed relative, but the couple's eyes told a love story. The handsome, Irish immigrant dipped his blushing bride into a dramatic kiss; two crazy kids wildly in love, and dirt poor, mugged it up for the camera.

Bernie McGinn brewed his wife Mae's coffee every day for forty-five years. In the early days, the lovebirds lived in Brooklyn. The shoebox-sized apartment over the deli was not a palace, but all theirs. On the night of their second anniversary, Mae, eight months pregnant with Sean, suggested the pair go out for dinner at their favorite restaurant, Giuseppes. In a rush to get home and be alone with his wife, Bernie ran a red light, and the couple's car collided head-on with a bakery van.

When Mae regained consciousness, the soft-spoken doctor held her hand and explained in order to stop her hemorrhaging they delivered her twins prematurely.

Their girl, Meghan, did not survive, however the boy, Sean, was holding his own in the neonatal intensive care unit. Bernie was doing well after required surgery to repair a fractured pelvis.

In the long months that followed, Mae struggled to raise a newborn alone while shuttling back and forth to the hospital to visit Bernie. With the help of her mother she managed to get through the difficult time. However, each trip through the busy city streets brought horrible flashbacks. Familiar noises, once her nighttime lullaby, left Mae unable to sleep. Each car horn and siren brought fear and forced her to reevaluate the safety of her longtime home for a small child.

A week prior to Bernie's discharge, Mae came to a difficult decision. Wanting a fresh start, far from the city commotion, once he was out of the hospital the couple packed the little they owned and moved to Rhyme—a quiet town ideal for raising a family.

Bernie and Mae thrived as their family grew. Their public displays of affection embarrassed Libby as a child. As an adult, she envied them. Until the day he died, Bernie referred to Mae as his bride.

Libby touched the photo and said, "So what's this *blip* with your bride, Daddy?" Pulling back to the chore at hand, she reached the top of the stairs, greeted by a half-naked Charlie. "Hey bud, no pants today?"

Charlie justified the wardrobe. "Sam and I need to wear our soccer shorts today, but I can't find mine."

"They're in the wash."

His freckled face crumpled. "But I need them! Sam said this is the only way our plan will work."

Libby loved Charlie's best friend Sam. Common sense, however, was not the boy's strength. The prior year, Ms. Stapleton, the boys' kindergarten teacher, decided to retire after her experiences with Sam and Charlie. She was thirty-seven.

"Charlie, I know I'm going to regret this, but what plan?" Libby asked.

"Sam was online last night and found out our soccer shorts are made of the same stuff as parachutes." Charlie dutifully explained. "All we have to do is get real, real high on the swings, jump off, and float down. Cool, right?"

Ivy League colleges, Libby thought to herself, *would not recruit Sam anytime soon.* "Very cool," she said, "but the air show is going to have to wait another day." *Or never.* "We don't have time to dry the shorts this morning. Throw on something else and hustle down for breakfast."

"Fine," he stamped a foot in frustration. "Sam's going to be mad."

"He'll forgive you on his way to the orthopedic surgeon. Get dressed."

Charlie stormed off in search of substitute pants. Looking at the hardwood floor, Libby noticed droplets of water forming a trail from the bath to Shannon's closed door; the sound of pounding bass competed with the hum of the hairdryer as the teen primped and prepped.

Libby knocked. "Shann, are you about done?" No reply. It was time for reinforcements. "Okay, Stump,"—Libby bent to the dog—"you're going in."

Shannon, the only O'Rourke capable of overlooking the odor, was Stump's champion. The abandoned dog had joined the family as Shannon entered an awkward, and yet to pass, pre-teen phase;

16

the pair bonded instantly. The pooch worshiped her at a time Shannon most needed worshiping.

Libby nudged Stump through the cracked door.

"Hi buddy!" Shannon gushed as the dog's entire body vibrated in delight. "How's my baby boy?"

"Success," Libby whispered before raising her voice over the music. "Stump, where are you? It's time for breakfast."

"He's in here, Mom!" Shannon bellowed.

Libby entered the purple and zebra print refugee camp. "Aw, you love your Shannon, don't you, boy?" Mission accomplished. "Are you about ready to go, kiddo?"

Shannon double-checked her reflection in the mirror and rubbed on a dab of lip-gloss. "I have to do my eyebrows."

Eyebrows? What eyebrows? "Okay, five minutes. We have oatmeal or toaster thingies. Which one do you want?"

"Thingy."

Back in the kitchen, Libby fed Stump, digestive medication included, and packed lunches for the kids. Bob scurried about grabbing up paperwork and gulping orange juice. Libby grinned. Bob was sexy in lawyer garb with his chestnut hair and pewter eyes. He projected the competent hero of the common man. Little did opposing council know underneath the stern exterior lay a Worlds Best Daddy T-shirt and accidentally pink boxers.

He landed a quick kiss on her before bolting for the door. "Got to go, home around five. Pizza okay tonight?" Wednesday was Bob's night to cook; he rarely did.

"Pizza is fine, Cicero's, okay? Last time we had Tony's I had heartburn for a week."

Bob defended Tony's no-good son-in-law on a regular basis; the result, gratis pizza.

"No problem." He grabbed his briefcase and opened the door. Familiar hydraulic brakes echoed down the street.

"Bus!" he yelled. "Move it, or miss it!"

Storming the kitchen like a heard of sneaker-clad buffalo, Shannon and Charlie grabbed their respective toaster thingies and made a dash for the bus stop.

"Bye, Mom!" They hollered in unison.

Libby followed as far as the front porch. "Learn lots. Make our outrageous taxes worth it!"

Taking her coffee out to the front porch, Libby looked around the yard. October was beautiful in Rhyme—bright foliage, doorstep pumpkins, and brisk autumn breezes coming in off the water. Appreciating a moment of quiet, she sat down on one of the two dark-stained oak rocking chairs crafted by her father only months before he died.

Often she and Bob rocked away stress with morning coffee or evening wine. And someday, when they were old and gray, grayer than they were now, Libby imagined soothing grandbabies to sleep in the same spot. The sound of a shovel breaking ground pulled her from the daydream.

"Morning, bella." Dominic Genovese, the O'Rourke's next-door neighbor greeted her from his knee-deep spot in his end-of-season tomato garden. "You're doing some deep thinking over there?"

"Hey Dom." Libby smiled. "Didn't see you down there, how's the crop? Any more rabbits saddle up to the buffet?"

"No serious casualties that I can see, but I may borrow Stump again for a few more deposits."

Dom read a gardening blog that suggested letting dogs mark a vegetable garden kept small animals away. Images of tomatoes speckled in Stump urine ruined Libby's love of Caprese salad.

"Glad he could be useful. Did you get any feedback from the Society on your trim colors?"

Dom's 1890 Saltbox-style home was in need of painting, and his color choices were up for review by the Society. "They have a tentatively approved Hunter Green as authentic to the period," he groaned. "Spruce, however, is still under discussion."

"Well of course," Libby teased. "Spruce could upset the historical balance of the entire neighborhood."

Bob and Libby hit the neighbor jackpot with Dom. A widower and retired police officer, he had no children of his own and patience for thirty. His tall, imposing stature gave the impression of authority, but beneath the gruff exterior was one of the kindest people Libby had ever had the privilege of knowing.

After Bernie's death, Dom stepped into the role of surrogate grandfather, spoiling Shannon and Charlie accordingly. Fortunately, for Stump, Dom had a deviated septum and loved to take the gassy canine on afternoon walks. A blessing in all regards, Dom was a tremendous addition to the O'Rourke extended family.

Checking her watch, Libby sprang. "Shoot, have to make a move. Don't need to be late for work."

"Hurry, Libby," he teased. "Dolores may give you a tardy note!"

Libby's boss, Dolores Watts, was many things,

including Dom's unrequited love.

"Wouldn't want that," Libby laughed. "Feel free to grab Stump anytime. Word of caution, he stole coleslaw last night, take a lot of pooper scooper bags. It could get messy."

Waving a goodbye, she popped inside for a quick shower and toaster thingy and headed to work. Although it was her day to open the library, Libby knew Dolores would arrive first.

Chapter Three

Dolores's sensible, beige sedan was first in the employee parking lot.

"I think she sleeps here," Libby mused.

Pulling in alongside her uber-punctual boss, Libby climbed out of the minivan and started toward the entrance. Maura Horton, Shannon's soccer coach, was popping returns into the drive-up drop slot, and the women exchanged a wave.

"Did you see that?" Dolores pounced on Libby. "She thinks no one saw, but the joke's on her! I got her this time!"

Arriving five minutes early each day to apprehend felonious lenders sliding overdue material into the slot, delinquency was Dolores's number one crime on the Library List of Offenses. The quirky behavior amused Libby at first, but lately she began wondering if Dolores might benefit from anger management classes.

"And hello to you, too, Dolores. Are you on a stakeout?" Libby said between laughs.

Rushing to the slot's catch bin, Dolores rejoiced. "Well, look here, three books and a DVD! Audiovisual loans are going to cost you extra, Miss Late Borrower. That's another twenty-five cents in the penalty jar."

Single and sixty-five, Dolores lived for books, organization, and the enforcement of late fees. Retirement was not an option. Her small frame was capped by a gray bob held away from her face by a pair of wire-rimmed glasses resting atop her head. Earth-tone sweater sets, single-strand pearls, and elastic-waist pants were her wardrobe staples. On celebrations, she mixed in a scarf.

After almost ten years at the library, Libby knew there was more to Dolores than what she allowed others to see. Hidden under the conservative facade was a lonely woman with an artistic passion and a guarded heart.

It cost Libby thumbscrews, but Dolores eventually confessed the unsigned paintings in the lobby were her creations. The beautiful landscapes of Rhyme and stunning portraits of families and lovers walking the shoreline were always from the perspective of the observer, never the participant—much the same as Dolores's life.

Passing through the swinging half door of the circulation desk, Libby turned to Dolores. "Any sign of Dewey this morning?"

Dolores followed and turned on the main desk computer. "Not yet. Probably still sleeping in the stacks."

Dewey, the black and white library cat, permitted the women a few minutes of his valuable time every day, but never hung around long enough to chat. Dolores found him napping in the donations bin a snowy, winter morning five years earlier and brought him in for some milk; he never left. By law, Rhyme prohibited animals in municipal buildings, but Mayor Burnette, a veterinarian, looked the other way in Dewey's case.

Libby switched on the overhead lights. "I'll head

back to the office and refill his food bowl in case he decides to grace us with his presence."

Her eyes glued to the computer screen, Dolores motioned Libby away with a sweep of her hand. "You go; I'll check the database for overdues. Meet me out here when you finish, we'll set up for book club."

Per Dolores's type A obsession with order, their shared office was neat as a pin. Each nook and cranny coded and crosschecked for effectiveness. Dewey's food was in the top right drawer of the file cabinet marked "Cat, Dewey." Even the pet was alphabetical.

Libby scooped food into the cat's bowl and sat down to boot up her computer. The screen saver, a picture of her entire family gathered on the dock outside Mae and Bernie's house was the last with her father before he died. The picture said it all. Charlie, vaulting the railing toward the water, at Shannon's encouragement, as Libby and Bob struggled to restrain him; older brother Sean, scowling; Kevin, the youngest McGinn with an arm around his tube-top wearing girlfriend, now wife, Suzanne; and finally Mae and Bernie, front and center, hand-in-hand. This was Libby's family, God help her.

The photograph reminded her to return Mae's call. Noting the time, she picked up the phone and dialed, visualizing her mother rolling out the last pink foam curler and cementing her salt and pepper hair in place for senior yoga.

Mae picked up on the second ring. "Hello."

"Hi Mom." Libby knew her first Mae-pacifying step was an apology. "Sorry I didn't call you back last night, I had a PTO meeting."

"No worries dear," Mae answered. "If it were an

emergency I would have called Sean." Sean—the perfect son—had yet to marry and produce grandchildren making Libby the reigning champion of the McGinn Offspring War.

Libby continued through clenched teeth. "Tell me why Dr. Cooper thinks you need to see the neurologist?"

"Dr. Cooper is an alarmist," Mae scolded.

"Go on."

"Part of my little checkup was this silly memory test, a demeaning experience for an adult, to say the least. It was similar to one of Charlie's little card games. I kept waiting for the nurse to yell 'go fish.' Anyway, I did poorly, and Dr. Cooper wants me to have a follow up test."

"Was that it, just the memory test thing?"

Mae hesitated.

Libby pushed, "Mom, what else?"

"He made a fuss about my eyesight and something or other about spatial issues, whatever that is. And to top it all off he had the audacity to suggest I shrunk! For the love of Mike, I am seventy years old, what does he expect, a super model with x-ray vision? I tell you, I gave that boy quite a talking to."

The "boy" was sixty-three, and despite a degree from Harvard, he underestimated the Wrath of Mae—a common mistake. Her apple-cheeks and a purse full of butterscotch presented the image of adorable Granny, but underneath lurked the Dirty Harriet of the gin rummy world.

"I'm no doctor," Libby said, "but eyesight and memory problems sound fairly normal for your age. Are you sure, there wasn't something more? Maybe he wants to get a baseline on your crazy meter before you go too far around the bend."

"Respect your elders, Elizabeth Margaret." Mae had Mom-tone down to a science. "He wants me to see this ethnic woman doctor in Hartford, Dr. Rosh Hashanah or something like that."

Libby winced. This was bad. First, Mae was from the archaic mindset that although competent, women physicians were inferior to men. Second, and the far bigger issue, Dr. Jewish Holiday was "ethnic," implying foreign descent. Mae bought only *Made in The USA* items, even doctors. This did not bode well for the doctor-patient relationship.

"Did you make the appointment?" Libby asked.

Mae harrumphed. "Eager Dr. Cooper made it for me while I was in his office. I go next Thursday at four o'clock. If you can't take me, Sean will close the office and make a special trip."

"And walk on water all the way there," Libby mumbled.

"What?"

"Nothing. That's not a problem. I have Thursday off and the kids are covered with afterschool sports. I'll grab you at three o'clock in case we hit traffic." Before Mae could make an excuse, Libby firmed up. "Email me the doctor's name and address so I can put it in the GPS."

In Mae's eyes, technology as a whole was the work of the devil. However, email, she quickly discovered, was a necessary evil besides being a foolproof way to communicate with her children.

"Well then, I guess I'm all set," Mae said. "I'll see you next week. Thank you for fitting me in dear, and call me between now and then if you have time."

"Will do," Libby checked in daily, but Mae never missed an opportunity to remind her to do so. "Love you. See you soon."

"Love you, Lib."

Conversations with Mae drained Libby. Her patience needed recharging. Opening the top desk drawer, she dug to the back and pulled out a contraband bag of chocolate-covered peanuts. Excluding book club, Dolores enforced a strict No Food or Drink policy. Libby bit the end of the bag and ripped. Some days call for rebellion.

Chapter Four

It was fifteen minutes before the kids stormed in from school. Libby used the downtime to her advantage and called Sean. In his defense, her brother had never campaigned to be Mae's favorite, but wore the crown nonetheless.

On top of his inability to do wrong, Sean was supermodel handsome. While Libby and Kevin swam in the red hair and freckles end of the McGinn gene pool, Sean's shocking blue eyes and ink black hair had Libby's childhood friends begging to be her lab partner. The exception to this rule was Caroline—coincidentally, the only one to see him naked. Granted she was nine, and the nudity was the result of an ill-fated belly-flop/swim trunk accident. Once the goods came out, the magic died.

Libby settled at the kitchen table and dialed Sean's office.

"Mae Day Construction, how can I help you?" Debbie Rugger kept Mae Day running. Originally a part-time bookkeeper, she signed on as office manager when Mae discovered constant togetherness was a sure fire path to murdering Bernie.

"I'm looking for the golden child," Libby said.

"Hi Lib," Debbie laughed. "How goes things in your camp?"

"Still standing," Libby answered. "How's Walt

doing?"

Laid off as a mechanic, Debbie's husband Walt had decided to be useful and clean the gutters. He ended the chore with three broken bones in his right leg.

"He's moaning about the ladder having a faulty rung," Debbie said. "Heaven forbid the old fool admits *he* screwed up."

"But you adore him?"

"I do. Guess I'm the bigger fool. Hang on a second and I'll grab Sean for you."

Smooth jazz filled the receiver, a definite improvement from Debbie's early cover-the-mouthpiece-and-scream method.

Sean's baritone picked up. "Hey."

"Hey to you, too." *Ever the conversationalist,* Libby thought. "I wanted to let you know I'll cover Mom's doctor appointment next week."

"Thank God. I owe you." Sean loved his mother, but her appointments ate up a sizeable deal of his time.

"You make it sound like I saved you from a burning building," Libby laughed. "It's not that bad, you big wimp!"

"You didn't draw the short straw last time! It was the gynecologist, for Pete's sake! No man should take his mother to the gynecologist. It's not natural."

"Come on, you didn't go in the examination room. All you had to do was read old magazines and wait."

"You weren't there, Lib, it was a nightmare." She could hear the frown in his voice. "Twenty women talking about birth plans, stretch marks, and some crap about mucus corks or something like that. There was nowhere to run."

"Oh, that's priceless. The man who gets dry heaves

changing a diaper surrounded by body fluid talk. I bet you went home and showered."

"It gets worse. On the way, Mom started blathering on about The Change. I got a twenty-minute unsolicited lecture on creams for vaginal dryness. Swear to God my ears bled. She has no boundaries—"

"Stop before I hear something I can never unhear," Libby interrupted. "You win a Get Out of Gynecologist Free card. Out of curiosity, did Mom say anything more about this neurologist thing to you?"

"No, just left a message on the machine about needing a ride. Why?"

"Nothing I can pinpoint, but I have this weird feeling there's more to the story she's not sharing. Mind you, I'm not borrowing worry until she sees the doctor, but I got the feeling she's not telling us something."

"Don't make too much of it. We know she's nuts, but it's *happy* nuts. I'm sure the doctor's just covering all the bases. We all lose it at some point—aging is not for the weak."

"True." Libby checked the clock. "I better get dinner started before the savages arrive. Don't stand a chance when they double team me. Are you going to Kevin and Suzanne's this weekend?"

"Like I have a choice?" Sean moaned. "It's a christening; Mom will crucify me if I don't go. No pun intended. Hell, she still harps on the fact that I didn't fly back from spring break for Uncle Al's funeral, and that was twenty-five years ago."

Religious events were mandatory in Mae's book. She took attendance and prayed for the souls of the absent. "I feel sorry for the baby," he continued. "Who names a kid Saratoga? She's a week old, is it too late to change it? Poor kid's going to get the snot beat out of her in school."

"I know," Libby agreed. "But at least they shorten it to Sara. Did Suzanne share their icky conception story with you?"

"Lib, I'm getting a little tired of women in this family sharing their fertility junk with me. Am I wearing an I Love Estrogen T-shirt?"

"Suck it up, this is priceless. On their way home from Suzanne's cousin Rita's wedding—"

"Rita?" Sean tried to put a name with a face. "Floating eye?"

"That's Emma, Rita's the pitchy giggle. Anyway, the car breaks down outside Saratoga Springs, and Kev and Suzanne decide to spend the night."

"Got it."

"Suzanne was pushing for a baby, but Kev wasn't quite on board. Long story short, wedding, open bar, Kev's low alcohol tolerance, Suzanne thinks the car is fate's way of intervening and *bam*, Saratoga's in the oven."

"Are you telling me Suzanne got Kev loaded and tricked him into knocking her up? Then named our niece after a racetrack?"

"Suzanne's a ditz, but far from an evil mastermind. It could be a lot worse than Saratoga."

"How?"

"The car might have died in Yonkers."

"Bad," he chuckled. "Very bad, Lib."

"Yes, but you know I'm right," she said.

"Scary," he agreed. "Listen, I need to run, but if something happens and you can't go to Mom's appointment, call me. Fill me in later on the details, you know she'll never tell me if it's something big; vaginal dryness, yes, major stuff, no."

"I'll touch base after, but I'm sure it's nothing to worry about." Libby knew under the rough exterior, Sean was a momma's boy at heart. "Go build some yuppie an overpriced house, and I'll talk to you later."

"Thanks for taking this one. See you at Staten Island's baptism."

Chapter Five

On the post-baptism drive to Kevin and Suzanne's house, Libby examined Saratoga's carefully selected puppy-themed invitation. "Family and friends are asked to contribute a side dish," she read aloud. "Rookie mistake. First rule of entertaining an Irish family, *assign* side dishes or prepare for a potato salad monsoon."

Bob chuckled. "They will learn."

"That Father Rodriguez was interesting." Mae piped in from the backseat. "All that dark hair and skin, he reminds me of that dashing actor fellow, you remember, he lived on an island with his small friend. What was his name?"

"Here it comes." Bob muttered from the driver seat. "Kids, put in your earbuds, Grandma is talking." *Interesting* was Mae-speak for illegal immigrant. Luckily, Shannon and Charlie were too busy fighting to notice.

Unable to shake the image of Father Rodriguez in a white tuxedo holding a Mai Tai, Libby tapped Bob across the armrest. "We are almost there, how bad could she be in five minutes?"

"I wonder what country he's from," Mae continued. "His English is quite good. Maybe he went to seminary in the United States?"

"Mom," Libby bit back frustration. "Father

Rodriguez is Carlos Rodriguez, the same Carlos Rodriguez I went through nine years of elementary school with. And the same Carlos who took Caroline to the Valentine's Dance in seventh grade."

"No, no," Mae corrected, "You're thinking of the Molino boy, he was the Latino at Immaculate Conception. I distinctly recall the Parade of Nations assembly. He held the Mexican flag and wore that giant hat."

"God, help me," Libby whispered. "Mom, Sister Collette made us pick our countries out of a paper bag for that stupid parade—I was Africa! And for the record, Jimmy Molino's family was from the Philippines, not Mexico."

"It's the same, dear."

Kevin and Suzanne's Cape Cod style home lay in a quaint development of cookie cutter houses, each more vanilla than the next. Offset by rose-colored shutters and pale pink trim, the white bungalow fit Suzanne's penchant for cuteness perfectly. Window boxes, intertwined hearts carved at their centers, were filled to the brim with pink chrysanthemums on either side of the light oak front door.

"This place gives me cavities," Libby's head shook.

"Be nice," Bob said and turned to the backseat. "Okay gang, everybody out, it's time for family fun and long buffet lines and let's all remember it's Saratoga's big day. No matter how bored you are, hiding in the van is not an option."

He glared at Libby.

"What?" She raised a brow.

"Like you don't know."

"Fine." She grabbed the vegetable tray. "One time I sneak off to watch a movie, and you never let me live it down."

He grinned. "Lib, it was Easter, and you were gone for three hours."

The family piled out of the car and headed to the front door. Mae stopped to chat with a visiting cousin as Charlie rang the bell. A medley of harmonized flutes and harps announced their arrival.

Libby smiled. "That never gets old."

Bob shook his head. "How does your brother put up with this much, this much...*girl*?"

Before Libby could answer, Kevin yanked open the door.

"Thank God"—Kevin took the vegetable tray—"a guest without a God-damned potato salad." He ushered them into the house. "Sorry about the potty mouth, kids. Uncle Kev's had a long day."

"No problem." Shannon replied. "Mom swears much worse than that in traffic."

"That's not true." Libby feigned shock.

At thirty-nine, Kevin looked more like Libby's uncle than kid brother. A financial planner, he survived life with handfuls of antacids and too many post-happy hour calls to the cab company.

"Suzanne's out back taking pictures of Sara and setting up the piñata," Kevin explained. "I was dispatched to find a weapon to pummel it with—I'm thinking nine iron?"

Libby frowned. "Baptism piñata?"

"Yeah, I know." He peered outside over Libby's shoulder at Mae. "Mom's going to blow a gasket. Bunch of kids whacking the hell out of a crucifix full of chocolate; we're all going to burn in hell. I'm playing the Suzanne's-an-Episcopalian-and-didn't-know-better card. Maybe Mom will buy it after a few glasses of merlot."

Among other inaccuracies, Mae believed Episcopalians were Catholics unable to do the right things—stay in dismal marriages, ordain men only, or throw a decent bake sale.

Bob grinned from ear to ear. "Good luck with Mae, Kevin. Now point me to the beer."

"On the porch under the gift table," Kevin said. "Grab me one while you're at it, will you? Suzanne's keeping tabs on me, she's afraid I'll drink too much in front of her relatives and do something dumb—as if anything I could do would surpass the toll inbreeding already took on that bunch."

Suzanne's relatives were an acquired taste; like black coffee for the cream-and-sugar-lover. All blonde, beautiful, and alarmingly cheerful, there was not a token black sheep in the bunch. The *entire* family was perky—a quality Libby found nerve-grating, but she'd made a vow to try to get along once Sara arrived.

Shannon and Charlie ran out the back door with Bob and Kevin trailing behind. Mae, through chatting up the cousins, joined Libby and proceeded to the kitchen to help set out food.

Elaine Brewster, Suzanne's mother, was popping a tray of ziti in for warming. An older version of Suzanne, Elaine was in a heated battle with Father Time. Her youthful look was maintained by several layers of high-end cosmetics and routine touch-ups at the plastic surgeon's. Yellow heels offset her tasteful black and white striped dress. This month's hair color was tomato.

"Hi Elaine." Libby air kissed. "Your hair looks fantastic! I love that color with your skin tone."

Libby learned early on to lead with a compliment when dealing with Elaine. And never use big words.

"Libby! Mae!" Elaine beamed. "It's so super to see you! Isn't this just a super day?"

"Super." Mae sneered. She did not tolerate Elaine's bubbliness well.

"Suzie has been working herself to the bone getting ready for Saratoga's big party!" Elaine continued. "I'm so proud of her. We planted all the mums in the window boxes yesterday. Don't they make the house look super cute?"

Libby made a mental note. *Select Elaine in Christmas grab bag—buy thesaurus.*

"The flowers look great," Libby spoke up. "You seem to have things covered in here. Why don't Mom and I head out to the yard and see if we can help there?"

Libby took Mae by the hand and slowly began backing out of the room. Years of family functions taught her one thing: Linger with Elaine too long and suffer teeth-grinding fashion and makeup talk.

Elaine slid in another tray. "Oh I'm sure Suzie needs a few helpers. There's a ton of food to put out, and all the pretty little decorations. You run along, and we'll have girl chat later!"

I'd rather have a pap smear, Libby thought.

In the yard, Mae spotted the piñata and froze.

"Play nice, Mom." Libby warned.

"Whatever do you mean, dear?" Mae said. "You wait here. I'm going to tell Suzie how marvelous everything looks."

"Mae McGinn, I know that look. Keep your opinions to yourself. This is not your party."

"Do not scold me, Elizabeth. I'm not a child."

"The way I speak to you is based on a lifetime of experience. Zip it."

Mae bee-lined to Suzanne and Libby prayed for the younger woman's life. Various Brewster and McGinn relatives gathered in polite conversational groups. Chatter ranged from weather, sports, and medical ailments to which family members died, divorced, or remarried since the last party. Stampeding children toppled drinks and dishes while their parents made halfhearted attempts to calm their unruly spawn.

Libby found Sean at the kid's table playing cards with Charlie and Shannon.

"Were you assigned this seat or are you hiding from crazy Mindy?" Libby asked him.

Suzanne's younger sister, Mindy, made her interest in Sean known from their first meeting at Kevin and Suzanne's wedding. Beautiful, with rocks for gray matter was not his type.

"She's a nice girl," Sean said, "but the family tree is a little shy on branches."

"What's the deal Uncle Sean?" Charlie chimed in, "You in or out?"

"In. I'll see your pretzel, and raise you two cheese balls."

Libby raised a brow. "What are you teaching my impressionable young son?"

"Five card stud. Your juvenile card shark here wiped me out at Texas Hold 'Em last time I babysat, figured I'd try another game."

"Of course," Libby laughed. "Silly me, nothing

says *baptism* like poker."

"You're bluffing," Charlie glared at Sean. "I call."

"Show me what you got, short stuff." Sean said.

"Full house," Charlie spread his cards on the table. "Take that!"

"Ouch! You got me kid." Sean tossed his cards down and took a sip of beer. Turning to Libby he said, "Where is baby Rochester, newest soldier of Christ?"

Libby pulled up a chair. "Judging by how she wailed through church, my guess is napping."

Bob walked across the yard and joined the group. He took Libby's hands and placed them on his temples. "Rub please."

"Uh-oh," she massaged small circles. "Which relative gave you a migraine?"

He groaned. "Remind me never, ever to ask Suzanne's father anything remotely political."

"Dare we ask?" Sean questioned.

Bob rolled his eyes. "All I said was 'how's business?'"

Ed and Elaine Brewster owned the Brewster Shoe Horn, a discount shoe store in Norwich. Their company logo was a sling back shaped like a saxophone. Elaine thought it was *super cute*. Libby thought it was phallic.

Ed made no secret of his political views, often hosting enormous sales on Bush family birthdays. Conservative power made him *hot*; the proof: Suzanne and Mindy—both conceived during Reagan years.

"And?" Sean inquired. "What did big Ed have to say?"

Bob gently pulled Libby's hands away and kissed them in appreciation. "Democrats are all communists set on ruining the shoe sale business, welfare is an urban myth, and—as if he hadn't told me a thousand times already—my career as a public defender is feeding a corrupt government. Oh, and apparently I free killers and terrorists set on world domination."

"Poor baby," Libby patted his hand. "I'm going out on a limb here and guessing you used the tried and true, 'I better check on the kids' exit strategy?"

"I went with 'nature's calling.' Seemed more plausible with the amount of beer I consumed during his rant."

"Good call." Libby gave Bob a peck on the cheek.

"I thought so." He leaned back and perused the yard. "Where's Mae? Not that I'm not enjoying the momentary calm, but I haven't seen her in a while."

"With Kev," Sean pointed to the piñata. "Someone needed to convince him to repent for the candy sacrilege. I see confession in his future. *Bless me Father; it's been six months since the blasphemous piñata.*"

Bob grinned, "I knew she wouldn't let that one slide."

After mass quantities of overcooked pasta and potato salad consumed, Suzanne brought out the cake. Kevin presented Saratoga to the gathering crowd with a flourish as family, friends, and drunken neighbors snapped pictures of the pink infant's blotched, and nap-lined, face.

Libby saw the cake and inhaled sharply. She grabbed Sean and pulled him in for a look. "Houston, we have a problem."

He scanned the crowd for of Mae. "Shit. We need to distract her until they cut it up."

It was too late.

"Sean Bernard," Mae shoved him aside. "Move over so I can get a picture of the baby and the cake." Then, she saw it.

There were sins Mae pardoned. However, all components of religious celebrations were to be recognized with respect; even baked goods. A pink puppy cake with glitter icing and various dancing cartoon friends was inexcusable. Scribbling "God Bless Saratoga" under the polka-dot kitty shimmying under a limbo pole would not erase the offense.

Libby whispered to Sean. "The piñata was bad, but this is going to get ugly."

"We should do something," Sean stammered. "She's got that cheetah-bringing-down-antelope look."

"Isn't that a *special* cake, Suzanne?" Mae smiled through gritted teeth. "*Wherever* did you find it?"

"It's adorable, right?" Suzanne squeaked. "I saw it at Annie's Bake Shop a while back, and I knew we had to have it for Saratoga! I asked the girl to add lots more glitter and write something Jesus-y on it. It came out perfect!"

"Oh God," Libby assumed combat position. "Duck and cover, duck and cover!"

"Jesus-y?" Mae sneered. "Of course. And what a clever way to include Christ on such a momentous occasion, it's always nice to toss the son of God in as an adjective. I'm sure he loves that."

"Mom, don't do it." Libby begged.

"One minute, Lib," Mae continued and zeroed in on her prey. "Suzanne, as lovely as the sparkly puppies are, don't you think there was a more appropriate choice? Perhaps something a bit more 'Lord and Savior' and less 'spay and neuter'?"

A hush fell over the crowd.

Suzanne's lip quivered. "I, I..."

Damage done, Suzanne bolted toward the house in high decibel sobs, Kevin trailing close behind.

Bob joined the commotion. "What'd I miss?"

"Damnation on a sheet cake." Libby answered.

Sean spread his arms wide and signaled a field goal. "And, it's good! Another shot between the uprights for Mae. I *love* family drama. It gives Mom something to obsess about besides my bachelorhood for a few weeks."

"What?" Mae's doe eyes widened. "I *said* the cake was lovely."

"Seriously," Libby glared. "Are you going to stand there and pretend that was a compliment? I can't believe you. This is the Fourth of July picnic all over again."

"That American flag bikini *was* offensive! For the love of God, Suzanne had stars on her nipples. That disrespects our country!"

"Made *me* feel patriotic." Bob said

"Me, too." Sean added.

Mae hit Sean in the back of the head. "You boys think with your privates. Grow up!"

"Hey," Sean pointed to Bob, "why didn't you hit him?"

"He gave me grandchildren!"

"Come on, Mom," Libby continued. "Suzanne is family. Do you honestly want to risk missing Saratoga grow up because you alienated her mother with your snarky comments?"

As much as it pained Mae to admit, Libby was right. Suzanne was here to stay and as much as she disapproved of Kevin's wife, it was not worth risking losing a grandchild.

"Fine," Mae said. "I'll call her tomorrow and apologize, but I'm only doing it for Sara's sake. I swear that cake breaks at least two commandments."

"Even if it does," Libby said, "I'm glad you're going to be a grown up about this and make things right. Now, let's go eat some butter cream cartoon characters and boost our cholesterol levels. I'll even make sure you get a piece with something Jesus-y on it."

"Oh, the cholesterol reminds me, I need one of you to take me to a silly neurologist's appointment next week in Hartford. I should cancel, you two are always so busy anyway."

Behind Mae, Sean and Libby exchanged glances. Neither spoke, but it was clear they were thinking the same thing.

Opting for humor, Libby said, "How much wine have you had, Mom?" Sean laughed along to add levity.

"You know very well I never have more than one glass," Mae answered firmly.

Libby proceeded with caution. "I guess the Anti-Christ cake threw you off. You already asked me to take you to the doctor. I'm picking you up at three o'clock, remember?"

A small shadow of fear crossed Mae's face but quickly vanished. "That's right, you have the day off so you can fit me in,. Just slipped my mind. Sean dear, make sure you keep that day open, you know Libby tends to cancel if something more important comes up."

Chapter Six

Monday was Libby's late day for work, and with the kids off to school and Bob at the office, she relished her early morning solitude. No laundry, no cleaning, and she could finish an entire cup of coffee without a single trip to the microwave for reheating. Reading the paper from headlines to car advertisements, she treated herself to a quick horoscope check and a few minutes sharpening her vocabulary on the crossword. This was Libby-Time and no one messed with it.

The phone shattered Libby-Time.

"Hello?" Libby answered.

"Mrs. O'Rourke?" A woman asked.

"Yes."

"This is Amanda Simon, the school social worker at Acorn."

Why is she calling? Libby thought.

"I visited with Charlie last week, and I wonder if you have a second to discuss some concerns I have?"

Libby met Miss Simon at the Acorn Open House. From what she remembered, the young social worker was tall, pretty, and fresh out of graduate school. Libby kept mayonnaise in the fridge older than Miss Simon.

"Is there a problem?" Libby asked.

"Not a problem per se," Miss Simon explained. "I'm calling about a red flag behavior Charlie has exhibited as of late."

"I'm all ears."

"Wonderful. It's always refreshing when a parent shows a vested interest in their child. In my experience, that is not always the case."

Libby fought off laughter. *How much experience is that, six months?* "Please continue," she said.

"Thank you," Miss Simon droned on. "As part of the first grade curriculum Charlie attends art class every afternoon. This month's project is very simple, crayon drawings of family moments. Most students submitted vacation themes and holidays; Charlie's images were darker."

Libby frowned. *How dark?*

She continued, "Charlie's last three pictures are solely in black crayon and depict some sort of battle scene. When the teacher reiterated the assignment was family life, Charlie assured her his pictures were just that. It goes without saying, we are concerned."

Okay, maybe there is something going on, Libby thought. "That is unusual for Charlie. Any suggestions as to what it may be?"

Grateful for the opportunity to highlight her authority, Miss Simon explained. "Art is an outlet of expression for much deeper psychological issues. In fact, a study at the Bronx Zoo recently showed that chimps given fingerpaints were able to rudely sketch cages, displaying their anxiety and fear of confinement."

Libby's jaw dropped. Did this pubescent social worker just call Charlie a crazy monkey?

Continuing her diagnosis, Miss Simon's tone bordered condescending. "Overall, Mrs. O'Rourke, I feel Charlie is a wonderfully empathetic child who may simply need more positive reinforcement at home. However, if you feel he needs to speak with a child psychologist, I have several in the area I can recommend."

"Well, this is genuinely unexpected, Miss Simon." Libby reigned in temper. "Charlie's father and I will have a discussion before he comes home from school today and set a course of action right away."

"Wonderful. Please keep me informed, and know that I will continue to monitor Charlie's behavior for signs of distress."

"I truly appreciate that." *No, I don't you meddling wench!* "Again, thank you."

Ringing off, Libby counted to ten before dialing Bob.

He saw the caller ID and answered on the second ring. "Hey honey, what's up?"

"Charlie is a potential sociopath."

He took a deep breath. "Everyone needs a goal. What happened?"

Libby recapped her conversation with Miss Simon.

Bob said, "So he draws in black and likes violence, big deal, he's a boy. I ate paste and liked to staple my fingers at his age, it all worked out in the end."

Bob had a way of boiling down problems until they seemed silly. Libby appreciated his soothing capabilities, but wished he shared a little of her rage instinct, just for company.

"It's not a big issue in my eyes," Libby said. "But I think Little Miss Shrink has him pegged for a life of crime. Do we need a conference?"

Bob likened school conferences to root canals, the meetings were always the same. He crammed his six-foot frame into a leprechaun chair and listened to teachers blather on for an hour about his child's strengths and weaknesses. Libby refuted everything on the ride home and insisted he do a criminal background check on the teacher. No one ever won.

"Please, no conferences," he lamented. "Can't we just ask Charlie what the deal is? I'm sure it's something simple."

"Fine," Libby said. "But the social worker said we have to ease into it. Not hit him between the eyes when he gets home."

"I'll take him out for ice cream tonight on the way back from soccer and see what I can get out of him."

"Good idea, and leave the lawyer voice at the office, no cross-examination."

"Will do, and are we having dinner together tonight or is it fend for ourselves?"

Libby tried to plan dinners around the mayhem of soccer nights, but the edible factor was always a question. "I fired up the slow cooker with something resembling beef stew. Toss it over some microwave rice before you head out to the field."

"Mm, sort-of- stew. Have to run. We'll talk later. Love you."

"You too."

Hanging up, she still had a few minutes before work and called Sean.

"Mae Day Construction," Sean barked.

"Where's Deb?" Lib asked.

"Walt has his first physical therapy today. I hate it when she's out; I have to *talk* to people."

Baffled by her brother's success, Libby wondered if Sean truly possessed any interpersonal skills.

Apprenticing under their father for seven years, Sean easily stepped into the role of company president when Bernie passed away.

At the time, Mae Day was doing well, but not fabulous. Within two years Sean turned the small family-owned construction company into the leading builder in the county. Unlike their father, he had a strong head for business and swung a hammer each day alongside the crew in an effort to stay connected with his employees. They respected him, and Sean knew the importance of happy staff.

"Do you want me to send Shannon over after school to cover the phones? It'll cost you a drive to the mall?"

"That would be great. I'll be here all day, but I have to chain myself to the desk to get through a stack of invoices."

"Don't sweat it, she likes coming in." Libby switched gears. "I called to get your take on Mom's little memory lapse yesterday."

"You mean the doctor appointment thing? Yeah, it was weird."

"This is pure speculation, but Grandma Shannon died pretty young, from a stroke I think. I'm wondering if that's one of the things the doctor is concerned about with Mom."

In the brief time the McGinn kids had with Shannon Finn, she was the best grandmother kids could ask for. Full of contagious energy, and a former showgirl, Shannon's trademark fire-engine-red lipstick and oversized costume jewels made her a showstopper. Libby adored her grandmother's vitality. Their fantastic summer visits to Brooklyn were full of dress-up games in eye-catching dance costumes and afternoons spinning and twirling the day away in a vintage black and white kitchen while big band music blared in the background.

Shannon's two-story brownstone smelled of butterscotch and oversized velvet furniture. China knick-knacks filled every square inch of space. The front parlor held a glossy, ebony baby grand piano. Its closed lid displayed countless black and white family photographs from generations past and present.

One summer, without warning, the trips to Brooklyn stopped. Heartbroken, Libby didn't understand exactly what happened. Within a year Shannon passed away.

"I miss Grandma Shannon," Sean said. "She was a riot. It's hard to believe our straight-laced Mom is her daughter."

"Genetics are a mystery," Libby laughed. "Do you remember how old we were when Gram died? I couldn't have been more than five."

"That sounds about right. I remember coming home one day after school, had to be first grade, right before summer break and asking Mom if we were going to Brooklyn to visit Gram over vacation. She got weepy and told me Gram was in a special hospital, and we were too young to visit. It must have been a nursing home. She never really talked about her after that."

"To this day Mom avoids talking about her. What do you think happened back then?"

"Beats me; maybe they had a fight or something? Mom might feel guilty about never settling things with her before she died. Guilt does weird stuff to people."

"Maybe, but I think there's more to the story." She

checked her watch. "I'll let you get back to work. Shannon will be in the office by three to help out with the phones."

"Great. Hey, did you ever tell Shannon about her wild and crazy namesake? It could be where she gets her love of loud music and all things theatrical. Gram was a sequin hurricane."

Chapter Seven

Shannon Finn retired her dancing career soon after she met and fell in love with a young soldier, Matthew Finn. Their storybook romance began on a dance floor, raced to the wedding chapel, and died the night Matthews's plane disappeared over the Pacific, leaving Shannon a young widow with two children, Mae and William, to raise alone.

A free spirit in every regard, Shannon's uninhibited love of singing and dancing away the days away garnered years of unwanted neighborhood attention. Transforming the front porch to center stage, her zealous performances featured Mae and William as audience and supporting cast.

Unaffected by the next-door gossip, Shannon filled her children with an appreciation for the arts and a respect for all things creative. Growing up Finn was an adventure, and Shannon saw to it the Mae and Will's lives were surrounded by art.

As a young mother herself, Mae was only able to sneak away and visit Shannon once or twice a year. They spoke daily, but trips to Brooklyn were impossible to manage while running a business and raising three small children. Mae was happy, but harried.

In the summer of 1974, Mae and Bernie packed the car while Sean, Libby, and Kevin ran around the yard anticipating a fun-packed visit to Grandma Shannon. One weekend every June the children stayed in Brooklyn while Mae and Bernie enjoyed some time alone, the break was all-around heaven.

"Mom, mom, mom," Libby tugged at Mae's blouse. "Is it time to go yet?"

Mae smiled down at her daughter's toothless grin. "Daddy's finishing loading the car. Do you need to tinkle before we go? It's a long trip."

Libby debated. "Nope, I'm ready."

"Go make sure Sean and Kevin don't have to go, and then we can leave."

Libby screamed across the yard. "Do you gots to go tinkle before we to Grandma's?"

Sean shook his head. Kevin dropped his pants and watered the rhododendrons. Too tired to stop her three-year-old from using the shrubs as a urinal, Mae waited for him to finish.

"Everybody get in the car and buckle up." She said. "Brooklyn, here we come."

Two hours later the road-weary family pulled into Shannon's driveway. The once pristine brownstone's facade wore signs of serious neglect. Mae and Bernie exchanged concerned looks across the front seat.

"All right, you bunch of troublemakers," Bernie teased, "go ring the bell, and don't jump on your poor Grandmother all at once. She's not used to your...energy."

"Do you think Mom's okay?" Mae said to Bernie. "The house looks a mess."

"Don't panic, maybe she's just a little short on cash." He opened the car door. "Come on, I'll grab the kids suitcases and put them on the front porch before I go fill up the tank. I want a quick getaway once our natives are settled with their captive."

Mae climbed out of the car and met the kids at the door.

"Did you ring the bell?" she asked.

"I pressed it three times," Sean said. "Grandma isn't coming. Are you sure this is her house? It doesn't look right?"

Mae silently agreed. "It's the right house, sweetie. Grandma must be having it painted or something." Ringing the bell a fourth time, Mae checked the doorknob; it was unlocked. "Mom," she cracked the door, "we're here."

"Mae?" A soft voice called from the back of the house. "Is that you honey?"

"It's us, where are you?"

"Give me a second, I'm in the kitchen." Shannon rounded the corner. "Sorry, I had the radio on and didn't hear the bell."

Mae gasped. At fifty-nine, Shannon's formerly brilliant red hair was stark white, and her sun-freckled, peaches and cream complexion appeared sickly yellow.

"Gram," Libby spoke first, "you look funny."

"Well," Shannon feigned insult. "That's a polite way to say hello to your favorite Gram! Get over here and give me a giant squeeze." She opened her arms wide, all three children ran into her embrace. Kissing her grandbabies madly, she turned to Mae. "And how are you my darling girl? Come give your old Mom a hug."

Mae wrapped her arms around her mother. Gone was the curvy, jaw-dropping figure capable of grabbing the attention of every man she passed; in its place, a collection of jutting bones. Shannon pulled away first.

"Who's hungry?" she asked. "I have it on good authority there are cupcakes in the kitchen and the first one there gets the biggest..." The children vanished before she could finish her sentence. "It's so good to have some life back in this old place," Shannon continued. "Kids are truly the fountain of youth, especially the boys. Lord how they keep us hopping, and our little princess is turning into a beautiful young lady. She is going to break some hearts one day with those enormous blue eyes and mop of red curls. Meghan is just precious."

"Libby," Mae's expression hardened. "You mean Libby, Mom."

"That's what I said, dear."

Tears welled in the corners of Mae's blue eyes. "You said Meghan."

Mae and Bernie's first child, Meghan Rose died before her first breath. Sean's twin had not survived the devastating car accident six years earlier. Mae and Bernie chose to keep Meghan a secret from their children, knowing they had no way to comprehend death, or a sister they would never know.

Horrified with the error, Shannon pulled Mae into her arms and whispered. "Oh sweetheart, I'm so sorry I said that. I didn't mean to upset you. I have had her on my mind so much lately; I always do when I know you are coming to visit. Are you and Bernie going to stop at the cemetery on your way home?"

"We always do," Mae wiped her face. "Bernie is filling up with gas, but as soon as he gets back we'll get the kids settled in and head over to St. Patrick's with some flowers."

"Why don't you cut some of the roses from the backyard? Remember when we planted them?"

Mae smiled. "I remember Will planting them and you and me supervising from the porch."

Shannon's face lit. "Your brother was quite the gardener, a talented young man able to nurture just about anything to bloom."

"Where is that talented young man?" Mae frowned. "I'd like to talk to him. No offense, but the house looks kind of shabby. He said he was taking care of that for you."

"It's not Will's fault. He travels quite often for work these days, and the man he hired to do the work never shows up. Will can handle all the yard nonsense when he gets back from his trip, it's a house, not a bowl of ice cream, and it won't melt if you leave it alone for a few months."

"Fine," Mae sighed. "I'll leave the house to Will, but what about you? I'm concerned you are too thin. Are you sick?"

Shannon threw her head back and laughed. "When did my spit-fire daughter turn into such a Nervous Nellie? Honestly Mae, I may be your elder, but you are by far the older soul." She took Mae's hand. "Don't worry about me; that is an order. I want you to focus on my beautiful grandchildren and that loveable brute of a husband. Nothing else matters. Can you do that for me?"

Mae knew arguing was futile. "Yes, but promise to at least get a checkup; I'd feel a lot better if you did."

"Oh you are such a pain in my bum," Shannon teased. "But if it makes you happy I'll schedule one next week. Will that be sufficient for you?"

"That will be fine," Mae smiled. "Now, why don't we go see if my cherubs left any cupcakes for the rest of us?"

Arm in arm they followed the blissful sounds of feuding siblings into the chocolate-covered kitchen.

****

After a romantic dinner in the city, Mae and Bernie arrived home and settled into the front porch swing. Made by Bernie's hand, the mahogany black slat was a gift to his bride on their fifth anniversary. Mae rested her head on his shoulder.

"Do you think they're okay?" she asked.

He looked at his watch. "Ten minutes."

"What are you talking about?"

"Since we've been home, it took you exactly ten minutes to bring up the kids. I thought I'd get at least fifteen. Woman, you are easier to read than a box score."

She laughed and punched him in the arm. "I worry. You saw Mom. She looks exhausted, and you know what our kids are like. They may have killed her by now."

"True, but she's enjoying the time with the little hellions so leave them be."

Standing, he reached out his hand. "Now pay attention, I've got two full days to romance my girl, and I intend to use every minute—no more talk of children, mothers, or any matter of domesticity. Is that understood?"

Mae saluted. "Understood, sir!"

"Good." He slapped her behind. "Now get into that bedroom, soldier. Let's start the romancing."

****

Sunday afternoon Mae and Bernie arrived to pick up the kids. Will's car was in the driveway.

"Good, my brother's here." Mae said. "I haven't seen him in ages, and I can ask him about the house. He's got to hire someone more reliable to keep up with this place."

Will exited the front door and walked over to greet them.

"Hello gorgeous." He wrapped Mae in an enthusiastic hug before turning to Bernie. "And hello to you too, you big Irish lush." The men embraced.

"Always good to see you Will," Bernie said. "No matter what your sister says when you're not around. She's an evil woman...not sure why either of us put up with her."

"I tried to convince Mom to swap her at the flea market when we were young, but no one wanted her. Big mouth, no skills, she was a tough sell."

"I hate you both." Mae took the ribbing with ease. "Now get out of my way so I can go fetch my children."

"Hold on a second." Will called. "I want to talk to you without Mom around."

"Good," Mae crossed her arms over her chest. "I wanted to talk to you, too."

"And that's my cue." Bernie stepped away. "When my lovely wife gets that give-you-a-piece-of-my-mind tone, I know to run. I'll see you both inside."

"Before you get mad at me," Will started, "there are a few things you need to know."

"I'm listening." Mae said.

"First, I've been away for three weeks and just got back last night. I know the house looks awful, and I want you to know I hired a landscaper, a good, dependable landscaper to do the job while I was gone. I introduced him to Mom. We set up a plan for him to come every Saturday and I left thinking everything was all set. Obviously, when I came over here to see the kids I was furious and called him right away."

"Good, I hope you gave him hell."

"No," Will sighed. "He came here as planned, and when he started on the lawn Mom came running out of the house screaming at him, yelling to get off her property and threatening to call the police. He tried to remind her who he was, but she called him a liar and refused to listen, so, he left. Honestly, I don't blame him; I would have done the same thing."

"She didn't remember meeting him?"

"No, and I don't want to dump this on you all at once, but that wasn't the first time she's acted strangely. It's not every day, but I'm concerned"

Mae spun toward the house. "I should check on the kids."

"Relax, they're fine," Will said. "I stayed over last night. Mom was okay, and I got a time to spoil my niece and nephews rotten." Mae exhaled.

"What do you think we should we do?" she asked. "We can't leave her alone if something is wrong."

"I agree, and I spoke with Mrs Norton from church. She and a few of the women are going to take turns checking on Mom once a day, and for now I'll keep coming by a few times per week, but that's all I can manage and still keep my job. If she gets worse, we have to figure out something more permanent."

****

Summer turned to fall, and Shannon's once-amusing behavior became troubling and inappropriate. Anger-fueled outbursts directed at family and friends became everyday occurrences, and simple tasks— locking the front door, turning off the sink, even basic hygiene turned problematic.

Will, attempting to keep Shannon in her own home as long as possible, increased his visits and prepared meals she could reheat on the days he was unable to stop by. After three weeks of throwing away untouched food, he called Mae.

Mae had concerns of her own, explaining the daily phone calls between she and Shannon had dwindled to once a week with Shannon rushing her off the phone. When they did speak, Shannon slid from present day to the distant past, speaking about long-dead friends and family in the present tense. With each conversation, Mae heard their mother's mind disappearing by inches, each call bringing fewer recollections of the people and places she held dear.

One bright November morning Will planned to surprise Shannon with lunch at her favorite diner. After a two-week business trip, he wanted to check in on her in hopes the fall air and delicious food would boost her failing health.

He opened the front door and froze. Seated by the picture window, in her favorite emerald wingback, Shannon was dressed in a red taffeta sequined gown. A once beautiful dancing dress, the costume hung off her skeletal frame like a wet bed sheet. Fire-engine lipstick, smeared across her mouth as though applied by a child, gave her the appearance of an eerie funhouse character.

She did not acknowledge his presence, her stare locked blankly on the window.

With tears in his eyes, Will knelt down in front of her. The smell of urine was overpowering.

"Mom?" he whispered.

Shannon turned in the direction of his voice but gave no response, no recognition. Her brilliant blue eyes remained empty and lifeless, and in that silent moment, Will knew his vibrant, full-of-life mother was gone. Only a shadow remained.

Mae caught the next train to Brooklyn and together she and Will took Shannon to the hospital where the attending physician completed a thorough exam.

Determining a series of small strokes were to blame for Shannon's impaired cognitive function, he stressed the likelihood of worsening symptoms and suggested Mae and Will consider long-term nursing home placement as a means to ensure both their mother's safety and the best possible care.

After wrestling with possible solutions, Mae and Will admitted Shannon to St. Joseph's Nursing Facility in Brooklyn hoping the caring and structured environment would bring their mother a sense of peace.

One month later, a week before Christmas, Shannon died with William at her side. When he called Mae to relay news, they agreed it was a blessing.

Chapter Eight

Sort-of-stew smelled fantastic when Libby walked in from work. Stump greeted her at the door.

"Hey pal." She gave him a scratch. "Tell you what, I'll slip a few bites in your food, but you have to eat outside. I'm low on stink tolerance tonight."

Dog fed and properly ventilated, Libby scooped out her serving and sat down at the computer to check email.

Four new messages. Jesus Loves You: Delete. Coffee Hut coupon: Print. Stacy Warner—Kiddie Kardio update: Copy Sender Email Address to free erectile dysfunction sample. The last was from YogaGranny123.

Hello dear, it's your mother. Was there a doubt? *The doctor's name is Vandana Rashan on Capitol Avenue in Hartford. I will expect you at three on Thursday. Call me if you have the time between now and then.*

Libby did an online search for Dr.Rashan; her bio was impressive. One of the top neurologists in New England, Dr. Rashan specialized in the treatment of degenerative cognitive diseases. She had published several articles in the New England Journal of Medicine on hereditary links in Alzheimer and dementia patients.

Does Mom's doctor suspect Alzheimer's? Seems like a big leap from memory bumps to life-altering disease. Maybe he's just covering his bases; the neurology consult could be precautionary. She printed a copy for Sean and shut down the computer.

In the kitchen, she washed her bowl along with the haphazard dishes scattered from Bob and Charlie's dash for soccer practice. A thump drew her attention out the window. Stump swatted an empty food dish around the yard with his front paws.

"He's such a happy dog." Libby said. "Not bright, but happy."

Past Stump was the cottage. Libby and Bob had ideas for the little structure, but time and money always squelched the plans. Filled with dusty furniture, sports equipment, and several boxes of Christmas decorations, the cottage had potential, but no immediate purpose. Shannon lobbied to convert the space into a Sweet Sixteen mega-gift. Bob was not biting. She had three years to appeal his "hell no" verdict.

As Libby put the last dish in the dishwasher, Sean and Shannon entered.

"Hey Mom," Shannon plopped her backpack down and headed for the computer. "What's for dinner?"

"Stew," Libby answered. "Would you like rice, or no rice?"

"Is it that new rice or the regular stuff?" Shannon's nose wrinkled. In an attempt to spice up the O'Rourke's lackluster diet, one Sunday dinner Libby had introduced wild rice in place of the standard white. The sticky wholegrain lump went over like a burp in church.

"Regular rice," Libby replied.

"Ok, I'd like rice, please." She turned to Sean. "Tell Mom about José!"

José Ruiz was the senior foreman on Sean's crew.

A married father of four, José worked hard and rarely spoke more than "hello" and "goodbye." He was Sean's kind of guy.

"I hope he comes back to work tomorrow," Sean said on a sigh.

"What happened?" Libby asked.

"You remember the Lerner project; big farmhouse on the ridge?" Sean asked.

Libby nodded.

"Well the owner's wife is um, lonely and taken a liking to José. She walks around in skin-tight, skimpy dresses when he's on the job site. Trust me Lib; skimpy isn't an appetizing look on Mrs. Lerner."

"This is going to be good, I can tell." Libby smirked and sat down at the kitchen table. "Continue."

"So the crew finished up," Sean explained, "and Mrs. Lerner asks José to stay behind to look at the grout in the master bath—some B.S. about not being happy with the shade. Poor guy follows her up, sticks his head in the bathroom, and it seems okay to him. When he turns around—Bam!—she's bare ass naked and on him like peanut butter on jelly."

"Holy crap, what did José do?"

"He had no clue what to do! He ran out of there like a bat out of hell and slammed into my office ten minutes later. He's was so frazzled he kept switching from English to Spanish, and I only got every other word. I picked out 'quitting', 'grout', and 'naked.'" He sat with Libby at the table. "I think I talked him down, but I'll find out for sure tomorrow."

"Your life is full of excitement," Libby teased. "I'm sure José will be back. Though to be on the safe side I'd put Irene in his place on the Lerner project."

A true force of nature, Irene was one of Sean's best employees and her crew loved her. Built like a platinum lumberjack, Irene ran a top-notch job site; taking guff from no one. People meeting her for the first time often misjudged her tough exterior for a hard soul, but in reality, Irene's heart was pure cotton candy.

"Irene can handle crazy Mrs. Lerner, that's for sure," Sean agreed. "I've got to run—playing basketball tonight with a bunch of the guys down at the gym."

Shannon walked past and started up the stairs. "Do you need help again tomorrow, Uncle Sean?" she asked.

"I'm set." He answered. "Thanks for pitching in today."

"José's story made it worth it." Shannon disappeared up the stairs leaving Libby with Sean.

"Do you want to take some stew home?" Libby asked.

"Thanks, no." Sean smiled. "I'm still recovering from your lasagna."

"There was nothing wrong with that lasagna!"

He put an arm around her shoulder. "Dear, sweet baby sister...I know you try, but lasagna shouldn't be crunchy. Yours tasted like tomato-covered wood shavings."

"Here"—she hit him in the stomach with the printouts from Dr.Rashan's webpage—"take these with you."

"What's this?"

"Some info on the doctor I'm taking Mom to on Thursday. Just some background for you to read through."

Sean scanned the bio photo and raised an eyebrow.

"Hot."

"Married."

"Figures."

He stuffed the papers in his back pocket and left. Bob and Charlie burst through the door from soccer practice minutes later.

"Hey Mom, guess what!" Charlie yelled on his way to the pantry for a snack. "Coach Tony said I can play goalie on Saturday!"

"Great!" Libby said. "Dom will want to see that. Go let him know before it gets too late."

Snack in hand, he ran to share the momentous news with Dom. As the door slammed, Bob wrapped his arms around Libby and said "hello" properly.

Leaning into him, she asked, "Did you gather any insight into our dark, disturbed artist during your father-son bonding time?"

"Damned if I know," Bob pulled back. "He seems happy, no signs of killing us in our sleep that I can see."

"Weird."

"Yeah I know. Maybe it's just a phase. The social worker probably overreacted." He went to the fridge for his mint chocolate chip nightcap. Some men drank to escape pressure-cooker careers, but Bob's addiction put dairy farmers' kids through college.

"You're right," Libby said. "I'll call Miss Simon tomorrow and ask her to send the pictures home and we can take a look. I'm sure it's nothing."

"Good plan." He put the carton back in the freezer. "Did I miss anything today?"

"Not much. Groceries, dry cleaner..." Libby smiled. "A little indecent exposure."

Bob frowned. "Will I have a new client tomorrow

morning?"

"Let's put it this way: if the name Lerner comes across your desk, run."

Chapter Nine

Post-bedtime negotiations, Libby discovered Bob dozing in Old Stink with Stump snoring contentedly at his feet. She slipped away to call Caroline.

"Hi Lib," Caroline answered.

"I wrestled the natives to sleep and figured I'd give you a call before tackling the Himalayan laundry pile," Libby said.

"That reminds me, do you have my royal blue sweater? The V-neck with the good boob placement?"

"Yes, I dropped it off with the dry cleaning on Monday. Do you want it back?"

"Before Friday, I've got a big date with Richard, the CPA."

"Remind me how you met this one?"

"He does the agency's taxes. Gail set us up."

Gail Miller, Caroline's boss, owned Redwood & Sterling Advertising. There was never a Redwood or a Sterling, but Gail, a woman attempting to break into a man's profession in the 1960's, named the firm for the tallest tree and strong metal hoping the name, albeit fictitious, created a rugged image.

"Wait a second," Libby continued. "Richard wasn't the guy we went out to dinner with? Cute, funny, chronic ear hair?"

"No, that was Ron. I broke that one off after he started sending mushy, late night text messages and calling Trevor 'sport.'"

"Ew!" Libby laughed. "Where is Richard the CPA taking you?"

"Higami Sushi, nothing says 'first date' like raw fish."

"Besides the perfect bust-accentuating sweater, what's the rest of the ensemble going to be?"

"Depends," Caroline debated. "If I stick to salad and water between now and then, jeans, but Trevor is selling candy for soccer, so most likely black stretch pants. By the way, you bought three chocolate almond bars. I didn't want to look like a pig and put myself down for ten."

"Good to know," Libby chuckled. "How many did I eat so far?"

Caroline confessed, "Two."

"I still remember selling candy for cheerleading when we were Trevor's age."

"Ah yes," Caroline grinned, "the days when our pompoms stayed put without underwires."

****

Libby and Caroline met in second grade. Sister Agnes, Immaculate Conception Primary's principal, appointed Libby as Caroline's tour guide after the Duffys moved to town from Georgia.

A one-story brick school, from a bird's eye view IC looked like a thermometer. The long central corridor housed K-8 classes, gym, lunchroom and library. At the tip of the building was a round outcropping of offices for the nurse and teacher's lounge. Libby's tour began at the most prominent spot.

"This is the lunchroom," seven-year-old Libby explained. "My mom makes my lunch, but you can buy if you want."

"Why don't you buy?" Caroline asked.

"I buy the chocolate milk, but the food is gross. Tommy Mancuso threw up the mac-and-cheese in math class last week. Sister Barbara had to leave the room; I think she barfed, too."

Libby was a wealth of knowledge; Caroline was fascinated.

The tour progressed past the bathrooms, library, and gym and finished at the nurse's office. The sterile white walls, covered in eye charts, overly graphic scoliosis photos, and dancing food groups ate up the entire room. A lime-green vinyl couch lined one wall, and on the desk, glass jars held cotton swabs, tongue depressors, and varying sizes of adhesive bandages.

"Go to the nurse in the morning if you don't feel good. She'll call your mom and send you home." Libby explained. "After lunch Sister Edwina fills in, and you don't want Big Ed."

Caroline laughed. "Does she know you call her that?"

"Of course not!"

"Why's she so bad?"

"She's *crazy* in a penguin suit. No matter how sick you feel she gives you an ice pack and sends you back to class to pray. My brother Kevin ate a pencil, and all she did was give him the ice and ten Hail Marys. He could have died!"

Caroline frowned, "What if you feel really, really sick?"

"Doesn't matter. Big Ed only dismisses early for barf."

****

At thirteen, Libby and Caroline made an earth-shattering discovery—boys. Although many of their classmates failed to break free from the shackles of *disgusting*, a few were shaping up quite nicely.

Tearing through Speils Department Store, the girls searched for eighth grade graduation dresses meeting Immaculate Conception dress code: high neck, full sleeves, and nothing remotely flattering. The pickings were slim.

"Did you see Jimmy Shea's hair cut?" Libby snapped her grape bubble gum.

Caroline pulled a pink, lace gown. "He looks cute; you should totally talk to him."

"Yeah, right," Libby wistfully ran her hand down the seam of a blue satin strapless and shoved it back in the rack. "What would I say, Hey there Jimmy, nice haircut. Want to make out?"

Caroline giggled. "What time is your mom picking us up?"

"We have to meet her at the Cine Time entrance after Sean's movie lets out at four o'clock. "She checked her watch. "I've got two hours to find something. If we leave empty-handed, Mom has threatened to make my dress again. Once was enough."

"Aw," Caroline teased. "But you looked so cute at Tommy's birthday party."

"I looked like a pilgrim after a crop fire."

At four-fifteen, armed with appropriate dresses and matching accessories, the girls met Sean.

"Is Mom here yet?" Libby asked.

"No, she's always late." Sean paced in front of the theater's glass doors.

"How was the movie? Did your girlfriend like it?"

"None of your business," he snapped.

"Oh boy. Somebody's testy."

"Grow up, Lib."

"Ignore her," Caroline chimed in. "She's just jealous because you're allowed to date and she's not."

"I am not jealous!" Libby snapped.

"Yes, you are." Caroline took her by the arm. "Let's get a snack while we wait for your mom. You get cranky when you're hungry."

On line at Pretzel Pagoda, Keith Wallace—a former IC student now freshman at St. Margaret Mary High School—slid in behind the pair.

"Well if it isn't the dynamic duo?" Keith said. "Lib, Caroline, how's things at good old IC?"

Keith always skirted the edge of trouble. He was the kid everyone *knew* toilet-papered the neighborhood on Halloween, but no one was caught in the act.

"IC's fine," Libby answered, stepping back to put distance between the girls and their unwelcome visitor. "How's high school? Sean seems to like it."

Hearing his name, Sean turned and caught sight of Keith's too-familiar proximity to Libby and Caroline. Abandoning his lookout duties, he made a beeline for the girls.

"High school rocks," Keith answered. "I got totally wasted last weekend at the football party." He shifted his attention to Caroline, stepped closer and leered at her chest. He licked his lips. "Duffy, you're looking mighty good. Seeing anybody?"

"Wallace..." Sean wedged in between the thug and Caroline. "Something I can help you with?"

A sneer crossed Keith's face. "Just talking to the ladies, O'Rourke. You got a problem with that?"

"No problem...yet."

"Good. Now how about you and Lib take a little walk while I talk to Caroline for a few minutes, alone?"

Sean turned to Caroline. "You want us to leave?" She shook her head. "Seems Caroline would prefer us to stay, Wallace. So why don't you be a decent guy and leave her alone?"

Lips curled in an unhappy snarl, Keith leaned into Sean and growled low, "Take a walk O'Rourke. The little bitch doesn't know what she wants. Get lost, and let me take a shot at her."

****

Sean discovered the Tri-County Mall security office had surprisingly comfortable chairs. An ice pack over one eye, he barely made out Mae's blurry silhouette as she spoke with the officer behind the glass partition. Libby and Caroline gripped each other and waited for the fallout.

Five minutes later, Mae stormed the waiting area. "All of you," Mae bellowed. "In the car, now!" Before the last seatbelt clicked, she exploded. "I have never been so humiliated in all my life." She turned to the passenger seat, "Sean Bernard, what in God's name were you thinking?"

She cut him off. "No! Do not open your mouth, not one word until we get to the office. I want you to explain this disaster to Daddy and me at the same time. I only want to hear it once."

She met the girls' terrified glances in the rearview mirror. "I am dropping you off at Caroline's house. Libby, Mrs. Duffy will bring you home after dinner."

By the time Mae deposited the girls, her temper had reduced to a low boil. "Sean, that boy needed nine stitches. What got into you?"

"I'm sorry, Mom. I know I shouldn't have hit him, but after what he said to Caroline the asshole had it coming."

"Language!" Mae pinched the bridge of her nose. "This isn't like you, you're not a violent boy, and you're darn lucky the pretzel salesman saw who threw the first punch, otherwise you'd be at the police station right now. Tell me what the boy said to make you angry enough to react like that."

Sean recounted the ugly conversation, and for several minutes, Mae said nothing. Torn between pride in his chivalry and a growing concern, she also wondered if Sean's feelings for Caroline's were developing past friendship.

"Mom?" Sean interrupted her thoughts. "Are you going to say anything?"

She pulled into the Mae Day parking lot and killed the engine. "What that boy said was reprehensible. Any child who uses language like that needs confession and a lesson in what it means to be a Christian, but you were dead wrong to hit him." She paused. "No matter how much the little bastard deserved it."

"Mom!"

"I never said that,"—she winked—"and if you tell anyone I did you'll be cleaning the bathrooms for a month. Now go inside and wait for me. Daddy and I need to figure out how to punish you."

Head hung, he exited the car and walked to the front door like a prisoner facing the gallows. Alone, Mae's eyes began to mist.

"How did I miss it?" she whispered. "I blinked, and in that split second my little prince stopped protecting the backyard from dragons and started defending the honor of damsels in distress."

She closed her eyes in prayer. "Lord, please keep Sean's tender heart locked away for a while longer, it's going to be a few years before Caroline Duffy realizes she holds the key."

Chapter Ten

Thursday morning Libby phoned Mae to confirm the doctor's appointment.

"I'm not sure why you keep calling, Elizabeth?" Mae grumbled. "I said I'd be ready at three and I will. Are you afraid I'll skip the country or something?"

"Siberia's nice this time of year," Libby snapped. "Need a ride to the airport?"

"There's no need to get snippy."

"There's no need to get defensive."

Mae sighed. "Just be on time, I'll be ready."

Hanging up, Libby clicked a leash on Stump and set off for a mind-clearing walk. Rhyme's postcard-perfect shoreline was the ideal spot to regain composure and prepare for a day with Mae.

A mile from home, Nichols Lighthouse stood surrounded by caramel sands and deep blue surf. Built in 1880, the weather-beaten red and white striped building was Libby's resting point. She let Stump off leash to run in the surf. Splashing madly into the waiting tidal pools, he sniffed out a pile of rotting fish and began to roll.

"No!" Libby yelled, but it was too late.

As Stump rejoiced in his fragrant discovery, a black and white police SUV pulled into the parking lot.

"Crap," Libby said. "This day keeps getting better and better."

Anticipating a hefty fee for breaking Rhyme's leash law ordinance, Libby breathed a sigh of relief as Jimmy Battaglia stepped out of the cruiser.

"A-freaking-men," she muttered.

A lifelong friend, Jimmy grew up next door to the McGinn's and coincidentally had two Labradors of his own. His tall, muscular frame commanded attention, and his striking Italian features strongly resembled a young prizefighter's. Fortunately he sounded nothing like a guy who'd received repeat blows to the head.

"Libby." His gaze traveled to Stump. "Nice day for a walk on the beach."

"Nice to see you, Officer Battaglia." Libby said. "You look mighty snazzy today. What is with the full dress blues? Is there a parade?" Rhyme's finest typically dressed in jeans and golf shirts; not much need for formality in a small town.

"Meeting with my CO later," he said. "I'm up for a pay grade review. Hoping for the big bucks."

"What?" She feigned shock. "Are you saying my tax dollars don't already pay you six figures? That can't be."

He grinned. "Oddly enough, no."

"Go figure," she laughed. "Are you busting me for allowing my vicious canine to roam?"

Jimmy looked at Stump; the dog's head was a mop of seaweed. "You've got no chance of keeping a Lab out of the water. The Pope will convert before that happens." He pulled a citation pad and started writing, "Here's what I'm going to do. I'm pretending to write you up in case anyone is looking, but this is my buddy Dave's address. He has a place on the water a bit further down the road and only uses the place during the summer. Stump can run off the energy down there since it is private property and ordinances don't apply. I take my dogs there at least once a week." He ripped off the form and handed it to Libby.

"Jimmy Battaglia, you big softie." Libby grinned. "How has no woman snapped up your sweet soul?"

"They've tried Lib, they've tried. I guess I'm too much to handle."

"So *not* true, you're all heart!"

"Shh, not so loud, you'll ruin my Bad Cop image."

"Won't say a word, I promise." Libby crossed her heart. "Hey, did Sean finish the job over at your mom's place?" Jimmy's mother Lucinda had Multiple Sclerosis. Sean converted much of her ranch-style home to handicap accessible living.

"Yeah, looks great," he answered. "Mom loves being able to stay in her own house. The thought of assisted living was giving her nightmares—I owe Sean big time."

"He was glad to help, and he adores your mom. After all, she kept him fed through most of our childhood." Libby drooled over the mouthwatering smells wafting from the Battaglia's house every Sunday. Lucinda jarred homemade marinara each summer from her herb and vegetable gardens. Night breezes brought the smell of fresh basil and rosemary through Libby's open bedroom window.

"Like my Sicilian mother ever lets anyone out of her house without feeding them?" Jimmy grinned as he closed his citation pad and turned toward the parking lot. "I'll catch you later, Lib, and good luck getting the stench out of that hairy beast of yours."

Jimmy climbed into the cruiser and waved

goodbye.

Libby whistled for Stump. He charged toward her. "Whoa, buddy." She held her breath as she clipped on his leash. "We're breaking out the extra strength doggie shampoo when we get home."

Twenty minutes later Libby strolled up the driveway and noticed Cha-Cha snoozing on the roof of her car.

"Uh-oh," Libby whispered and firmed up her hold on the leash. Unfortunately, Stump had the memory of a lima bean, and forgot he and Cha-Cha were friends with the start of each new day.

"Here we go; three, two, one."

Spotting the cat, Stump launched onto the hood of the minivan and howled uncontrollably. Unfazed, Cha-Cha stretched and began a tongue bath.

Dom flew out his front door. "Sorry, Lib," he yelled. "She must have snuck over while I was in the shower."

"No problem," Libby yelled over the howls. "Stump likes to prove his big, brave guard-dog skills once in a while. Bob thinks it's because we let the vet emasculate him—his words, not mine."

"Makes sense," Dom laughed. "Cha-Cha! Get your lazy behind over here, troublemaker."

With a final lick, Cha-Cha leapt to the ground, inches from Stump. The *fearless* canine whimpered and rolled to his back and allowed the cat to pass without further fuss. Libby shook her head.

"Big wuss." She giggled. "Some protector you are. Come on; you've got a hot date with the hose." Stump trailed Libby to the backyard and willingly subjected to a good scrub.

Two lather-and-repeats later, she tossed him a doggie treat and left the dripping pooch sleeping in the sun to dry. On her way into the house, she turned back to check his water dish and caught Cha-Cha sneaking in. Before she could scoot her away, the cat curled up alongside Stump and settled in to nap.

"I swear, you two are an old married couple with tails," Libby said.

Entering the house, she checked the time, two o'clock. After a quick shower, she left for Mae's, purse loaded with patience-strengthening supplies: Chocolate, antacids, and more chocolate.

****

"You can do this," Libby gave herself a pep talk in the parking lot outside Mae's condominium. "She's your mother, be supportive."

Autumn Hills, a fifty-five-and-over complex, had been Sean's first solo construction project. Mae took immense pleasure in bragging about the exceptional artisanship to all who listened.

The six conjoined structures resembled New England-style ranch homes with dove gray exteriors, white trim, and black shutters. Although each occupant's front door was identical dark oak, the tenant's board, of which Mae was president, encouraged residents to decorate their entryways to reflect individual tastes.

No one would confirm or deny the rumor, but there was an implied competition between neighbors to display the most eye-catching entryway. Mae's porch, decorated with matching oversized red urns, was full to overflowing with yellow and orange mums. The front door opened, and Mae exited.

"Smile," Libby told herself. "Don't let her get to you."

Mae stormed to the car, climbed in, and slammed the door.

"You're in a hurry," Libby commented and backed out of the drive.

"This is nonsense," Mae harrumphed and picked specs of lint off her sensible navy blue velour tracksuit. "I'm old, what does the doctor expect to find? I think it's just another way to get more money out of me."

"Mom," Libby soothed, "I'm sure there's a valid reason Dr. Cooper wants you to see this neurologist."

Digging into her handbag, Mae pulled out a hubcap-sized pair of sunglasses and slid them on. "Cooper and this Rashan doctor are probably in cahoots," she speculated.

Libby shook her head but remained silent. In addition to her other strong opinions of medical professionals, Mae often indulged in conspiracy theories. "All those fancy specialists are the same," she continued. "They milk helpless seniors for unnecessary tests and spend the profits on fancy cars and vacations, while we struggle to survive."

Mae painted a picture of herself begging for change in the subway. Libby prayed for patience.

"You are hardly destitute, Mom," Libby said. "Daddy left you comfortable, and Dr. Cooper just wants to cover all the bases." She shifted approach. "It's okay to be a little afraid about today's visit. That's normal."

"I'm not afraid, Elizabeth," Mae protested. "The appointment is simply a waste of time, and I resent natural aging being treated as some type of dire illness." She tugged at the delicate necklace peeking from beneath her jacket.

"Mom, I can tell you're anxious, you're playing with your locket." For as long as Libby could remember, Mae fiddled with the heart-shaped locket in times of stress.

In the early years of their marriage, jewelry was a luxury Mae and Bernie could not afford. Despite the cost, Bernie had the delicate locket hand-crafted in honor of their late daughter Meghan, and engraved with her initials, MRM. Mae kept the treasured remembrance of their lost daughter close to her heart at all times. Holding the warm metal in her palm, Mae's voice shifted to a more neutral pitch.

"Enough about me and this ridiculous doctor visit," she said. "Tell me what's going on with the kids. How are they doing at school?"

After the academic and sports recap, Libby recounted the call from the school social worker.

"For the love of God," Mae boomed. "Charlie is six! How can that twitty woman diagnose him as a mass murder? For heaven's sake, he hasn't even got permanent teeth yet, let alone murderous instincts."

Libby tried to explain. "I know but—"

"But nothing! Kevin went to the bathroom outside until he was nine. Does that make him an exhibitionist? We only convinced him to use the toilet after that awful bee sting." Kevin's obsession with urinating everywhere except the bathroom affirmed Mae and Bernie's parenting skills.

"I'm not agreeing with the social worker," Libby said, "Bob and I want to see the artwork and if it raises concern, we'll decide whether or not to get Charlie professional help."

"Huh! Professional help." Mae scoffed. "Charlie is a sweet-natured little boy. Leave him be."

Spoken like a grandmother, Libby thought.

Mae went on. "Now that Sam friend of his," Mae continued, "he's got Connecticut Penal System written all over him. I bet a few dozen Hail Marys and a dose of those ADVD drugs would work wonders. Do you know if his parents take him to church? They should register him at Immaculate Conception. Catholic education would settle that mischief-maker right down."

"Sam's Jewish."

"Even better," Mae brightened. "Jews know how to raise successful, upstanding children. I think it's the Hebrew school, sucks the hellion right out of them."

Chapter Eleven

Mae checked in with Dr.Rashan's receptionist and sat down next to Libby.

"I told you," Mae whispered. "The ethnic doctors always make you wait. This wouldn't happen in an American waiting room." Libby cringed and bent at the waist.

"Did you drop something?" Mae asked.

"No." Libby answered.

"Then what are you looking for, dear?"

"A hole; I need a place to curl up and die when your commentary get us kicked out of here."

"Don't be such a drama queen."

Decorated with inspirational photographs, the sunny, bright waiting area wrapped patients in a welcoming atmosphere. Mae did not agree.

"This place is dismal," she scanned the room. "Like death's checkout line."

"I think it's kind of nice," Libby picked up a senior-driven magazine. "But that's probably because the only doctor's office I've been in lately has puppets—plus someone's always screaming, or leaking body fluid."

"Must you share everything in such vivid detail?"

"Must you be so negative?"

Neither spoke until a smiling, heavyset black nurse opened the waiting room door. "Mae McGinn?"

Mae stood.

"I'm Olivia, we're ready for you. Your daughter can come with us if you'd like?"

Mae hesitated. "Will I be naked?"

"Um, no," Olivia stammered.

"Well then,"—Mae turned to Libby—"do you want to come in, or is that magazine more important?"

Libby stood and followed. Mae's privacy was an integral part of her personality; Libby knew sharing something this personal was a silent plea for support.

Trailing behind Olivia down the beige hallway, Libby noticed each examining room door painted a different color.

"Here we are," Olivia said, "the blue room." She opened the door and ushered the women into the exam room.

It was not at all, what Libby expected. Alongside the exam table, a quaint cherry table and three matching chairs sat in the corner.

"Have a seat," Olivia said. "Can I get either of you something to drink while you wait? Water, coffee?"

"None for me." Libby replied.

"I'm fine," Mae answered. "Thank you, Olivia."

"My pleasure. Dr. Rashan will be in shortly." She shut the door behind her.

"Something to drink?" Mae shook her head. "What is this, a buffet?"

"Be nice," Libby scolded. "She wants you to feel comfortable."

"I haven't been comfortable since 1976. How is a paper cup full of stale coffee going to change that?"

Libby gave up and walked the room. Several framed magazine and newspaper articles hung on the walls.

"Did you see these?" she asked. "Dr. Rashan has been written up in some pretty impressive places; New England Journal of Medicine, New York Times."

"Good, I don't want some quack with a mail-order medical degree poking and prodding at me." The sound of clicking heels sounded just beyond the examining room door. Dr. Rashan—all four-foot-eleven of her—entered the room.

"Mrs. McGinn?" She closed the door and extended her hand. "I'm Dr. Rashan, sorry for the delay." Points for Dr. Rashan. Any wait warranted an apology, in Mae's book.

"Nice to meet you, doctor." Mae shook hands and gestured to Libby, "This is my daughter, Elizabeth O'Rourke."

"Call me Libby, please." She shook the physician's hand. "Thank you for seeing us today."

"My pleasure," Dr. Rashan joined them at the table. "Let's take some time to get acquainted, shall we?"

The women sat around the small table as Dr. Rashan placed Mae's chart in the center. Leaving the file unopened the doctor looked at Mae. "Mrs. McGinn, did Dr. Cooper explain why he referred you to me?"

Mae's eyes rolled. "He gave me some basic reasons—memory problems and such, but in truth, this seems like a waste of your time. I'm old. Forgetfulness is part of the package. There's no need to borrow worry over something that happens to all of us eventually."

"You are absolutely right," Dr. Rashan continued. "Many people obsess over worst case scenarios when memory becomes even slightly impaired." She opened the file and a small frown crossed her face. "My concern, however, is, in looking at your tests results—although typical for a woman in her early seventies—you have some underlying factors that put you at a higher risk for neurological problems."

Mae was indignant. "What *factors*?"

"Results from your physical show high blood pressure, marginally elevated cholesterol and your last cardiac work-up showed a condition called atherosclerosis, essentially a buildup of plaques on your artery walls. These factors, coupled with the results of the cognitive tests Dr. Cooper ran warrant today's visit."

Dr. Rashan closed the file and looked at Mae. "Mrs. McGinn, none of these results are uncommon individually, but together they can pose a problem. I need to take a full family history to rule out any genetic predispositions for stroke, dementia, and other varying conditions."

Libby recognized the elephant in the room. "Is Mom at risk for Alzheimer's?"

"Alzheimer's Disease is only one of many forms of dementia," Dr. Rashan calmly explained. "People mistakenly assume memory lapses in older adults must be Alzheimer's, but that is untrue. Dementia has multiple faces, but with the right diagnosis and treatment, symptoms and their impact on a patient's quality of life can be less severe. Most wait until it's too late to start treatment. Dr. Cooper rightfully recognized your early symptoms and sent you to me for a consultation. "

"And he got all this from a few little memory tests?" Mae was doubtful. "That seems like jumping the gun if you ask me."

The doctor's response was patient but firm. "I prefer to think of it as being cautious." She stood and removed a packet of forms from the file cabinet. "I have to admit, though, after reviewing your case, I have an ulterior motive."

"That sounds sinister." Mae said.

Dr. Rashan laughed. "Actually, I was hoping to convince you to take part in a research study I'm conducting."

"I'd be a senior lab rat?" Mae raised a brow.

The doctor's laughter intensified. "No, no." She passed the literature to Mae. "I'm on the board of St. Sebastian's Hospital and we are seeking volunteers for a study on aging, specifically, the effects lifestyle and diet play in the process."

"You want to study how people get old?" Mae grinned. "That sounds rather futile. Let me save you the grant money: we get old, we wrinkle, and we die. End of the study."

"To the contrary," Dr. Rashan answered. "Aging is fascinating. In particular, I would like to examine lifestyle choices, especially those of active seniors, and your profile fits the study precisely on target. I believe, and hopefully the study will conclude, activity reduces stress and diminishes the severity of age-related illness, dementia in particular."

Libby watched Mae for signs of reluctance, but none came.

The doctor continued. "Mrs. McGinn, based on Dr. Cooper's earlier tests, you have certain physical and cognitive signs that indicate dementia-related illness could be in your future. That is in no way certain, but the possibility exists. However, with the right tests and follow-up care, your prognosis is quite good. That's why I would love for you to be part of the study; your current health and active lifestyle make you an ideal candidate."

Looking down at the packet of information, Mae took notice of the people depicted in the glossy color photographs—happy, sipping iced tea on outdoor patios, surrounded by potted plants.

"You say this is a study on aging, and how it relates to dementia," Mae said. "But the people on these pamphlets look don't look looney."

"Mom!" Libby scolded.

"It's okay." Calmly, Dr.Rashan addressed Mae. "Mrs. McGinn, dementia is highly misunderstood. Undiagnosed, the illness can become overwhelming, but it does not have to be. It all depends on the individual and their treatment plan. Many people in their nineties only experience a hint of symptoms, while others much younger suffer debilitating consequences. I believe this may relate to their lifestyles and warrants a significant research study."

Having given this speech hundreds of times, the doctor knew fear when she heard it, and chose to answer honestly, and with simple-to-follow basics in hopes of diffusing patient concern. "At this point," she continued, "we are fact-finding. In your particular case, I see no reason for alarm."

"So, you want me to be part of your study because my case is potentially mild?" Mae questioned.

"Yes and no. Your case, if there is one, is early. With your permission, I am going to do some additional tests and take a detailed family history so we can get an accurate assessment. Is that okay with you?"

Nodding, Mae folded her hands together and waited for the questions.

"These are all fairly routine, but knowing your family history will give me vast insight into those risk factors we discussed earlier. In fact, family history might be the single most crucial piece of a puzzle when making a diagnosis. Let's start with your father."

"Irish." Mae said.

"That much I guessed." Smiling, the doctor continued, "I'm going to list some common medical conditions. If you know that your father had one of them, stop me, and we'll make a notation. Ready?"

"Yes."

For ten minutes, Dr. Rashan listed medical conditions, noting only that Mae's father, Michael Finn had minor medical issues and died in his thirties while serving his country.

"Now we'll move on to your mother."

Dr. Rashan methodically moved through the same lengthy list of medical conditions as Mae's patience waned. Although her perception of the doctor was one of competence and caring, Mae could not help but become frustrated. Talking about her mother was always upsetting.

"And what was your mother's cause of death?" Dr. Rashan asked. "And her age, if you remember."

"She died when she was sixty-one, it was a stroke." Mae started to stand. "Is that all? Are we done?"

Libby noticed Mae's increased tension. "Mom, sit down and let Dr.Rashan do her job. This isn't a race."

"I would appreciate it if you refrain from speaking to me like one of your kids, Elizabeth." Mae glared at

Libby.

Defusing the situation, the doctor continued. "This questioning can be very monotonous," Dr. Rashan explained. "However, it truly helps me get the most accurate accounting of your medical history."

"I'm sorry doctor," Libby interjected. "We tend to be a little oversensitive in our family."

"There is never a need for either of you to apologize. The fact that you asked your daughter to come with you today, Mrs. McGinn, shows me your family is supportive. Believe me, that is often not the case. Now I need a little bit more information about your mother's stroke. Was she ill, or was the attack sudden?"

"She wasn't eating and lost a tremendous amount of weight toward the end," Mae explained. "Mom stopped taking proper care of herself. My brother William and I felt it was best to place her in a nursing home so someone could keep an eye on her."

"Grandma Shannon was sixty-one?" Libby frowned. "I thought she was much older than that when she died."

Grateful for her daughter's question, Mae answered, "You were six, Libby. Thirty seems old when you're that age."

Dr. Rashan took vigorous notes. Mae's posture and tone of voice spoke volumes, cluing the doctor in to the fact her patient was withholding critical information. "Still," she said, "even with weight loss and malnutrition, stroke in an otherwise healthy adult that age is far younger than the norm. And you say she was in a nursing home?"

"Yes." Mae said.

"A skilled nursing facility most often requires a diagnosis other than what you have described in order to admit a patient. Can you remember any other reason your mother may have needed supervised medical care?"

Painted into a corner, Mae took a moment to compose her thoughts before answering. For a lifetime, she had shielded Libby and her sons from the extent of her mother's peculiar behaviors and mental decline. They were too young at the time of her death to understand, and she wanted the children to remember their grandmother as the fun-loving woman they adored, not the empty shell of madness she had become.

Coming clean now left her with a feeling of unease, she needed time to weigh out how best to share the complicated history without causing alarm over her own current symptoms. "My mother died a long time ago," Mae stalled. "She had a difficult life, losing a husband and raising two children alone couldn't have been easy. She never went to the doctor or did any type of exercise, she never had time. I assure you, Dr. Rashan, Mom may have been young when she died, but her soul had lived a hundred lives by the time the mental exhaustion caught up with her. I can't recall a specific diagnosis other than the stroke. Her physician at the time claimed a nursing home was the best place for her; William and I agreed."

"I completely understand." Dr. Rashan said. "You mentioned a brother, William? Is he still living?"

"Yes."

"Would it be all right if I spoke with him?"

Mae's hackles rose. "Why on Earth would you

need to speak with Will?"

Libby jumped in. "Mom, there's no need to get angry."

"I'm not angry," Mae said. "I just don't see why she needs to speak with Will. He has nothing to do with my health."

"I'm sorry. Let me explain," Dr. Rashan said. "I would not, under any circumstances, share confidential information regarding your treatment with William. Anything that transpires between you and me falls under doctor-patient privilege and remains private regardless of what William and I discuss. However, his recollections of your parents' medical histories could include details you may not be privy to, especially during your mother's end-of-life care."

She clicked her ballpoint pen and slid it into her pocket. "In addition, on a selfish note, should you decide to participate in the research study, I would love to include your brother, as well. Siblings have similar DNA, and yet the aging process may be dramatically different. Your brother may not follow your excellent example and schedule yearly physicals, and it's always beneficial for families to encourage each other to stay on top of their health, asking him to participate in the study may force him to do that."

Mae grabbed at her locket. "I suppose it would be all right," she said, "but Will lives in Florida. I don't have his phone number with me."

"Wait a minute..." Libby dug into her purse and pulled out a cell phone. "I have it."

"Of course you do." her mother muttered, as Libby relayed both Will's and her own contact information.

"William is a homosexual," Mae said with a

glare—daring Dr. Rashan to say something derogatory. "Does that disqualify him for your study?"

"Oh God," Libby moaned. "Please, Mom, I'm begging you…"

"Quiet." Mae held up a hand. "I'm talking with the doctor. This does not concern you."

Dr. Rashan cleared her throat and kept a firm grasp on her professionalism. "Sexual orientation does not factor into the study," she answered. "If William is interested in participating, I would be pleased to have him."

"Oh, well," Mae stumbled, "it's perfectly acceptable if you include his gayness. He won't mind, and neither will my family. We are tremendously proud of him as a person. William is an accomplished artist. A few of his gentlemen friends have a lovely gallery by the beach, very upscale, all the celebrities shop there." Mae loved her older brother to the moon and back. "His lifestyle is welcome in Key West. That's why he left Brooklyn; it's hard to be homosexual in Brooklyn."

"I'm sure William is a wonderful person." Dr. Rashan smiled and closed the file. "I look forward to speaking with him. Now, let's run a few basic wellness tests for a baseline. Have a seat on the exam table and we'll get started."

Mae sat stock still as Dr. Rashan performed routine visual, reflex, and auditory tests.

She uploaded the findings to a handheld computer.

"What would you young people do without your gadgets?" Mae said.

"Smoke signals," Libby teased. "Pony express…the possibilities are endless."

Mae glared.

Dr. Rashan placed the device in the pocket of her lab coat. "Tracking my patients this way works well. The possibility of misplaced results is minimal, and many patients find it reassuring to know their test results, and confidential information is only being accessed by me, or my nurse. Privacy is paramount in our office."

"Well, that makes perfect sense." Mae stood. "Are we finished? May I go?"

"Mom, you sound like Charlie after his dental check-up. There's no rush." Libby said.

"I'm sure Dr. Rashan has other patients, Elizabeth," Mae lectured. "We need to show respect for her valuable time and let her get on with her day."

My, how the tables have turned, Libby thought, *the ethnic woman doctor is now Mae's champion.*

Dr. Rashan said, "We are done. However, before you leave, Olivia will draw some blood. And we'll schedule an appointment to go over the test results." She excused herself.

Without so much as a flinch from Mae, Olivia had the vial drawn, and the group met Dr. Rashan at the appointment desk.

"Olivia," Dr. Rashan said, "let's find Mrs. McGinn a spot two weeks from now." The nurse scrolled the computer for an open appointment.

"Was Thursday convenient for you, Mrs. McGinn, or would you prefer another day?" Olivia asked.

"Keep Thursday," Libby, answered. "I'm off that day."

Mae pounced. "Why don't I wait until I get home to schedule? I'll call Sean. I'm sure he can find the time to do the next appointment." She patted Dr. Rashan's hand. "My son always makes room for me in his schedule, even though he's so frightfully busy with his successful construction company."

Libby groaned. Mae wife-shopped for Sean at every opportunity.

"I'm sure Sean would be happy to help, Mom," Libby said. "But he may be busy healing the lepers that afternoon. I'll bring you."

"Tone, Elizabeth."

Olivia bit back laughter. "That puts us on November seventh; any time preference?"

"Mom?" Libby said. "I'm free all day."

"We have four o'clock available again," Olivia offered.

"That's fine." Mae sighed and turned to Dr. Rashan. "Will I need to bring anything with me?" Her voice hushed. "You know, like a urine sample or bowel movement? I wasn't sure, so I didn't bring any this time."

Whenever Libby thought her mother could not say anything more to surprise her, she did. "Speaking as your chauffer," she teased, "I appreciate not having those little gifts in the car with us. Poop in your purse would have distracted me the entire drive."

"Really Elizabeth, your mouth is more and more like your father's every day."

Dr. Rashan could not help but smile. "Samples are not necessary at this point, but thank you for thinking ahead." Extending her hand to Mae, she continued, "It was a pleasure meeting you, Mrs. McGinn. I look forward to getting to know you better."

Mae shook her hand. "Thank you doctor, I'll see you in a few weeks." Keeping her grip in place, she asked, "By any chance, are you married, dear?"

"Yes, I am. Why do you ask?"

Libby groaned. "Do you have no limits, Mae McGinn? I'm sorry doctor, God love her, Mom is attempting to marry off my bachelor brother."

"Oh." Dr. Rashan chuckled. "It's very sweet of you to ask; I'm sure your son is lovely."

"Just thought I'd check." Mae reached for the exit door before spinning back. "Do you have a sister?"

Chapter Twelve

Saturday was soccer day. Without fail, Shannon and Charlie had games at the same time on opposite ends of town. Libby and Bob decided who attended which game over breakfast. Shannon's match-ups were decidedly more fun to watch, but Charlie's team provided circus-like entertainment, spontaneous cartwheels, and dandelion-picking contests were common. No one kept score, and no matter how hard Coach Tony tried to strategize, the team was always more interested in the postgame snack than athletics. Libby drew the short straw.

Packing the van with children, folding chairs, and one smelly dog, she headed to the field. Charlie and his partner-in-crime, Sam, huddled together in deep, backseat plotting. "What plan are you two masterminds hatching back there?" Libby asked.

Charlie met his mother's stare in the rearview mirror. "If we're really, really good can we go to The Shack after the game?" he pleaded. Home to the finest clog-your-arteries food in the world, The Shack's cuisine was taboo. Healthy soccer moms shunned those who partook.

When pregnant with Charlie, Libby's Shack french fry cravings rivaled methadone addiction, going so far as to borrowing Sean's company truck and scarfing down lunch incognito. Little did the snooty soccer moms know Libby was indulging her inner grease diva.

Drooling at the thought of fries, Libby snapped back to reality. "I don't know," she said. "Don't you get a snack after the game?"

Sam answered. "It's Mrs. Swanson's turn to bring a snack; raisins."

Agnes Swanson was a hardcore healthy mom and Libby welcomed her oranges or other fruits, but she drew the line at raisins. Raisins were grapes someone forgot in the crisper.

At the field, Sam and Charlie jumped out of the minivan and ran to join their teammates. Libby popped open the rear door and freed Stump as he charged off at a gallop to tackle the boys. Grabbing her travel coffee mug and folding chair, she walked over to join the crowd.

At the end of the first quarter, the team took a water break and Coach Tony gave the traditional pep talk. "You guys are doing fantastic!" He beamed. "Good teamwork, and even better, nobody cried yet. A little more work on our offense and I think there's a decent chance we may even get a goal today." The team had yet to score this season, but Tony was optimistic.

As the players headed back to the field, Libby's phone rang; the display read "Hubby."

"Hi," Libby answered.

"Hey hon, what's the report?" Bob asked. "Will anything make the Rhyme Top Play Run-down tonight?"

"Not unless all other organized sporting events take the day off." Libby watched Charlie block a shot on goal. "Nice one, Charlie!"

"Did he find a dandelion?" Bob teased.

"Nope, he actually touched the ball." Libby laughed. "Wonders never cease. How's Shannon doing?"

"Still nothing-nothing. However, I did learn another valuable parenting lesson."

"Do tell."

"In addition to the new drop off/pick up procedures at school, I am no longer allowed to cheer at her games. Apparently this is social homicide."

Libby grinned into the phone. "Did she tell you to be quiet?"

"No, I just got the look-of-mortification." Bob took his shortcomings in stride, but Shannon was still his baby. "Are we all meeting back at home for lunch?"

"I've been solicited to hit The Shack."

Bob let out an appreciative groan. "How about it?"

Libby needed little convincing. "It's okay with me. But I swear to God, Robert O'Rourke, if you give Stump even one bloody french fry, I'll kill you in your sleep!" Human food always exaggerated Stump's issues.

"Consider me warned."

"I'll be there first. Tell me what you want and I'll order."

"Such service! I like this."

"Don't get used to it. It's the lure of the fries that makes me accommodating."

Bob placed his order and rang off.

Postgame, Libby packed the troops in the minivan and headed down Main Street. Each storefront was marked with a yellow Halloween Parade Participant sign and festively decorated for the town council trick-or-treat display contest. Pumpkins, hay bales, and cornstalks ate up small window spaces in an effort to tempt children in for sweet treats. Ironically, as Libby passed the dentist, Dr. Tyler, he too had a trick-or-treat sign.

"Job security," she mumbled.

At The Shack, Libby spotted Caroline's car. Glancing around, she located her friend on line with Trevor. Charlie and Sam ran over to meet them as Libby strapped a leash on Stump. The smell of grilling meat and fry oil had his massive jowls dripping with saliva.

"Not pretty, Stump." She wiped him down with one of the many sports towels in her backseat. "Behave yourself. No food snatching, got it?" The dog looked at her, his large brown eyes begging for a treat.

Joining the group, Libby was stunned at Trevor's latest growth spurt. The spitting image of his father, Trevor had more charisma than he knew what to do with, evident by the swarm of giddy teen girls competing for his attention.

The groupies broke away as Libby spoke up. "I see you suckered your mom into grease today, too?"

"Hi, Aunt Libby." Trevor's voice had not fully changed and tended to rotate octaves. "It was Mom's idea. She said she needed 'comfort food,' whatever that means."

The moms exchanged a look. Libby said, "Trev, can you take Stump to a, um, private area for me so he can make a deposit?" Trevor loved dogs, but with Caroline's schedule and his afterschool activities he knew they did not have the time a pet needed.

"Sure." He took the leash from Libby. "Come on buddy, let's go drop a bomb somewhere and blame it on that snotty poodle over there."

As Trev headed away, Libby turned to Caroline. "Okay, spill it"

"What?" Caroline feigned urgent interest in the menu board overhead.

"Don't give me that. I've known you too long." Libby stuck her face in front of Caroline's view. "You don't need 'comfort food' aka 'crap' unless it's man trouble; dish it." The jig was up, and Caroline knew it. Libby could spot avoidance a mile away.

"It's no big deal," Caroline said. "My date with Richard was...hmm, I guess the best way to put it is...flat. No wow factor."

"So," Libby giggled. "Dick was a dud?"

Caroline burst out laughing. "How long have you been working on that literary gem?"

"It just came to me now. I should write greeting cards." Caroline's order came to the window. Libby grabbed a french fry off her tray. With the first bite, she moaned. "Did you let Richard down easy or stomp his bean-counting heart?"

"It was mutual." Caroline slid down the counter and grabbed napkins and condiments. "There's a rule when you date over forty; if at first there is not spark, run, and run away."

"Got it," Libby placed her order then joined Caroline at the ketchup. "Any other man-prospects on the horizon?"

"I'm taking a hiatus; thus fat and salt for lunch." Caroline popped a fry into her mouth. "I'm instituting Big Pants November. I'll let myself gain a few pounds of self-pity then jump back on the horse in December."

"Sounds like a workable plan." Libby's order

arrived, and the friends snagged a spot at the largest picnic table available.

"There is a plus side to dating in winter," Libby said. "Big sweaters hide all."

"My thoughts exactly." Caroline scanned for Trevor. He was surrounded by short-skirted girls feigning interest in Stump. "Your pooch is a chick magnet for my hormone-driven son."

Libby turned in Caroline's direction. "That won't last. I saw Stump scarf a hot dog off the ground. Any minute now the smell will send them running for higher ground."

"Poor Stump, he still has tummy problems?"

"Yeah, but we love him anyway."

Libby called the kids over for lunch. Charlie and Sam inhaled without a break for breath while Trevor, a close second, managed to work in a few text messages between bites. Caroline assumed the mildly disruptive texts were coming from the pint-sized super model batting her eyes from the adjacent table.

Catching on quick, Libby met her friend's eyes in silent amusement. "Tell me, Trev," she asked, "got a girlfriend yet?"

His cheeks reddened. "Nah, I'm cool right now. " He flipped his blond bangs back in his best pop star impression. "I'm playing soccer and hanging out, nothing serious, ya know?"

"Yeah, that's cool." Libby did her best not to chuckle. "How was your game today?"

Mouthful of burger, he replied. "I got a sick goal in the second quarter."

"Good for you, Trev, great job!"

"Yeah, thanks." He swallowed. "Coach said I got a

good chance at varsity next year."

Caroline frowned. Trevor had been hitting the brag button a little hard lately. "Don't get ahead of yourself," she warned. "JV is just as competitive as varsity."

"Mom." Trevor's you-just-don't-get-it expression said it all. "Varsity is a completely different gig." He patted his mother tolerantly on the shoulder and walked away to join a group of friends that had just arrived. Caroline's jaw hung open.

"Did he just say gig?" She moaned.

"I believe he did," Libby answered.

Caroline watched her baby boy swagger to a group of teenagers gathered at the opposite end of the picnic tables. Ten years had passed since she dropped him off for his first day of kindergarten; the frightened blond-haired, blue-eyed little boy had turned into a sullen teenager overnight.

Physically he resembled his father, but that is where the similarity ended. Caroline's ex-husband, Steve, was a wad of balding arrogance, and his behavior alienated friends and family at a rapid rate. A massive ego left him poor in relationships as well as love, and Caroline prayed Trevor took a better path in life.

The sound of tires on the gravel parking lot made Libby turn around. "Damn, Bob's here," she said. "I was just about to eat his fries."

Caroline motioned to the order window. "There's no line, get more. You can borrow my fat pants."

"No. I'll look like a pig getting seconds."

"But plowing through Bob's fries before he gets here is better?"

"That's sharing. Gluttony rules don't apply."

Shannon sat down at the table. "We lost."

Libby put her arm around her shoulder; losing was a common occurrence. "Too bad," she consoled. "Was it close?"

"Final score was two to one."

"They had a great game!" Bob interjected between gulps of chocolate shake. "Shannon was a rock star, really brought her A-game!"

"Geez, Dad, A-game?" Shannon winced. "You're weird. Can I go sit with my friends, Mom?"

"Go ahead." Libby answered. "Take Stump with you, I don't want your *weirdo* father sneaking him any food."

Shannon grabbed her meal and walked off with Stump to join the group of chatting teenagers. Bob took the ketchup bottle from the center of the table and added a healthy squeeze to his fries.

"Now I'm weird." He shoveled in a mouthful of fries. "I wonder when she'll like me again. Was Bernie ever weird, Lib?"

"Always," Libby said. "But I loved him to bits." Sneaking one of Bob's fries, she turned to Caroline. "How about your dad, was he a constant embarrassment?"

"Total geek," Caroline said. "I believe I was a freshman in college when I started to like him again. High school was rough, and my hormones were insane. Dad didn't have a clue how to talk to me."

"Great," Bob said. "I've got a minimum of four more years of disdain to look forward to."

In the time it took the group to finish lunch, several cars packed with hungry grease hunters came and went. Shannon and Trevor wandered back to their parents, and Sam and Charlie returned blessedly empty-handed from their search for dead stuff on the beach.

Slurping up the last bits of chocolate shake, Bob remembered a phone message. "I almost forgot to tell you, Lib. I called home; there was a message from Uncle Will. Call him back when you get a minute."

Libby adored her mother's brother. Family trips to his home in the Keys were some of the O'Rourke's most treasured memories. Will took Shannon and Charlie out on his boat in search of dolphins and other adventures while she and Bob relaxed on the beach, frosty drinks in hand. Will's home was a classic beach cottage, walls covered in beautiful watercolors and tapestries designed by area artists, the same talented people featured in his gallery. The entire atmosphere was open, inviting, and conducive to relaxation. Recalling their last visit, Libby could almost smell the coconut-scented sunblock.

"I miss Uncle Will," she said. "Did he say what he wanted?"

"Nope." Bob wiped the shake dribble from around his mouth. "He just asked you to give him a ring when you can."

Wrappers and cups gathered and trashed, the group broke and headed home. Libby had to return Sam to his mom, so she sent Stump home in Bob's car. It was about time her husband enjoyed the after-effects of canine irritable bowel.

At home, Sean's truck was in the driveway and a ladder leaned against the side of the house. Deathly afraid of heights, Bob had asked Sean to tack down a few roof shingles for him after the last rainstorm. The group followed the sound of hammering to the backyard.

Charlie spotted him first. "Hey Uncle Sean! Can I come help you?"

Bob grabbed the back of Charlie's sweatshirt. "No way, bud. Uncle Sean can handle this all by himself." He sniffed his son's head. "You smell like old socks—go shower."

"Fine." Charlie hung his head and went into the house. Shannon trailed behind him, eager to check her email.

Turning his face toward the roof, Bob spoke. "You didn't have to come out here right away, this could have waited."

"I had time." Sean answered. "How were the games? Any goals for the kids? Or scantily clad single moms for their uncle?" Libby came around the corner of the house just in time to hear her sexist brother.

"I heard that," she scolded. "And even if there were any loose soccer moms, you wouldn't let me set you up anyway."

"I didn't ask for you to set me up." He fired a nail. "They're just fun to look at."

"You are a pig."

"It's a gift." He gathered up his tools and climbed down the ladder. Stump waited at the bottom rung.

"Hey there, Stump." He wiped the dog's affectionate kiss from the back of his hand. "How do you keep yourself from tripping over that yard of tongue?"

"He couldn't be better." Libby answered. "We hit The Shack for post-soccer lunch, and he feasted on fallen hot dogs."

Sean's brow rose. "That will be fun later."

"Yeah, lucky us." Libby tossed her purse down on the porch and took a seat on the bottom step. "So, did José end up coming back after the Mrs. Lerner debacle?"

He set his toolbox down and took a seat next to his sister. "Oh yeah, he came back." Wiping the sweat from his face, he continued. "I had to swear a blood oath never to ask him to go back there. Poor guy was traumatized."

"Can you blame him?" Bob asked, "He's shy to begin with. He'll probably need therapy, better check your workers comp policy." Heading up the porch steps, he asked, "I'm getting a beer, anybody want one?"

Lib raised her hand.

"I'll take one, too," Sean answered. "Hold on—it's not that girly beer Kev gave me yesterday, right? Some Pumpkin Harvest crap. Beer and pumpkins should never be in the same bottle—defies the rules of manhood."

"We've got plain old draft," Bob said. "Will that keep your manhood intact?"

"God bless you."

Beers in hand, Libby, Sean, and Bob sat on the back porch enjoying the late fall afternoon. Two days before Halloween, the yard looked like an orange and yellow patchwork quilt. Tall oaks shed their leaves at a rapid pace. Four misshapen pumpkins waited for carving on the back step.

"Uncle Will called today." Libby said to Sean.

Sean's face brightened. "How is crazy Will?"

"Don't know, he left a message. I need to call him back."

"I should go down and visit him." Sean finished his beer and threw the bottle into the nearby recycle bin. "A little sun and R&R sound good right about now. Just thinking about that grouper place down the street from his place makes me drool."

Charlie crashed onto the porch. "Mom," he panted, "can we carve the pumpkins now? You said 'later,' and it's later."

Pumpkin carving was Libby's least favorite holiday tradition. Each year it was the same story; Charlie and Shannon, bursting with excitement, drew intricate faces to carve on their individual pumpkins, but when Libby would cut the tops off to scoop out the guts, poof, the kids vanished. She got the guts and none of the glory.

Taking her final sip, Libby tossed the bottle into the bin along with Sean's empty.

"Go get the big knife and newspapers to put underneath," she told Charlie. Bob stood. She grabbed his arm. "Don't even think of leaving me to do this alone, you're helping."

"Your wish is my command," Bob answered. "But I'm getting another beer first." Libby released him and set her sights on Sean. "How about you, want in on the pumpkin carnage?"

Sean inched toward the driveway. "As fun as it sounds, I'm going to pass this time." Charlie came out, supplies in hand. Sean said, "Do me a favor pal, save me the dark chocolate from your massive Halloween haul."

"Will do," Charlie answered, "You want the chocolate raisins? I hate those."

"No way, I hate those too, they look like rabbit

turds." Raisins were a mutual McGinn hatred. Fishing his keys out of his pocket, Sean headed toward his truck, "I'll talk to you guys later, and Libby, when you touch base with Uncle Will, tell him I said hello."

****

True to form, Charlie, Shannon, and even Bob disappeared for the gut-scooping portion of the carving process. Staring down four decapitated pumpkins, Libby decided the dirty chore would pass faster with a distraction and rang Uncle Will. Setting her cell phone down on the step beside her, she pressed the speaker button. Will answered.

"Is this my exceptionally smart, and equally beautiful niece, Elizabeth?" Will gushed. A native New Yorker, his voice had never absorbed the Brooklyn inflection and, somewhere down the road adopted a refined, southern distinction

"None other," Libby answered. "How are you Uncle Will? It's been ages since I've seen you!"

"Now whose fault is that, Mrs. O'Rourke?" he scolded. "I invite you to my little piece of heaven constantly, yet you rarely grace my doorstep."

"One of these days my jailors will let me run away and join you for a nice long visit." She scraped pumpkin guts and smiled at the possibility. "But until then you'll have to tolerate my witty emails and far-too-infrequent phone calls."

"I suppose I'll forgive you, but come soon, dear. I'm older than dirt, and you never know when my expiration date will be due."

Libby smiled, mentally picturing Uncle Will and his little beach house.

His small frame settled into one of the tattered

wicker chairs on the back porch overlooking the surf. Adjusting his wire rim glasses, he prepared for a nice chat. "Onto the reason for my earlier call," he said. "Who is Dr. Rashan, and why does she want the sordid details of our family medical history?"

Libby paused mid-scoop. "I take it she called you?"

"Yes, lovely woman," Will answered. "However, I informed her I needed to speak to you first before answering any questions."

"She's great, very well respected, *and* crazy enough to sign on as Mom's neurologist."

Will released a small laugh. "I am sure Mae is thrilled with an *ethnic* woman doctor."

"You know Mae so well." Libby chuckled. "Believe it or not, Mom likes her. She even tried to set her up with Sean."

"That poor boy," Will admonished. "My sister has no shame when it comes to potential grandchildren." He cleared his throat and changed to a more serious tone. "Tell me, what's happening with Mae? My sister has yet to return my call, rude woman, so I have no idea why she needs a neurologist."

Libby brought Will up to speed. "I don't think Dr. Rashan is overly concerned, but the more family history she has to work from, the more she can rule out. Mom told her Grandpa died in the service, and Grandma had a stroke, but very little else. To tell the truth, Mom was somewhat odd about the whole thing, and kept rushing to get out of the office. I've never seen her in such a hurry to leave somewhere."

Will was quiet and Libby assumed the connection dropped. "Hello? Uncle Will? Did I lose you?"

"No, no dear," he answered. "I'm here, just pondering a bit."

"Care to let me in on your pondering?"

He took a moment to gather his thoughts. "I'm curious sweetheart, has Mae ever spoken to you about your Grandma Shannon's last few months, before the stroke?"

Libby thought a minute. When was the last time her mother had spoken about Shannon? "No, now that you mention it, Mom hasn't talked about Grandma in years. All I know is what I remember from when I was little. God, Gram was a character, funny, great dancer. I still remember those visits to Brooklyn. We had a ball back then, but all of a sudden, I don't know what happened, the visits stopped."

"Mother loved having you kids for those visits," William reminisced. "We went to the market before you arrived so she could stock up on chocolate, cake, and all the other sugar-laden treats Mae forbade."

"Mae loved having a break from us," Libby said, "even if we did come back in candy withdrawal."

Will laughed. "I remember the first time she left you three with Mother. Mae had all these lists with what you liked to eat, when bedtime was, and the like. As soon as she left Mother tossed the lists and set out to spoil all of you rotten."

"Hey." Libby feigned insult, "I'm not rotten. I turned out fairly well-balanced."

"Yes dear, you certainly did."

"It's funny, I remember Mom giving Grandma those lists. She was so retentive, even then." Libby paused for a second. "She never stayed overnight with us. She and Dad headed back home right away. I guess they needed the break."

"Once your mother left Brooklyn, she rarely came back." He paused. "It was easier that way."

"You make it sound like coming back was a punishment?" Libby said.

"Not a punishment, per se, Libby. But coming into the city brought sad memories for your mom."

"From the accident?"

"Among other things." He quickly shifted topics before Libby could probe further. "So you say Mae rushed through the appointment with the doctor?"

"Yes." Libby said.

"But she answered the questions?"

"Minimally; Mom got defensive when Dr. Rashan asked if she could speak with you. At first I thought it was because she was thought the doctor didn't trust her answers, but then she mentioned her research study and Mom seemed to settle down and be receptive to the idea."

"I see." Will had a decent idea why Mae was defensive, and suspected Dr.Rashan knew her patient was withholding information. All the pieces of the puzzle started to come together. His sister deliberately withheld their mother's mental decline from Libby and her doctor out of fear she was suffering the same fate. Mae obviously did not want him to convey the full truth to the physician, but Will knew that early intervention was critical.

"Uncle Will," Libby questioned, "What am I missing? Obviously you want to tell me something, but you're holding back."

"Not holding back dear," he answered. "Deciding where my place is. I'm not your parent; I'm the adoring eccentric Uncle. I must tread carefully." Will took a sip of his iced tea and pinched the bridge of his nose. "I'm going to share a few elements your mother omitted, for whatever reason, regarding Grandma Shannon."

"Elements?" Libby asked.

"Yes sweetheart," William explained. "Before I continue, I want you to promise not to jump all over your mother for being evasive. I'm a feeble old man; Mae scares me, always has. I don't want her showing up on my doorstep in brass knuckles. Moreover, she's your mother. The choices she makes are her own and she owes no explanations. Agreed?"

"Okay, now I'm a little scared."

"Absolutely no reason to be," Will said. "But since this doctor is going to speak with me too, and—channeling my inner George Washington, 'I cannot tell a lie'—the cat will be out of the bag soon enough. You need the entire picture."

William patiently explained Shannon's end of life challenges. Traveling down that particular stretch of memory lane brought pained feelings to the surface but provided Libby with an accurate accounting of the family history.

Seeing his mother's rapid decline had devastated Will, and knowing there was a chance he and his sister were genetically predisposed to the same condition left him feeling unsettled.

Irritated, Libby questioned him. "Jesus Christ, why on earth would Mom not tell me this?" Libby exploded. "If she witnessed her mother go through what sounds like significant dementia, wouldn't she want to be proactive in her own care and give the doctor all the information? Hell, even if she doesn't want to face it, what if I'm at risk—or my kids?"

"Don't get ahead of yourself, Libby," Will stated. "I don't think Mae is misleading you intentionally. Her thought process, if you can call it that, I assume was to shield you from anything bad."

Will cut Libby off before she could interject. "She's your mother, she doesn't want you to worry about her. It's *her* job to worry. And before you blow a clot, I'm sure the other factor here is fear. You were not there, Libby, my mother's decline was rapid and frightening. Mae is probably terrified she's destined for the same fate."

"For the sake of argument," Libby said, "let's say Mom thought she was protecting me. That still does not explain lying to Dr.Rashan; how can she help with preventative care if Mom gives her half-truths?"

"She's not thinking clearly, Libby. And that's not to imply her mind is failing. She is afraid. Mae is intensely private when it comes to her personal matters, and whether or not you agree with her methods, you must respect her wishes."

Libby's feelings were a jumble. She was angry with Mae for keeping secrets, and yet helpless to do anything to convince her mother to share her anxiety. Mae maintained control in her life, even in the most chaotic of circumstances. The possibility of losing that hold must be unbearable. "All right, Uncle Will, I'll take it slow. For your safety I'll speak to Mom calmly and without a hint of Irish temper."

"Good girl," Will answered.

"Is there anything else I should know before I talk to her? Was I adopted, born a boy, anything?"

Will laughed at her knack for lightening the darkest

mood. "As far as I know you were born with the same equipment you have today. And as far as adoption, not a chance. You have your father's awful frizzy hair."

"Flattery will get you nowhere."

"Honestly Elizabeth, cream rinse, that's all I ask."

"You blatantly feed the gay stereotype monster so many people try to destroy."

"I came out of the closet in my late fifties. There's a lot of pent up homosexual humor to release."

"I love you, Uncle Will. You keep me sane in this family asylum."

"Glad to help. Now I've got to ring off, but I'll call the doctor back on Monday, and of course prepare for my sister's verbal beating on Tuesday. Approach with caution, Libby, Mae is small, but explosive when cornered."

"Good advice and we'll chat after I speak with Mom. Take care of yourself Uncle Beach Bum."

"You too, honey. I'll be in touch, give my love to your brood and those delinquent brothers of yours."

Disconnecting, Libby realized she needed a few days to figure out the best way to approach Mae. One thing was for sure, the conversation would require extreme sensitivity and a large, pink box from Annie's Bake Shop.

Chapter Thirteen

Charlie stormed into the kitchen, after school on Monday, concern on his face. Tossing his backpack onto the table, he took a seat next to Libby.

Sipping from her ever- present coffee mug, she greeted him. "Hey buddy, how was school?".

"Okay." Charlie's small voice was laced with apprehension. "Miss Simon sent home a big envelope for you. Did I do something wrong?"

Poor kid, Libby thought, *notes home usually mean punishment.* "Nope," she answered. "Miss Simon thought your artwork was interesting and sent it home so I could take a look at it."

"Oh, I guess that's okay then." He slipped his sweatshirt over his head and tossed it onto the floor. "Do we have any good snacks? Please don't say granola bars." *Good snacks* for the O'Rourke family involved a chocolate or cheese coating.

"Check the pantry. I don't think Dad polished off all the cookies yet."

"Cool."

Libby reached into Charlie's backpack and extracted the so-called *disturbing* artwork. At first glance, the pictures looked like any young boy's imaginary life—battles and castles. But the theme of the assignment was family.

"Charlie, come over and sit with your old Mom

while you chow down." He sat and bit into a cookie.

"These are kind of stale." Charlie said.

"That's because your father cannot seem to master closing the bag when he's done snacking."

She looked closer at Charlie's pictures. "Miss Simon says these are supposed to be about family, but I must not pay close attention to the backyard. When did we get castles and wolves?" Charlie erupted in giggles.

"What's so funny?" She asked.

"That's not a wolf!" he said. "It's Stump."

Well, that makes sense, Libby thought silently. "Okay, it's Stump. I can see that now." She continued. "But why is he eating this, um, is that a deer?"

"No, Mom," Charlie sighed in frustration. "That's Cha-Cha. Stump is chasing him out of the sandbox. See?" He pointed out the sandcastle and the cast of characters. Relieved, Libby had the answer to the dark nature of the pictures, Stump and Cha-Cha were family, albeit four-legged, but she still had no explanation for the black color scheme.

"Did you pick all black for a reason?" She asked.

"I don't understand? Did I do a bad job?" His lip quivered.

"No, sweetie." She hugged him. "I think these are fantastic pictures; you're a great artist!"

"Then what did I do wrong?"

Libby put a hand on his baby soft cheek. "You didn't do anything wrong. I was just wondering why you didn't use any other colors. Like maybe orange for Cha-Cha, or some yellow for the leaves."

"I can't," he whispered, refusing to meet her eye to eye.

Is this a bullying issue? "Why can't you use

different colors?" She asked. "Is some kid telling you can't have the crayons?" He shook his head. She kicked herself for tossing all the parenting magazines directly into the recycle bin. "Do you feel sad, Charlie? Is that why you draw with black?"

"No," He started to shake. "You are going to be mad, really mad. This is my fault."

Oh God, this is bad, Libby thought. *There is something terribly wrong; Charlie has some deep dark issue buried under his cute little moon-pie face.*

"What is it Charlie?" She asked. "You can tell Mommy anything, I won't be mad."

"You promise?"

"Yes, please tell me."

"It was Sam's idea."

Uh-oh. "Go on."

"Well, art class is after recess, but before snack," Charlie began. "When we come in from the playground and put our coats in the cubby room Sam and I wait for everyone to go into art, and...you really won't be mad, right?"

"Yes Charlie, you have my word. Spit it out."

"Okay, when everyone goes into art, Sam and I stay behind and go in the other kids' backpacks and see if they have better snacks than us, and switch them."

"Charlie, someone's mom or dad packed those snacks. How would you feel if someone did that to you?"

"Bad, I guess."

"Yes, you would." Libby continued, "But I still don't understand. What does stealing snacks have to do with coloring in all black?"

"Oh, sorry, I forgot." Charlie's mood perked up

considerably after the confession. "By the time Sam and I get to art, the black crayons are the only ones left in the big box; all the other kids take the good colors."

Thank God. Charlie's not depressed. He's just a petty thief. She could not wait to share her findings with the all-knowing Miss Simon.

"Am I in trouble?" Charlie asked.

"I am very disappointed in you," Libby said. "But as long as you stop the snack switching, we'll let this one slide. That goes for Sam, too. Do I make myself clear Charles James O'Rourke?" Taking a branch of Mae's discipline tree, Libby broke out middle names when metering punishment.

"Thanks Mom." He hugged her, the scent of cookies and milk mixing with boy sweat.

"Go do your homework." Libby smiled at her freckled felon. "Coach Tony canceled soccer because of the rain."

"Cool! No practice." Charlie ran up the stairs to his room. Model cars were calling.

Libby finished her coffee and put the mug into the dishwasher. A night with no activities was a welcome change. Of course now she felt obligated to muster up a dinner consisting of more than hot dogs. She opened the fridge.

"Hmm, let's see what magically comes to me." Uninspired, she moved the milk gallon and revealed something that could once have been cheese. She dug deeper as Bob and Shannon came in the backdoor.

"Hey Mom, what's for dinner?" Shannon tossed her backpack by the door and kicked off her sneakers. Stump grabbed one of the discarded shoes and headed off for parts unknown.

118

"Dinner is up for debate," Libby answered. "I was just going to do hot dogs and apples before Charlie headed out for soccer, but they just cancelled practice. I'm thinking of something a little more substantial."

Bob and Shannon exchanged a concerned look. Taking in their apprehension, Libby said, "Don't panic, I'm talking about spaghetti and meatballs, not French cuisine."

Bob walked over to his wife, kissing her soundly on the mouth. "My stomach lining thanks you," he said. "We're still recovering from last week's Pad Thai experiment."

"That was good!" Libby shouted.

Shannon giggled. "Mom, even Stump wouldn't eat it. What does that tell you?"

"So I'm not a gourmet chef. Live with it."

"I'll be in my room, call me when dinner is ready." Shannon ran up the stairs. Within minutes music pounded through the floorboards.

Bob looked up at the ceiling. "I know I'm going to sound like my father, but how does she concentrate with all that noise?"

"She gets straight A's," Libby answered. "Let her rock-the-house if it gets the job done."

"True, I'm going to go get into my sweats. I'll be back to help with the salad."

Libby got the makings together for spaghetti and dumped the jarred sauce into a pot on the front burner. Her Irish heritage did not leave much room for creativity. A trip to the freezer produced ready-made meatballs.

As the meal came together, Bob returned and poked his head in the fridge. "Do we have salad stuff?"

"Bottom bin," Libby answered. "But I think it's time to toss the chunk of cheese on the top shelf." She paused. "At least I think it was cheese."

Bob saw the offending object. "Wow, I think we grew antibiotics on this one." He took it to the garbage before setting up shop at the chopping board. "So, how was your day? Any good library mayhem?"

"Nope," She put the pasta water on to boil. "Not even any late fees. That really annoyed Dolores. How about you, any good cases come up?"

"I wish." He added lettuce and tomato to an empty salad bowl. "A few small thefts and one disorderly behavior. Slow day for criminals."

"Always good to hear, seeing the majority of your clients live in the same town we do." Prep work complete, Libby went to the fridge for iced tea. She raised the pitcher to Bob. "Want some?"

"Sure, thanks."

Glasses filled, Libby remembered her earlier conversation with Charlie. "I got some insight into Charlie's *dark* artwork today."

"The potential serial killer sketch?" Bob asked mid-chop.

"Yep, that's the one; you will never guess what he told me."

She relayed the conversation, and although relieved, Bob's inner lawyer was not amused. Stealing was still stealing, and Charlie would get a lecture from him after dinner. In retrospect, he had to give his son points for creativity. Charlie never outright stole, he was more the snack Robin Hood of first grade; stealing from the rich in junk food, giving to the poor in apples.

Libby stirred the pasta. "I'm going to fire off a

heartfelt, yet slightly evil email to Miss Simon after dinner, and suggest we discuss her mislabeling of our son's mental stability."

"Be nice, Libby." Bob warned. "Charlie has seven more years at Acorn. Don't tick anyone off. The PTO's already put a target on your back; don't alienate the staff, too."

"Fine," she sulked. "You steal all my fun." Fifteen minutes later dinner was ready. Libby walked over to the staircase. "Dinner!" she bellowed.

Two sets of thundering feet pounded down the treads, and the entire family sat down to dinner—a rare treat for a Monday. Stump smelled the meatballs and came out from his hiding spot with Shannon's sneaker firmly clenched in his drool-soaked jaw.

"Charlie," Libby said. "Please feed Stump. I hate it when he sits here staring at us while we eat. It's like he's watching us on some doggie reality show, *When People Eat.* He never blinks, and it's unsettling."

Charlie dashed to the pantry, Stump fast on his heels. Quickly returning from his chore, he dug into his pasta with gusto. "Hey Mom, this is good."

"Thanks Charlie, it's an old family recipe." Libby winked at Bob. "I'll pass it down to you some day."

After dinner, the kids headed back upstairs, Shannon to finish a book report and Charlie to empty the hot water heater with his long shower. Libby and Bob cleared the table and loaded the dishwasher.

Stump stole a stray meatball from the trash, inhaling the morsel in one bite and followed up the theft with a contented nap on the living room rug.

Bob started the dishwasher. "Did you call your mom yet?"

After her conversation with Uncle Will, Libby had filled Bob in on the details pertaining to her late grandmother's condition. "No, I'm not sure what to say." She gave the counter a quick wipe down. "I mean how do I start that conversation without putting Mom on the defensive?"

He leaned back on the counter, crossing his arms and ankles and said, "Practice on me."

"You?"

"Yeah, I'll be Mae." Bob pursed his lips, stuck out his chest, and raised his voice to soprano. "Elizabeth, what do you have to say to me? Make it quick, I'm going to church to pray for your soul."

"I know your intentions are good, but that's disturbing. Stop."

"Fine, I'll drop the drag queen. But give it a shot. After all, you listen to my closing arguments all the time, let me return the favor."

After a little more prodding, Libby agreed to use Bob as faux Mae. "Okay, Mom," Libby said, "I spoke with Uncle Will the other day."

"Yes? And how is my brother?" Bob played along. "He never calls—must have better things to do than speak to his only sister."

"We talked about Grandma Shannon. He told me that, though the doctors did not diagnose it back then, she had dementia. At least that's what he assumed it was. Did you know anything about that, Mom?"

"Are you implying I kept secrets from you? That I lied?"

"Of course not, I'm just asking—"

"Do you think my mother was crazy? That I'm crazy? I should be locked away in some nut house full of droolers and screamers. Would that make you happy, Elizabeth?"

Libby signaled time-out. "Far too real," she said. "No more Mae tonight, I need my husband back."

"Sorry." He hugged her. "I did get a little far into character with the 'nut house' remark, didn't I?"

"If I know my mother, that was bland compared to what she's going to say to me. It could get ugly quick; I've got to choose my words carefully."

"So,"—Bob pulled away—"I'll ask again, when are you going to talk to her?"

"Tomorrow after work." Libby released a long breath. "The library's closing early for a town council meeting, and I have the afternoon off. I'll send Mom an email tonight. If I call, she'll balk. I'll swing by Annie's tomorrow for a carrot cake on the way over to her place. Cake helps everything, right?"

"Absolutely." Bob headed toward the living room for his nightly Sports Center and intermittent napping ritual. Settling into Old Stink, he popped the footrest. "Make sure *you* slice the cake. Mae with a knife probably isn't wise."

Chapter Fourteen

Tuesday morning Libby added a third cup of coffee to her routine in hopes the extra jolt would help muster her courage to confront Mae later that afternoon. The workday passed without a glitch, and no glitch meant no excuse to avoid her mother. Digging into her overstuffed purse for keys, she noticed the message light blinking on her phone; she pressed the "missed call" button—Mom.

"Oh no, you don't, Mother Dear." She tossed the phone back in her purse. "You're not getting out of this visit."

Annie's Bake Shop window displayed a "Trick-Or-Treaters Welcome" sign. "Damn," Libby muttered. "Mental note: pick up candy." She made it a practice never to buy Halloween candy prior to the thirty-first; it kept the temptation to a minimum.

Inside the bakery, she had a small carrot cake boxed and started over to her mother's condominium.

Mae's development, decked out in spooky force, begged for Halloween. Pumpkins, skeletons, and wispy craft-store cobwebs adorned residents' doors, each entry more outrageous than the next.

Pulling into the parking spot in front of her mother's unit, Libby chuckled. Mae's door not only displayed the expected Halloween garb, but an additional illuminated "Countdown to Christmas" sign.

Mae knew how to trump the neighbors. Throw Santa in the Halloween mix and kids would flock to her door. Libby was about to ring the bell when Mae tore open the front door.

"What are you doing here?" Mae scowled. Adorned in a fluffy pink terrycloth bathrobe with matching slippers Mae was visibly flustered.

"I love you too, Mom." Libby answered.

"I left you a message," Mae said. "I'm under the weather and not up for company."

"I won't stay long," Libby pushed. Mae reluctantly gave way and allowed her inside. "I brought cake. If I take it home, there's a good chance the kids will eat it all before I even get a bite. At least here, I stand a chance of getting an entire slice."

She walked into the living room. As usual, the space was neat as a pin; leaving her to question how she and Mae were related. Her mother's sense of organization was legendary. While most women delighted in shoe shopping, Mae's pulse raced over shoe racks.

Every meticulous inch packed with neatly displayed collectibles was freshly dusted and polished at all times. Mae's prize possession, the Spoons of the United States collection, sat on display in the glass-front corner cabinet. Idaho was missing. The potato mecca vanished after Mae volunteered to watch Charlie after preschool one afternoon.

Setting the teapot to boil, Mae selected two mugs from the cabinet. "If you insist on staying, I'll make tea," she grumbled. "Is regular okay, or do you want something fancy?"

"What constitutes 'fancy' tea?"

"I have a few. One to make you sleepy, one to boost your metabolism—"

"Sounds more like a medicine cabinet than tea."

"Smart mouth." Mae set the tea choices on the kitchen table.

Libby sat down and made her selection. "Do you have paper plates for the cake, or should we go nuts and use the real ones?"

"Paper." Mae grabbed the plates. "I know they are harmful for the environment, but less mess for me later. Mother Nature will forgive my shortcomings." The teapot boiled, and Mae filled the mugs. Taking a knife from the drawer, she brought everything to the table. Libby recalled Bob's warning and offered to cut. She plated the first piece and slid it across the table to Mae.

"Carrot," Libby said. "Your favorite."

"Mm," Mae savored the first bite. "Annie always makes the best cakes. Even Saratoga's christening cake was delicious, once you ignored the offensiveness." She patted her lips with a napkin. "So, tell me Libby, is this a special occasion or do you need something? There must be a reason; cake always comes with a catch."

"Why does there have to be a catch?"

Mae glared "Dear, do I look like a moron?"

"No," Libby said. "At the moment you look like one of those pink snack cakes with the twenty-year-old coconut."

"I told you, I'm ill; and this is my most comfortable robe."

"What's wrong? Do you want me to take you to the doctor?"

"No, no, nothing like that." Mae blushed. "I overdid it a little in yoga. Myrna Goldstein was on the mat next to me, showing off as usual." She rolled her eyes. "We were in downward dog and Myrna, dreadful woman, says to me, 'it's so nice that someone your age remains flexible.' My age, my age! I'm only two years older than that adult-diaper-wearing fossil. Anyway, I turned my head to give her a piece of my mind and tweaked something in my back."

Senior yoga can be cutthroat, Libby thought. "Have you taken anything for the pain? I can run home and get you some ibuprofen and a heating pad."

"I have all that. Rest is best." Mae took another bite. "But since I'm not doing any resting, are you going to tell me what brought you over with bribery disguised as cake?"

Libby took another bite of cake, and prayed for patience, before saying, "I talked to Uncle Will on Saturday."

"Oh," Mae stared into her tea. "He called here earlier. I've been too busy to call him back. How is my brother?"

"He's well. The gallery is booming. He'd like us to come again for a visit soon. The kids would love it, and Bob and I could use the break."

"You should go, he loves having you there."

Libby procrastinated, pushing cake around her plate. "He told me Dr. Rashan called him the other day. He was impressed with her."

"I'm sure he was. He's always had a soft spot for exotic women. Do you remember that singer friend of his? I think she was Vietnamese, sang in that little bar not far from his house." Mae put her finger to her pursed lips trying to remember. "What was her name?"

Her name was Larry, but Libby would keep that

little tidbit of information to herself. "Yep, Uncle Will has lots of exotic friends."

She shifted in her chair. "Uncle Will had some more information about Grandma Shannon's time in the nursing home. Important information I think Dr.Rashan should have. I know it's been a long time since she passed away, but do you remember much about the last year of her life?"

The minute Shannon's name came up, the air in the kitchen turned frigid. Mae's demeanor changed from hospitable to agitated in under ten seconds. "I was too busy with you kids to see a lot of her then," Mae snapped. "We were barely keeping Mae Day afloat. I didn't have time to take the train all the way to Brooklyn to visit Mom and race back here to take care of you."

Her impatience increased with each word. "Will took care of the nursing home and all the details. He was closer. I only saw Mom once or twice that year. Anyway, Will has a flair for the dramatic, I'm sure whatever stories he told you were exaggerated."

"Mom, be honest with me, okay?" Libby looked directly into Mae's frown. "Uncle Will told me about Grandma's dementia. It was the reason she needed to be placed in the nursing home, and it's the reason you stopped taking us for visits. Am I right?" She paused, but Mae did not answer. "Come on Mom, there's nothing to be embarrassed about. This is important. Why didn't you tell Dr. Rashan?"

"My mother was exhausted, not crazy. Will needs to stop playing doctor and diagnosing illnesses he knows little about. "

"He didn't say she was crazy, he said—"

"I know what he said, Meghan, and he's absolutely wrong! My mother was a tired woman who lived a hard life, nothing more. William's been on a beach too long; all that sun affected his memory."

"Who is Meghan?" Libby looked at her mother, puzzled. Mae went sheet-white.

"What did you say?" Mae asked.

"You called me 'Meghan.'" Libby said.

"I did no such thing."

"Yes, you did."

"Oh for Christ's sake, Libby," Mae slammed her mug down on the table. "I did not. And even if I did, it was a slip of the tongue. Probably a name from the program I was watching before you rudely barged in here."

Her eyebrows knitted as she wagged an accusatory finger. "Wait a minute, I see what this is. I see what you're thinking—'Mom can't remember my name, she must have dementia like her crazy mother'—is that it?"

"That never even crossed my mind." Libby fought for calm. "You're screaming at me and all I did was ask a simple question?" Her voice dropped to a soft, even tone. "Let's settle down and talk about this, okay? Come on, have a sip of your tea."

"Do not tell me to settle down." Mae screeched. "I am your mother, and I know damned well how to take care of myself. I'll decide what that nosey doctor does, or does not, have a right to know. You are all making mountains out of mole hills."

"Dr.Rashan is not nosey, Mom. She is attempting to help you. It's obvious from your reaction you either do not see a problem or don't want help—hers or mine. I came over here to see if you wanted to talk about this and you're being irrational."

Libby stood and picked up her purse. "I want you to know I'll be here if you're scared, but obviously you can't talk about it right now. Call me after you've cooled off. And if you don't, I'll see you next Thursday for your appointment as planned."

"Sean will take me," Mae spat.

"No." Libby reached the door and swung around to face her. "I'm taking you, like it or not. This is not up for debate. If you call Sean and insist on having him drop everything and drive you all the way to Hartford, plan on seeing me in that office waiting for you. Either way, I'm going."

"You have no right to come into my home and dictate where I go and with whom. I am still your mother, Elizabeth, and you will show me respect."

Libby heard Uncle Will in the back of her mind: *She's afraid.* "You're right, Mom. I don't have any right to tell you what to do. However, I'm going to take you to your appointment with Dr.Rashan, and I'm going to make sure she has our full family medical history. If that upsets you, I'm sorry."

She opened the front door and stepped outside onto the Halloween-engulfed porch. "The doctor can't help you unless she has all the facts, and if you want to stop seeing her after the next visit, I won't hold a gun to your head. At least she'll have all the right information if, or when, *I* am ever diagnosed. Of course, it would have been nice to hear all the history from you, but at least Uncle Will recognizes me as an adult, and knows the value of honesty."

Take that! You're not the only one who can dish out the guilt. "I'll see you next week. And, by the way," she pointed to the pumpkins on Mae's doorstep. "Myrna's are much scarier."

Libby climbed into the van. After a quick stop at Buy Mart for Halloween candy, three bags of mini-chocolate bars lay on the passenger seat. Two made it home.

Chapter Fifteen

It took three days to digest twenty-five bite-size candies. Libby learned this fact the hard way, but by Friday morning her appetite was back in full swing. On her way to work, she noticed Sean's truck at the Coffee Stop and pulled in. Greeted by the smell of dark roast and blueberry scones, she joined him on the line.

"I see the candy hangover wore off." Sean smiled. "Back on solid food yet?"

"Yes, thank you." Libby placed her order. "Got a minute to join me, or are you off to hammer something?"

They sat at a small table by the front door. Outside, the Main Street window displays were morphing from Halloween to Christmas. "Has Mom told you about our latest screaming match?" Libby asked.

Sean frowned. "No, must have been a whopper though, if she's still keeping it under wraps. She usually bitches about you every chance she gets."

"Odd." She sipped her coffee. "I thought by now for sure she would tell you what a wretched and ungrateful child I am."

"That's *old news*," he teased. "But you may be onto something, Mom's never quiet this long. Are you sure you didn't kill her?"

"She was alive, and fuming, when I left." Libby broke off a piece of scone and wondered what force of nature kept Mae silent.

"I know you're going to tell me anyway, but let me go ahead and sound like I care." He took the lid off his coffee and sipped. "What was the fight about?"

Libby recapped the conversation with Uncle Will, and her subsequent argument with Mae. Sean listened, not one bit surprised by the information.

"Well, at least I know what possessed you to eat your body weight in sweets," he said. "You know Mom, she likes to keep things private, and she probably does not want us to remember Gram as anything less than the wild woman we knew."

"Why? It doesn't make any sense?" She bit hard into her scone and chewed away frustration. "Shouldn't we know all the facts? Even if she didn't want us to worry, we still have a right to know; it's our medical history too. The risks are the same for us."

"Come on, Lib, Mom rarely makes sense. She never talks about her life before we moved to Rhyme. I think the accident with Dad scared the crap out of her— she just wants to leave it all in the past. Maybe she lumps what happened to Gram in with it. It was pretty much around the same time. "

He looked down at his watch and quickly finished his coffee. "I have to get moving; I've got drywall going up on a condominium project. Would it help if I call Mom later and try and smooth things over?"

"God, no, I'll never hear the end of it if you do. She's probably already called Uncle Will and ripped him to shreds for telling me about Grandma. Let's just give her a few days to cool off."

"Good plan."

Sean pulled away and Libby checked the clock on

her dashboard—fifteen minutes before work, she dug out her phone and called Kevin's job.

His proper business voice answered. "Kevin McGinn."

"Libby O'Rourke."

"Glad we cleared that up."

"What's eating you?" she said.

"Quarter end." He raised his voice to a dramatic level. "Unfortunately, I work with buffoons who do not recognize the term 'deadline.'"

Libby laughed. Aside from being a dictator, Kevin was highly respected in his office. "I see you still have your people skills finely tuned."

"So, what's up?" he asked.

"Has Mom called you? In particular to gripe about me?"

"Oh crap, am I going to have to deal with one of your famous cat fights to top off my already glorious day?"

"No, Captain Empathy, she's just ticked off at me because Uncle Will told me some things about Grandma Shannon; things that Mom, in her infinite wisdom, decided were not important enough to share with us." Libby explained the situation as Kevin listened intently.

"Is this something we need to keep an eye on Mom for?" Kevin asked. "Like is she going to start wearing her bra on the outside or something?"

"Honestly, I have no idea." Libby answered. "I'll find out more next week after the second appointment with Dr. Rashan. I'll give you a ring after and fill you in on what I find out."

"Okay, sounds like a plan," He paused to clear his

throat. "Lib, I know I get wrapped up in my own shit a lot of the time, but don't leave me out of this, all right? You and Jesus, I mean Sean, take up most the slack with Mom. I want to help."

Touched, Libby responded. "I promise I'll keep you in the loop, and for the love of God, keep Suzanne at arm's length. Mom's still hung up on the damned puppy cake."

Kevin laughed. "Yeah, I can do that. It's been a cold few weeks in my house since that fiasco. The sofa bed ain't all it's cracked up to be."

"I can imagine." Libby grinned and started her car. "I'll talk to you soon, got to get to work."

"See you later, and say hello to Delinquent Dolores for me." Kevin said. "I had such a twisted crush on her when I was ten."

"You are a sick, sick man, little brother," Libby teased. "I'll be in touch after Mom's appointment."

Libby pulled into the library parking lot and spotted Dolores. Her body was oddly positioned beside the overnight drop slot.

"Dolores," Libby called on approach. "Is everything okay?"

"No, everything is most certainly *not* okay!" Dolores shouted. On closer look, Libby saw Dolores's arm wedged in the slot.

"Are you stuck?"

Dolores nodded, and Libby asked, "Care to tell me what happened?"

"Some awful children stuffed the slot with garbage again. I was able to clean most of the trash out from the inside, but there was a pop can I needed to grab from out here. When I tried to dislodge it, my watch stuck on something. Can you go in and see what I'm held up on?"

Libby went inside. At the drop slot feed, Dolores' disembodied hand protruded from the wall like a B horror movie special effect. She moved books aside for a better look and heard conversation coming from outside. Dom was teasing Dolores.

"How the hell did you do that?" Dom laughed.

"Mind your own business, Dominic," Dolores fired back. "Go away and wait for Book Club to start. Not that you ever read the books—I know you only come for Ruth Liebowitz's oatmeal cookies, and nothing more."

Libby chuckled to herself as she eavesdropped on their banter.

"You know *nothing*, woman," Dom answered. "I *always* read the book, and Ruth coincidentally *just happens* to make a delicious cookie. Maybe you could take a lesson or two from her; seems to me you could use a little more sweetness in your life."

"I'm a wonderful baker Dominic Genovese—I need no lessons from the likes of Ruth, and no advice from you—thank you very much."

"Is that so?"

"Yes it's so."

"Prove it."

"What?"

"I said prove it. I'm making my famous lasagna for our Retired Officer's dinner next Wednesday, and we still need a dessert. None of us bakes. It's considered sissy work. Come to dinner with me, bring your best baked treat, and let me be the judge of your talents."

Oh, this is getting good. Libby snickered.

"My time is accounted for on Wednesday," Dolores stammered. "I work until eight o'clock—"

"Dolores," Libby interrupted through the drop slot. "I'm trying to get you undone in here, and I couldn't help but overhear your conversation."

"Hey there, Libby!" Dom shouted through the opening.

"Hi Dom." Libby said. "I can cover for you Wednesday, Dolores. Make Dom your pineapple upside-down cake. It is *sin on a plate*, Dom. The guys will love it!"

Dom smiled at a still-captive Dolores. "I like pineapple."

Jaw clenched, Dolores said, "Thank you Libby, how nice of you to offer to help." Obviously displeased, she jiggled her arm. "Have you managed to find the problem in there, or will you need to call for reinforcements?"

Libby unhooked Dolores' watch from a loose screw. "That should do it. Pull back gently."

Arm free, Dolores readjusted the clasp on her watch and turned her attention to Dominic. Every bit the stuffy librarian, she said, "Very well, I'll go with you to your police person dinner. You may meet me here. What time shall I be ready?"

"Dinner's at seven o'clock, I'll swing by and get you at six-thirty."

"I'll follow you in my own car," she snipped. "That way I can leave early if you decide to stay late and indulge with your friends. What is the attire?"

"By attire, you mean clothes, right?"

"I see your Word-A-Day Calendar is paying off in spades," Dolores scolded. "Of course I mean clothes."

"There's no need to get testy," he said. "The *attire* is informal. Don't get all gussied up or anything. It's a bunch of guys and their wives having a pleasant meal together. You'll like it. May even loosen you up a little."

"I do not require loosening," Dolores huffed.

"I beg to differ." Dom left her for Book Club and first crack at Ruth's cookies.

Dolores walked to the circulation desk, slid into her seat and fired up the computer.

Libby, unable to resist the opportunity to rib her, sat down alongside. "So," she whispered, "you have hot a date with Dom on Wednesday?"

"I have no such thing." Dolores continued to click away at the keyboard. "I'm accompanying Dominic to a respectable dinner with his fellow officers. I see none of the romantic connotations you are implying."

Libby could not resist. "Dolores and Dominic up in a tree, k-i-s-s-i-n-g!"

"I can fire you, Mrs. O'Rourke." Dolores blushed.

Chapter Sixteen

Libby was in a pickle; she needed to be in two places at one time. With no recent breakthroughs in cloning, she was out of options and phoned Caroline.

"Are you about to leave work?" Libby asked.

Caroline checked her watch. "Wow, I had no idea it was that late. Do you need me for something?"

"Bob called and he's going to be late. I need to pick up Shannon at Mae Day and get her to soccer practice at the same time Charlie needs to get picked up from model club. Are you available for either taxi assignment? I would ask Sam's mom, but he's home sick."

"Timing is your friend, O'Rourke. I was just about to call for a hair appointment tonight, but my roots can wait."

"Bless you. Sean's meeting with a client right now at the office and can't leave to shuttle Shannon, you're saving me, yet again."

"No problem, I'll talk to you later."

****

Twenty minutes later Caroline rushed into Mae Day, and ran smack into Sean—hitting him in the forehead with the front door.

"Hey Duffy," Sean said, rubbing his head. "Use a turn signal next time."

"Sorry," Caroline grimaced. "Are you okay? It's

freezing out there, and I just ran inside." A welt formed in the center of his forehead. "Damn, you're going to have a lump."

"No worries, not the first time I've run into a door." He led her in. "I called Lib. My meeting ended early, I can take Shannon. We must have got our signals crossed. Sorry you had to come all the way over here."

Caroline looked down at her phone. "Oops, it looks like Lib did try to get me. I had the ringer on vibrate." She slid the phone back into her pocket. "No big deal, I'm here now and I'm headed that way anyhow; I'll take her."

"Okay, that would be great; it'll give me time to wrap up stuff here." He yelled over his shoulder, "Shann, Caroline's here. Get moving or you'll be late."

An awkward quiet came over the room. At a loss for conversation the pair fumbled with mundane tasks. Sean sorted paperwork on Deb's desk while Caroline mindlessly dug into her purse for nothing in particular.

Since returning to Rhyme, post-divorce, Caroline had taken note of Sean's absence at many of the events she attended. She was developing a complex. Had she unknowingly offended him in some way? She broke the silence. "Okay, this is silly."

"What?" Sean asked.

"Don't give me that—you know exactly what I'm talking about. This..." She stirred the air between them. "You're avoiding me, and I want to know why?"

"What? You're imagining things. I'm not avoiding you." Adverse to confrontation, he yelled for back up. "Shannon, come on! Aunt Caroline is waiting."

"That is such bull, and you know it," she insisted. "We have a history—"

Shannon burst in the room. "I couldn't find my other shin guard...it was in my backpack." She grabbed her coat. "Bye Uncle Sean. Call Mom if you need me tomorrow." She ran out to the car.

Caroline turned to Sean before following. "We are not done here," she warned.

"Caroline..." Sean's easy-going expression turned to stone. "We were done a long time ago."

****

Caroline and Libby primped for the senior prom. A seven-month culmination of anxiety, the prom marked the highlight of the St. Margret Mary High School social season.

Smart gown shoppers adopted full hunt mode over Christmas holiday. Hair test runs, including proper length and highlight color, were February must-do's. They learned a valuable lesson from Mary Kozinski's unfortunate clumpy-bangs incident a week prior to Junior Prom. Prom dates, secured by April, were mandatory. Couples parting ways post-April first must attend the prom jointly. It was the law. Young love shattered, but prom contracts were iron-clad.

Caroline's boyfriend Mark attended the University of Michigan. Home for Easter break, Mark informed her was unable to attend the big dance. The relationship ended officially weeks later, but Caroline took it in stride.

Libby refused to attend prom without her best friend and offered up Kevin as a sacrificial date. A junior, and self-proclaimed nerd, Kevin needed all the social status points he could get and was happy to go. Not her first choice, Caroline reluctantly agreed, and plans were set in motion.

Sean, a University of Connecticut freshman, agreed to escort his on-again, off-again girlfriend Michelle to the dance.

The momentous night arrived. Caroline, Michelle, Libby's date Tom, and the three McGinns gathered in front of Mae's prized garden for pictures. Blooms of every hue framed the young couples.

Caroline's pale blue strapless gown matched the hydrangeas. Her shoulder length blonde hair was pulled back with a fresh yellow rosebud. Small diamond studs twinkled at her ears.

At Mae's insistence, Libby in her virginal white taffeta styled her curly red hair in a loose up- do. Grandma Shannon's pearls were at her neck.

In polar opposition, Michelle wore a low-cut black satin dress offset by a large rhinestone crucifix necklace. Black lace gloves and four-inch stilettos added to the rock star-inspired image while an over-beaded bag concealed lip-gloss, condoms, and a freshly rolled joint.

Mae positioned the friends for a group photo and lifted the camera to her eye. She caught site of Michelle's jewelry. "What a lovely cross, dear," Mae said. "Can you pull it up slightly for the photo? It's getting lost in your bosoms."

"Mom, don't go there." Sean warned.

Clueless, Michelle hiked up the rhinestones from her cleavage and smiled for the camera.

"Hush Sean, everyone smile!" They obeyed. "Okay, now just my three kids." Sean, Kevin, and Libby huddled together. The boys' white tuxedos matched Libby.

"We look like bowling pins," Kevin muttered

under his breath.

Libby smiled through clenched teeth for the camera. "More like a First Communion on steroids. Suck it up and smile so we can get out of here."

Pictures complete, they piled into the limousine as Bernie and Mae waved from the front porch. The clashing perfume, corsages, and unnecessary aftershave filled the car's interior. Michelle's berry chewing gum added a fruity aroma. Tom pulled out a flask and made the first toast.

"Bottoms up," he gulped, and passed the vodka. "Here's to a little liquid courage to get things rolling." Michelle temporarily removed her wad of gum and took the second sip. Each passenger followed suit, except Sean.

"None for you, bro?" Kevin asked.

"I don't need shitty booze to have a good time." Sean said.

"Well aren't you *too perfect*?" Libby teased. "Come on, Sean, have a little fun. I've got two weeks before I ship off to Camp Filthy Rich for the summer." Libby had accepted a summer counselor job at an exclusive sleep-away camp in the Berkshires. The prom was her last chance to have fun. "Can't you drop the big brother act, just for one night, please?" Sean ignored his sister and looked out the window in silence.

Michelle snapped her gum and giggled. "He's just pissed because he has to go with me tonight instead of hanging on campus with some hot college chick."

"Give it a rest Michelle." Sean said. "I told you I'd come to the damned thing, and I'm here. Don't make a big freaking deal."

Kevin started playing with the radio while Michelle

and Tom worked on finishing the vodka. Libby turned to Caroline. "You're quiet. What gives?"

Caroline welled up with tears. She pulled her hair behind her ears. "Dad gave me Mom's earrings to wear tonight. You know he's not a sentimental guy, but he choked up. Seeing him like that—I guess it just hit me how much I miss her on nights like this."

Evelyn Duffy had died in January of ovarian cancer. Her husband John was at her side until her last breath.

"I remember when your dad gave her those earrings." Libby said. "It was last year's birthday, right?"

The memory made Caroline laugh a little. "She was so mad at him! They needed to fix the roof and, instead, he bought her these." She touched the stones. "Mom wore them every day."

Overhearing their conversation, Sean recalled the days spent helping Mr. Duffy patch the roof so he could save money on a contractor to buy his wife a special gift. He wanted her to have something beautiful during her battle with the ugliest disease.

Sean glared at Kevin. Busy playing with the car radio, he was oblivious to Caroline's tears. *Hold her you idiot.*

At the school, the group piled out of the limo and into the gym. Decorated in a Roaring Twenties theme, the space resembled a back-alley speakeasy. Dim lighting and mobster murals hid the overhead scoreboard and basketball hoops. The tables, covered in crushed red velvet, were set with durable white plastic dishes and vases of lilies. Their fragrant scent was not fully able to mask the thirty years of phys ed.

Tom sniffed. "Looks good, but it still smells like wrestling mats."

"Hard to believe I was doing sit ups in here yesterday." Libby said. The photographer caught her eye. "Let's get our pictures done early. I'm not making the same mistake as last year."

At the junior prom, Libby over-indulged on both drink and dance. With just half an hour left at the dance, she and her date raced to the photo station for the formal picture her parents paid for in advance. The result haunted her.

"I looked like a homeless stripper." Libby shivered. "Mae was not pleased." Entering the picture line, she saw the portrait backdrop—three mafia-inspired gangsters gathered around a mahogany bar, guns at their hips, cigarettes dangling out of mustached mouths. The menacing caricatures, designed in keeping with the 1920's style, fell short of creating elegant keepsakes. Honoring St. Margaret Mary's true Catholic school image, painted into the mural, directly above the martini-clad bar, was a weeping Jesus on the cross.

"Classic." Kevin smiled. "Gangsters and God, these pictures are going to send Mae around the bend."

Libby nodded in agreement. "Last year's photo is going to look like the cover of Good Girls Quarterly after this."

Mug shots complete, they sat down to a dinner of overcooked chicken and cold green beans. Food was food. No one cared what it tasted like. The purpose of the prom was to mock others' dance moves, drink, and behave regrettably; it was a rite of passage.

After dry vanilla sheet cake topped with freezer-burned chocolate ice cream, the dancing began. Libby and Tom gyrated in one of the larger groups while Sean and Michelle huddled in a corner, locked in an intense argument. Kevin, rhythmically and socially stunted, took off in search of booze, leaving Caroline alone at the table.

An hour later Michelle vanished to smoke off her mad, Kevin disappeared in search of even more booze, and Libby and Tom slow danced to big-hair bands crooning of unrequited love.

"Hey." Sean dropped down in the seat beside Caroline.

"Hey." Caroline said.

"Kevin MIA?"

"Looks like."

"Kid drinks like a fish. Dad gave him hell last week, but he hasn't slowed down." Sean had his stern face on. Always the responsible one of the group, he felt the constant need to supervise. He took his role as eldest seriously.

Caroline smiled.

"What?" Sean asked.

"Nothing."

"It's not 'nothing.' What are you smiling at?"

Her grin spread. "You call Kevin a 'kid' like you're eighty or something; you're not his dad, Sean. Let him be an idiot, it's his life. You don't have to babysit anymore."

Sean shrugged. "Someone has to keep an eye on this bunch." He pointed to Libby and Tom swaying closer than wise. "She's going to be knocked up if she keeps it up with that guy, and you aren't much better. At least you wised up and broke it off with that shithead, Mark."

"You know, Sean, college turned you into a real asshole!" She stood. "If Kevin ever surfaces, tell him I left." She stormed out the gym door.

Sean swore under his breath and chased after her. He caught her at the edge of the parking lot and whirled her around to face him. "What's your problem?" he yelled.

Shaking free, Caroline blasted him. "I'm not your sister, Sean, or even one of your slut girlfriends! I don't need you to keep tabs on me. Go back inside and let your pothead date grope you."

"Nice mouth," Sean fired back. "Did your dumbass boyfriend get sick of listening to it, and that's why he dumped your ass?" He regretted the words the minute they left his mouth and instantly stepped forward to set things right. It was too late. Caroline's corsage-dressed wrist slammed into his jaw with a satisfying crack.

"Jesus Christ! You hit me! You fucking hit me!"

She wasn't done yet. Caroline shrieked at an inhuman level and continued to pound at his chest without hesitation or any sign of stopping.

"Knock it off!" Sean gripped her in a vice-like hold. "Shh. Take it easy, slugger. I'm sorry, okay?"

Caroline stilled and leaned into his hard chest, her voice eerie and detached. "The dumbass," she said between tears, "dumped me because I thought I was pregnant."

Sean froze. Her eyes held him captive.

"Don't worry, it was a false alarm. But the scare helped good old Mark realize he needed someone who wasn't, let me see if I can get the words right, 'a stupid, inexperienced bitch.'"

Sean's rage was a distant second to the

overwhelming need to apologize. He pulled Caroline firmly into his arms and held on as if the earth were ending.

She struggled to get free, yelling and pushing against his chest. His grasp tightened. "Let me go! I don't want your Goddamned pity."

Her efforts were futile. Sean's embrace turned from prison to haven, and her sobs released. As she cried, his hands ran up and down her back. He buried his face in her soft hair.

"Car, I'm sorry, I shouldn't have said those things." He looked down at her. "I am such an asshole."

Caroline pulled back only slightly, wiping the dampness from her cheeks. "You could never be an asshole. Anyway, I'm the idiot who stayed with him all that time."

He closed his eyes and rested his forehead against hers. "I hated that guy. He treated you like crap, and here I am acting just like him."

"You could never be like Mark." Caroline smiled. "You go into big brother mode at the first sign of trouble. I used to hate that, even when I was nine, and forced you to pretend-marry me."

Sean thought back to the day Libby and Caroline roped him into playing wedding in the backyard. Lib, the priest, broke gender rules right from the beginning. Stuffed animal guests watched as Caroline, sporting a pillowcase bridal veil, dragged Sean to the swing set altar, a bouquet of dandelions in her grasp. Even then, he gave in without complaint. If it made Caroline happy, Sean did it.

She brushed an innocent kiss across his cheek. "You always played my hero," Caroline said. "You protected me even when I didn't know I needed it."

His shocking blue eyes bored down on her. She swallowed hard. "You don't have to protect me, Sean. I'm not the *other* little sister chasing you around the yard anymore. I grew up."

Sean took Caroline's face in his hands. Staring back at her was someone new, someone Caroline felt like she was looking at for the first time. His eyes darkened, his expression, intense. She shivered. The air shifted between them and an intimate pull began to form—she felt an unrelenting need to be close to him.

"I can't stop protecting you. I don't want to." His voice dropped. "And trust me, I haven't felt like your brother for a hell of a long time." Stepping closer, he went on, "It kills me to see you like this. I physically hurt when someone upsets you."

His hands ran through her hair and down her back. His jaw clenched. "I want to go find that guy and…shit. Never mind. I shouldn't tell you in case the cops ever find the body. I think that would make you an accomplice or something."

A small, nervous laugh escaped Caroline. "Connecticut has the death penalty. I couldn't live with being responsible for sending you to the electric chair. Mae would never forgive me."

Sean locked on Caroline's gaze. "For you,"—he tightened his hold—"death is worth it." He traced the outline of her face with his free hand. Emotions he'd been wrestling with for years surfaced, and for the first time he let go.

His tender words were full of confusion. "I'm not sure what to do here." He wanted to kiss her more than take his next breath. "You've been through a lot, between your mom and how that dick treated you; I'm afraid if I do what I want to right now...God I don't want to mess this up."

"Sean?" Caroline's soft voice filled with awe as tears gathered in the corners of her eyes. The whisper of space between them shrank. "I've been waiting for you since third grade." She wiped away a stray tear, and placed her heart on the line. "I don't need a big brother, Sean; I need you."

His lips came down on hers with pure hunger. A lifetime of frustration released in a single, heart-stopping moment. Caroline groaned. As the kisses deepened, she expected to feel awkward or nervous, but a sense of completion overtook her as they touched—like finding a home, after years of searching, and never wanting to leave.

The comfort of knowing all the intimate details of each other's lives fed the passion erupting between them, no secrets, no restraint. Everything melted away. The music and conversations spilling from the gym disappeared.

All too soon bright headlights cut across the parking lot and broke the spell. Breathless, Caroline spoke first. "Sean, I..."

The sound of heavy, uneven footsteps intruded on the moment. Michelle stomped across the parking lot like a Clydesdale in sequins. "Where the hell have you been?"

Feeling exposed, they turned toward her like children caught with their hands in the cookie jar.

Michelle wobbled to a stop. Words slurred, the smell of marijuana surrounded her. "I went for a quick smoke, and you disappeared."

In spite of his date's sideshow appearance, Sean could not pull his gaze from Caroline. Her swollen lips and flushed cheeks made him ache to touch her.

"Go back inside, Michelle," he said. "I'll be there in a couple of minutes."

"Fine," Michelle said. "If you don't hurry up, I'm not putting out. Got that dickhead?"

Sean rolled his eyes. Caroline hid a smile.

"Go on," he said. "I'll catch up with you later." Michelle weaved her way back into the gym. Sean reached for Caroline, and she went willingly into his arms.

"Sorry about that," he said. "Just goes to show we've both been with the wrong people, at one point or another." Caroline nodded, but he could see the nerves were starting to set in.

He tapped a finger on her forehead. "I know that look, and this scares me too, Duffy. Don't pull away now. We'll take it slow, no pressure. This could be a really good thing if we let it."

He kissed her gently and smiled. "I'm just sorry you had to slug me to make me see it. You've got a mean right hook."

In spite of her anxiety, Caroline laughed. Her hands took on a life of their own, unable to stop touching him.

"Sean, I want this too, more than you know, but we're not just two people who met at a party or something. There's a lot more to lose here. If we open this door, there's no going back."

He pulled her to his chest and whispered in her ear. "I'm opening the door, come inside with me."

****

From the moment it began, Sean and Caroline knew a romance was risky and agreed to keep their relationship private. Caroline felt dishonest withholding the new romance from Libby, but with her best friend away for the summer at camp, the secret was best left between her and Sean.

In fall, Sean would return to the University of Connecticut as Caroline started her first year at Boston College. From the beginning they realized the transition would challenge their newfound happiness, but chose to live in the moment and let time decide if they would stay together.

The night before Caroline was set to leave, Sean asked her to meet him at the beach.

The moon was full, casting a glow on the sand. Looking out at the shoreline, Caroline saw Sean's silhouette. Building homes alongside his father, his frame had transformed from lanky teenager to muscular, well-defined man.

At the water's edge, he sat with broad shoulders slumped, head in hands. Before he spoke a single word, his defeated posture said the relationship was ending. Walking toward him, she felt sadness gnaw at her heart.

Seeing her approach, he stood and opened his arms. She ran into his embrace and buried her face in his soft sweatshirt. She loved his familiar scent— sawdust and freshly fallen rain. His grip tightened as she clung.

They came together at a point in her life filled with pain and uncertainty, and with Sean's support, Caroline had healed, and discovered what it felt like to love completely. She wept, knowing what was to come.

"Look at me, Caroline," he turned her face to his

and kissed her with softness only she knew he possessed. "Please don't cry. You know the distance thing never works."

Caroline's voice cracked. "Why? BC and UConn are close. We can see each other on weekends." She grabbed at him. "Why are you giving up before even trying?"

Lying was not Sean's strong suit, and telling Caroline he wanted to end things between them called on every ounce of acting skill he could muster. She needed time to experience life without him, to find her path in life. The very thought of being without her stole the life from his soul.

"Caroline, I don't want to hurt you, but be realistic. You are going to want to see other people in college; I'll just hold you back."

"I can't believe you are doing this," she sobbed.

"We've only been together a couple of months," he said. "It was a summer thing. We knew that," he lied. The truth was too difficult to confess. "We're friends, and always will be. Neither one of us is ready for anything serious right now. Let's not make this a big deal."

"A big deal?" She stepped out of his embrace. "Let me clear something up for you Sean. When I was at my lowest, when I hated who I was and didn't know how I was going to get from day to day, you were there, and you made that hurt go away. When you touched me, it wasn't sex. I've had sex. What we had was love."

Sean reached for her. She shoved him away. "And this pain you seem to think you are saving me from"— she touched her chest—"this pain I feel right here, right now, makes what Mark put me through feel like a paper cut. I'll make it easy for you, Sean, okay? You want to end this, fine. But before you walk away I want you to know something, I'm in love with you, I have been for as long as I can remember, I can't force you to feel the same way. You don't need to break out *older brother mode* and make it all better. I'm a big girl now, but know this...I will never be able to look at you, never be in the same room with you without remembering right here, right now...the moment you gave up on us. "

Before he could respond, she ran away from him, down the darkened beach, away from the life they might have had. All he could do was watch her go.

Sean drove by her house on the way home, determined to make sure she got home safe. Her rusty convertible sat in the driveway, a dim light shone from the bedroom window. Fighting the urge to run to the door and beg for forgiveness, he headed toward home.

Alone with his thoughts in the silent car, he realized he left Caroline with a broken heart and no one to console her. Libby was away, her mother was dead, and the guilt of knowing what he had done was eating him alive. No amount of time would lessen the feeling.

At home, he opened the back door. Bernie was at the kitchen table, a bottle of Irish whiskey ready to pour.

"Dad," Sean questioned. "Why are you still up?"

Bernie invited his son to take a seat and reached in the cabinet behind him for two glasses. He poured a generous amount of amber liquid into each. "Something told me you might need a bit of company tonight, and Lord knows I'm not naïve enough to believe this is your first tip of the bottle. Set your behind down and join me." Bernie grinned, "I believe it's time for your first official drink with your old man."

Sean sat down and reached for a glass. "What's the occasion?"

"Ah lad, the occasion will be on the day you finally come to your senses and marry that girl, but for tonight, we'll just have a toast." Meeting Sean's shocked stare, Bernie raised his glass and lowered his voice. "To love, and the women who make it worth losing."

Sean stared at his father. Were his feelings for Caroline that obvious? "You knew?" He covered his eyes with his free hand, shaking his head in disbelief. "Christ, does everybody know?"

"Drink up Pansy-boy, and then I'll answer your question."

Sean obliged, downing the liquid in one sip. Bernie did the same.

"Of course I knew," Bernie continued. "Hell, every time Caroline Duffy set foot in this house you all but peed a circle around her, marking your territory. Really Sean, it got to be a bit embarrassing."

Bernie poured them another drink. "No worries, your sister is too wrapped teaching those spoiled juvenile delinquents and dating that inbred I-talian, Mancuso, to notice anything. And Kevin's too drunk to see straight half the time. No son, no one else knows, it's between us."

"I had to end it, Dad." Sean sighed.

"You don't have to convince me son. I know you did what you had to...for now at least. She's got some growing to do, you both do. Give it time, see what fate has in store. It may surprise you."

Sean nodded and downed the second shot. Voice quivering, he surrendered the idea of holding his emotions in check; this was his father, there was nothing he couldn't tell him, "It's killing me, Dad. I feel like I'm going to die. I love her."

Bernie finished his drink, stood up and walked around the table wrapping his stoic oldest child in his burly arms. "I know son. I know." He ran his hand over the top of his head, much as he had when Sean was a small boy. "Our Caroline. She's one of the special ones."

Tears streamed down Sean's stubbled face as he met Bernie's understanding gaze. "Yeah? How do you know that, Dad?"

"Now, Sean Bernard, that's a dumb question from a smart man." Bernie smiled. "It's easy for me to recognize a truly remarkable girl when I set eyes on her; after all, I married the best one. Don't tell your mother that, it will go right to her head."

Sean cracked a faint smile. "Got any other words of wisdom?"

"As a matter of fact, I do. Never hesitate on your happiness, son. If the man upstairs grants you a moment's joy, no matter when or where it comes, grab on with both hands and hold on with all your strength. Whether fate brings our Caroline back to you or takes another path, life is a gift. Accept it as such, and never take a minute for granted."

"I won't Dad, I promise."

Bernie slapped him on the back. "Good, now get your sorry ass to bed, we've got work tomorrow. I don't need you falling off a roof and having me end up on the receiving end of one your mother's lashings. She's may be small, but the woman scares the crap out of me."

****

156

Caroline Duffy met Steve Schwartz in her first year of college; they were married four years later. *Fate,* Sean thought, *was a bitch.*

Chapter Seventeen

"That quarterback needs glasses!" Bob switched off the television and strolled to the kitchen desk to see what Libby was doing. "What are you looking at?" He rubbed her shoulders as she sat at the computer.

"Dementia symptoms." Libby moved her mouse around the glowing screen. "Although, in looking at some of these, I'm pretty sure most, if not all, of us have it already."

Bob read over her shoulder. "Language problems, misplacing items, getting lost on familiar routes, personality changes and loss of social skills—sounds more like the teenage years to me."

"All the symptoms sound fairly common until you get to the later stages; those are the frightening ones." Libby pointed to the computer. "I bet these are the only ones Mom ever saw in Gram; rapid weight loss, lack of proper bathing and grooming, inappropriate and offensive language, no recognition of family."

She let out a breathy sigh. "Mom was living in Rhyme, busy raising a family and Gram was all the way in Brooklyn, so I bet she never recognized the first signs. It could have been going on for a long time and Mom wouldn't have noticed."

She leaned away from the computer, rubbing her eyes. "God, it must have hit her like a ton of bricks when she went to see her in the nursing home that first time. I can't see Grandma Shannon as anything less than full of life. Will made it sound like she was an empty shell by the end."

Bob pulled up a chair next to Libby. "I'll bet Mae wants you to remember her mom that way," he said. "I'm sure that's part of the reason she kept the truth from you. Your grandmother was in her early sixties when she died. It was an extreme case, not the run-of-the-mill dementia—if there is such a thing. Mae is already in her seventies and takes excellent care of her health. That must tip the scales in her favor, right?"

"I wish I knew." Libby shut down the computer, took a deep breath and forced a smile. "I guess I'll know more after her doctor visit on Thursday. As for tonight, what are we going to do about dinner?" She bolted up and headed to the kitchen. Bent in the fridge, her voice shook. "Not looking too rosy in here. We have lettuce, peanut butter, mayo, shredded cheese."

"Libby," Bob shut the fridge and pulled her into his arms. "Remember that whole for better or worse thing we promised? There was big white church, long-winded priest, seven hundred of our family and friends griping about the heat." She smiled as he said, "I think we're past the point in our marriage where you hide the worst part from me."

Libby buried her face in his sweatshirt and let the tears flow. Her words came in a childlike whisper. "She's my mom," she said, as he held tight. "This isn't supposed to happen. She's supposed be one of those old ladies in the Rhyme Times over one hundred birthday list. I want her at Shannon's wedding, Charlie's college graduation. Hell, I want her to live to see my first hot flashes."

"I know, honey," Bob soothed.

"Even if Mom physically makes it to that point, her mind may be long gone years before any of those momentous events happen."

"Let's be optimistic, okay? Mae's case could be quite different from her mom's, or Dr. Rashan could try some alternative treatments." Bob's words aimed to appease, but he knew Libby's heart was breaking. Seeing her cry killed him. They both knew even the best medical treatments available could not stop the dementia process. Mae was in the beginning stages of the disease, but the end would come soon enough. The symptoms would progress to the point where she no longer recognized her own children, grandchildren, or perhaps even her own name.

Libby looked up into Bob's compassionate face. "This could be me someday," she said. "Twenty or thirty years down the road I could forget you, us, the kids."

Pushing her hair away from her face, he kissed her with total gentleness. "One day at a time, Libby. You and me. Better or worse, remember? After all, chances are your cooking will kill me long before you get dementia."

She slugged him just as Charlie came in the back door.

He saw Libby's moist eyes and stopped dead in his tracks. "Mom," his little voice quivered. "What's wrong?"

Wiping the tears, she bent over to hug him. "Everything is okay, pal, I just got sad for a minute. I do that sometimes."

"Like when Stump ate your necklace?" Charlie

innocently replied. "Poppy Bernie gave you it for your birthday when you were a kid, and you cried really hard when Stump didn't poop it out."

"Yeah, just like that." She laughed and switched gears. "How was your play date with Sam? Did his mom drop you off at home, or his dad?"

"His dad, and the new girlfriend, Melanie."

Bob and Libby exchanged glances. Sam's father, Lyle, a serial dater, was notorious for cruising the sidelines at soccer games; trolling for single moms to add to his list of conquests. It amazed Libby a man whose face so closely resembled a dried apple could still attract twenty-something girlfriends.

"What's Melanie like?" Libby asked.

"She's okay, I guess." Charlie's face squished. "Her lips are really, really big, and she laughs all squeaky."

"She sounds like a keeper," Bob muttered.

Libby turned back to Charlie. "Did you thank him for the ride home?"

"Yep."

"Good." Back on track for dinner, she re-opened the fridge. "Okay, what are we going to eat tonight? Charlie, Shannon is eating at Maggie's house so you get to make the call, what will it be?"

"Can we grill hot dogs, the real kind, not the turkey ones?"

"Sure, go wash up."

While Bob headed out back to light the grill, Libby got out the fixings for hot dogs, a quick salad, and some leftover mac-and-cheese. Setting up dinner, she decided to indulge in a big glass of Chardonnay and a healthy fistful of Cheese Bites; she'd earned it.

Bob returned and pointed to the glass in her hand. "Hey, pour me one of those."

She poured, and he took the glass.

"Is it white or red wine with hot dogs? I can never remember."

What would I do without this man? Libby wondered. Their life was far from perfect, but she knew with each passing day her decision to marry Bob O'Rourke was the smartest thing she had ever done. It may not be the relationship blockbuster romance movies depict, but the love they shared went down to the very heart of whom they were, and kept going when the world around them fell to pieces.

"Do me a favor?" Libby asked with a grin.

"Anything," he wiggled his eyebrows. "Does it involve sex? If not; can I *make* it involve sex?"

"There's potential," she teased. "But I can't commit until after the kids are asleep."

"I'm a patient man." He sipped his wine. "What's the favor?"

"Never stop making me laugh." Libby put down her wine and wrapped her arms around her husband. "Even if the day comes when I don't know who you are, or even who I am; make me laugh, okay? I'm always less afraid when you do, and I can guarantee even if I have no idea what's going on, I'll recognize the feeling—the one I get after you chase away all the crummy stuff with your goofy humor. It's one of my favorite 'better' parts in that whole 'for better or worse' thing. "

"I can do that." He held her tight. "So what are some of the other 'better' parts; perhaps my stunning good looks or unyielding sexual prowess?"

"Honey,"—she pulled back and took his face in her hands—"that's exactly the type of laughter I'm talking about."

Chapter Eighteen

Dolores was dressed to impress. Decked out in a maroon wrap dress, sensible black heels, and gold hoop earrings, gone was the gray sweater set and pearls of the drab librarian. Tonight, Dolores was on the prowl. Libby caught her boss putting on lipstick in the hallway mirror.

"Look at you, fancy pants," Libby teased. "Ready for the big date?"

Dolores brushed off the comment and returned to the circulation desk to continue date-stamping the new releases. "I'm not sure why you insist on calling this a date."

"Dolores, you are two adults, attending an organized function, where there will be food, wine, and possibly dancing. That's a date."

"The term is juvenile."

"I beg to differ. If I wanted juvenile, I'd say you're *hooking up.*"

"Good heavens Libby, we're not fish." The faint chime over the front door announced a visitor. Dominic, clad in navy blue suit, pinstriped shirt, and stylish red tie rounded the corner to the circulation desk, a bouquet of Gerber daisies in hand.

"Hello, ladies." He extended the flowers to Dolores. "These are for you...a little peace offering."

"Thank you." Dolores's hands trembled as she took

the flowers. "I need to get my coat. Please wait here; non-employees are prohibited behind the circulation desk." She walked back to her office, leaving Dom to chat with Libby.

"Well," Dom grinned, "I wouldn't want to break the rules. Thanks for covering for Dolores tonight, Lib. Seems to me she could use a night out on the town. Maybe she'll have a little fun for a change."

"Is Dolores the only one who needs some fun?" Libby asked.

"I suppose I'm entitled to a good time once in a while, too." His cheeks flushed. Dewey leapt on the desk.

"Well, hello sir," Libby stroked his fur. "Nice of you to visit. Let me guess, you're hungry?"

"That's a good-looking animal." Dom rubbed the cat under his chin. "I've never seen him in here before."

"You wouldn't have, Dewey's a shadow. He usually stays out of sight during the daytime hours, but at night he hangs out with us, especially Dolores. He loves her. He usually wakes up around now, eats a little something and starts his night watch duty." Dewey purred as Dom continued to scratch him. "He's not usually this friendly. You must be special, Dom."

Reaching under the counter Libby pulled out a bowl of cat food and set it on the countertop.

Behind her, the door to the office closed, and Dolores approached. Tucked into a gray overcoat and matching scarf, Dolores exited the circulation desk, an award-winning pineapple upside-down cake in hand.

"Sorry to keep you waiting, Dominic." Dolores said.

"No problem." He took the cake from her. "Do you

still want to take your own car?"

"Absolutely. Just pull around front and I'll follow you over to the Community Center." Dolores marched to the front door. "Come along, we don't want to be rude and keep your friends waiting." Dom shrugged his shoulders and hurried to the door.

Libby, feeling like a mother sending her kids off to their first dance, watched them go. Although Dolores pretended the evening was a nuisance, Libby knew her friend's stomach swarmed with butterflies. It was lovely to see two people she cared so much about finding a small piece of happiness. It was about time for both of them.

She returned to Dewey. "What say you and I do a little re-shelving before quitting time?" The cat ran off to the audiovisual section. "I'll take that as a 'no.'"

At seven-thirty, the phone rang. "Rhyme Public Library."

"Hi Mom," Shannon said.

"Hi honey." It was unusual for Shannon to call, especially given the fact Libby would be home in half an hour. "Everything okay?"

"Dad wanted me to call and tell you I got an A on my Susan B. Anthony report."

"That's great!" Libby heard Bob saying something in the background. Shannon giggled. "Okay, what am I missing? Obviously something's funny, and I'm not in on the joke."

"Dad said it was my job to soften you up with good news before he talks to you." Her laughter intensified. "Here he is."

This is not good, Libby thought. The last time Bob had one of the kids call her at work he accidentally booked a boys' golf weekend in Myrtle Beach the same date of Charlie's scout campout. In his absence, Libby took over den leader duty and slept in a rain-soaked tent with ten sneezing, homesick five-year-olds.

Bob picked up the extension in the bedroom. "Hi hon, how's work tonight? Enjoying your quiet time?"

"Cut the crap, O'Rourke," Libby growled. "We both know I'm not going to like whatever you're going to tell me; get to it."

"Okay, no small talk. I can respect that."

"Spit it out Bob."

At the risk of bodily harm, he said, "My mom called."

"Oh shit."

"Don't get upset, it's not *all* bad."

Shelia O'Rourke was a hairspray-drenched tornado, who typically blew into town with no warning, and took out everything in her wake. A widow, Shelia made the most of her single status. Men flocked to her like moths to a flame. Unfortunately, the caliber of men flocking to her flame had run the gamut—ranging from wonderfully dashing to bottom-feeding troll.

Taking meticulous care in maintaining her youthful appearance, Shelia often neglected to inform her suitors she was, in fact, a grandmother. On more than one occasion, she had taken Shannon or Charlie shopping, never outright claiming to be their mother, but not denying it when others assumed. Through strong genetics and regular trips to the spa, she could pull it off.

Shelia had yet to pay Libby a compliment without an accompanying suggestion on how to improve. She had a good, well-intentioned heart buried beneath an age-defying super bra.

"Hear me out," Bob pleaded his mother's case. "Mom was supposed to be on that Caribbean cruise for Thanksgiving this year."

"'Supposed to,' as in she will *not* be there now?" Libby's anxiety grew.

"Fred, the guy she was going with, broke his hip at swing dance class and can't go...Mom refuses to go alone, so"—he prayed Libby would not kill him in his sleep—"I asked her to come stay with us for a few days."

"Define 'a few days.'" Like spicy mustard, Libby loved Shelia in small doses.

"I pick her up at the airport on Wednesday, and she'll leave Saturday. I'll make sure we have lots of wine, red and white. You can accompany any meal or snack with alcohol." His lawyer tone came out, "I can also offer a full body massage with no inappropriate touching or lingering on your girl parts."

"Your proposal has appeal, counselor." Libby grinned. "I guess this means one more for Thanksgiving dinner? How many are we up to now?"

"I think we've moved past *quaint dinner* and into the realm of *mess hall*."

Between Libby's entire family, Caroline, Trevor, Dominic, Dolores, and now Shelia, Libby needed to roast an ostrich. "Okay, I still love you, and you know Shelia is always welcome, but you owe me big time!"

"I know." His relief was apparent. "Dear God, I know. Are you coming home soon?"

"I'm leaving here at eight on the dot. I'm exhausted. I need a decent night's sleep before the trip to the doctor with Mom tomorrow."

"Shoot, I forgot that's tomorrow. Sorry to pile more stress on you with Shelia. Have you spoken to Mae since the blow-up?"

"Only via email, I sent her a message confirming I'd pick her up at three. I got a one-word reply—'fine.' This is going to be a picnic."

"One step at a time. Maybe it won't be that bad."

"I appreciate the pep talk, but Mom only reverts to the silent treatment when she's good and mad. Should be an interesting ride to Hartford."

Libby could hear Bob sit down on the creaky old bed, their first purchase as husband and wife. The owner of the little antique shop they bought it at said it belonged to her parents, and their marriage lasted for sixty-four years, so the bed must be charmed. Libby could not wait to get home, climb in beside Bob and nod off to the sports channel theme music. Tomorrow was going to be hell.

Chapter Nineteen

Mae waited at the front door in her best purple tracksuit and giant sunglasses.

"Hi Mom," Libby said. "Are you ready to go?"

"No," Mae barked. "I thought I'd stand out here in the damp weather and wait for a bus." She slid into the car and slammed the door.

Libby called on every ounce of patience she possessed and got in beside her. "Do you need to grab anything before we leave?"

Mae reverted to mother role. "No, but you should try to go to the bathroom, it's a long ride."

At forty-one, Libby knew when she needed a restroom, but it never stopped Mae from asking. "I'm all set," she answered. "Let's get going; there may be traffic."

Underway, they made small talk; weather, town gossip, and general nonsense that did nothing to address the elephant in the backseat. Libby dropped Mae off at the front door to the office and went to park the van.

Mae checked in with the receptionist. "Mae McGinn," she said. "I have a four o'clock appointment with Dr. Rashan."

"It's good to see you, Mrs. McGinn," the chipper receptionist said. "Is all your information the same since your last visit? Address? Insurance?"

Mae nodded.

"Okay, have a seat and Dr. Rashan will be right with you."

Mae sat in the waiting room. Libby walked in and joined her.

"Let's see how fast, 'right with you' is?" Mae said, while digging into her behemoth purse for knitting needles. Judging by the purple yarn, the creation was for Shannon. Each year Mae knitted Christmas gifts for family in their favorite colors. Libby owned *six* green scarves and treasured them all.

"Mrs. McGinn?" Olivia, the nurse they had met at her first visit opened the door. "We're ready for you."

"That was quick," Libby said. "You didn't even have time to do two rows." She hesitated, "Do you want me to come in with you?"

Mae shrugged. Libby recognized the fear behind her mother's eyes and followed her into the examination room. As they walked, Libby saw the slump in Mae's shoulders and the way her feet dragged as she walked. It reminded her of a student on the way to the principal's office for punishment.

"Here we are." Olivia led them into the blue room. "You ladies have a seat at the conference table and Dr. Rashan will be right in. Can I get you some water or coffee?"

"No, thank you," Mae replied.

"I'm fine right now." Libby smiled. "Thank you, Olivia."

A thirty-year registered nurse, Olivia sensed their unspoken fears and said, "It's so nice that you come here together. So many of our patients are alone in the world. Does my old heart good to see some families aren't too busy to help each other."

She looked at Libby. "I lost my mama over twenty years ago, still miss her big opinionated mouth. *And* her pecan pie; Lord that woman had a gift with the pecans." She laughed. "You ladies need anything, just open the door. I'm right around the corner."

Mae dug into her bag and returned to her knitting. The needles moved at lightning speed, each movement precise and flawless. Libby did not inherit her mother's crafty talents.

"Damn." Mae dropped her project onto the table and shook her hand vigorously.

"Knitting casualty?" Libby asked.

"I poked my finger, now I'm going to bleed all over Shannon's scarf." She put her finger to her mouth and motioned to the tissues in the center of the table. Libby slid the box over.

"Good thing we're in a doctor's office." Libby peeked in the counter drawer. "There's a pretty good chance I can get you a bandage." With her back to Mae, she moved a few items and located a box of adhesive strips. "Jackpot! We have a variety here. Would you like blue, red, or one of the normal kinds?"

Mae did not reply.

Libby turned. "Mom, did you hear me? Do you want blue, red..." She saw an alarmed expression on Mae's face. "What's wrong?"

Still, Mae did not answer.

"Mom, you are starting to scare me, what's the matter."

"Tissues." Mae said and pointed to the box directly in front of her.

"Mom, they're right there? Is it your eyes? Can't you see them?"

"Of course I can see them Elizabeth. I'm not blind!"

"Then what is it?"

"They weren't here last time."

"Okay, now I'm just lost." Grateful Mae was not sick or injured, Libby exhaled, frustrated by her mother's lacking communication skills. "What the hell are you talking about?"

"You wouldn't understand. Once you reach my age you pick up on the little things, like tissues." Libby motioned for her to continue. "Fine, I'll explain, but you're going to think I've lost my marbles. Oh wait, you already do."

"Mom, I don't think—"

Mae raised her hands. "I'm not going to argue with you Elizabeth. I've had quite enough of that lately. Between our disagreement, Suzanne's constant nonsense, and my conversation with William on Monday—meddling old fool—I'm finished."

She took a breath and continued, "For your information, the last time we were here there were no tissues on this table. They were over there by the sink."

Libby gave a blank stare.

Mae groaned and went on, "Everyone knows if you have to give bad news, put tissues in arm's reach before you deliver the blow." She pointed to the tissues, "Obviously, this is not going to be a pleasant visit or the damned tissues wouldn't be sitting here, staring me in the face."

"Oh for God's sake, Mom, they're tissues, not a bomb. You are totally blowing this out of proportion." A knock sounded at the door and Dr. Rashan entered.

"Hello Mrs. McGinn, lovely to see you again. And

you as well, Libby." Dr. Rashan closed the door and joined them at the conference table. "I'm sorry for the delay. My last patient had a few extra questions, and I did not want to rush through his appointment; thus I appreciate your patience."

Mae plastered a superficial smile on her face. "That's no problem at all, I'm sure your time is in very high demand. I've just been catching up on my knitting while we waited."

"I wish I could do that. I've read knitting significantly reduces stress. My mother-in-law has tried to teach me several times, but it takes a gift I seem to be lacking."

"Mom tried to teach me, too." Libby added. "But the gift seems to have skipped me and gone directly to my daughter, Shannon. She picked it up the first time Mom showed her. Remember, Mom, at the lake that summer after Daddy retired? You two took Charlie and Shannon for two weeks." She turned to Dr. Rashan. "It was Heaven."

"I remember," Mae answered.

"It is always nice to see the younger generation learning something so timeless," Dr. Rashan said. "Most of my nieces and nephews are too busy electronically blowing up the universe to consider learning a craft."

"Oh, my kids do that, too," Libby confessed. "But we try and throw in a little unplugged time to balance them out."

"Good plan." Dr. Rashan sat at the table and turned to Mae. "How have you been feeling since we last spoke, Mrs. McGinn? Any changes, specifically, physical changes that I should be aware of?"

"None." Mae said.

"You feel well, no health concerns?"

"Fit as a fiddle."

"Wonderful." She opened Mae's file. "I have all your blood work; levels remain the same as your visit with Dr. Cooper. You take exceptional care of yourself, Mrs. McGinn. I wish I could say that for all my patients." She flipped through the test results. "I remember you enjoy yoga. Are you still participating in that?"

"Twice a week," Mae said. "Last week I missed—pulled muscle—I'm better now."

"Good, keep that up if you can," Dr. Rashan encouraged. "I am a firm believer in exercise combating many of the complaints my patients associate with aging, depression, and anxiety in particular. Yoga is a superb choice for building muscle strength. As we age, muscle mass naturally diminishes. However, whatever you are doing to remain fit is working beautifully."

Libby exhaled. Mae's physical health was sound, but it was evident Dr. Rashan had concerns.

"Mrs. McGinn," Dr. Rashan continued, "I was able to speak with your brother, William, late last week. He was wonderfully helpful, and a true pleasure. I can see why you are so fond of him."

Mae smiled.

"As I mentioned to you at our first visit, your family history is an integral piece of the puzzle when we look at all the factors concerning the possibility of dementia. William shared some information regarding your mother that by no means create a cause for alarm, but could pose a concern."

"I'm sure Will was exaggerating," Mae said. "He does that, he's very dramatic sometimes."

"Mrs. McGinn, I cannot diagnose your mother. She was not my patient, you are. Moreover, in that regard, you and only you are my concern right now. Based on my conversation with William, I was able to contact the nursing home that your mother resided in, St. Joseph's in Brooklyn, and pull her medical records. That in and of itself was a miracle. Most nursing homes purge records after ten years, but St. Joseph's is small and able to store records much longer."

Mae's face turned ashen.

"Mom, do you want me to get you some water?" Libby asked.

"No, dear," Mae said. "Let Dr. Rashan finish. Go on doctor."

As Dr.Rashan relayed the details regarding Shannon Finn's final year including high blood pressure, cholesterol problems, and various other conditions, they waited for the other shoe to drop. Libby could feel the small room closing in.

"I don't mean to interrupt, doctor," Mae said. "I already know all of this, and I take much better care of myself than my mother ever did. She cooked with lard, drank wine with dinner every night, and smoked two packs a day for twenty years. I don't do any of those things so I would imagine my chances of stroke are markedly reduced, simply based on my lifestyle."

"Absolutely," Dr. Rashan answered. "However, all of those factors just contributed to your mother's stroke. The underlying diagnosis was quite different." She pushed the tissue box close to Mae.

Damn it, Libby thought. She took Mae's hand and

squeezed tight.

"Mrs. McGinn," the doctor continued, "your mother was not simply aging, or exhausted, she was suffering from a condition called Vascular Dementia. This diagnosis qualified her for admittance into the nursing home. Although the condition itself is common, in your mother's case the onset and subsequent decline was extremely rapid."

Mae's voice quivered. "And you believe I have this vascular thing?"

"There is no way to be sure without a CAT scan. But given your family history and the test results we have already been able to read, yes, that would be my preliminary thought."

She went on, "I need you to be cognizant of a few things before we go forward. First, your mother was living alone, and again, she was not my patient. With many people I have treated, people who live alone, symptoms of this disease go undetected simply because no one is taking note of small day-to-day changes in behavior. I believe your mother's early signs of Vascular Dementia were overlooked."

"How is that possible?" Libby asked, "Wouldn't my uncle or her doctor have noticed?"

Dr. Rashan shut the file folder and folded her hands. "It would be extremely simple to miss. Your Uncle William has told me he traveled quite often, and obviously did not live with your grandmother. It would be difficult for him to notice if she missed a meal or had behavioral changes."

Turning toward Mae, she continued, "If he, or you, Mrs. McGinn, called your mother, and she seemed abrupt or defensive, it would be natural to assume you simply caught her at a bad time."

"That happened all the time," Mae responded. "I would call and she would tell me I was interrupting her. I couldn't imagine what was more urgent than talking with me for five minutes."

Dr. Rashan nodded. "Often patients with dementia become agitated when routines are altered. Let's say you rang to say hello and your mother was about to cook an egg. First she may be bothered at the change in routine, but more importantly, she may forget to finish cooking and skip the meal altogether. We will never fully understand what transpired in your mother's final years, Mrs. McGinn, but as your doctor, I believe it is wise to schedule a CAT scan for you, soon."

"And you are certain Mom has enough factors to put her at high risk for Vascular Dementia?" Libby asked. "I mean it couldn't be anything else, less"—she searched for the right word—"terminal?"

"Without the CAT scan, I can't be certain," Dr.Rashan said. "But a genetic predisposition coupled with Mrs. McGinn's earlier exam makes this a likely diagnosis. Before we go any further, let's do the scan.

Reaching behind her, she pulled open a file cabinet and took out a packet of papers. "I want you to take some information." She handed the packet to Mae. "This reading is going to be daunting at first, but there is some beneficial information in here about dementia. I believe knowledge is power."

"I agree," Libby interjected, taking the packet from her mother's trembling hand.

"Tremendous breakthroughs in dementia treatment are happening every day, Mrs. McGinn. Sadly, your mother went undiagnosed too long, and as a result, her lifespan was significantly shortened. Aside from minor typical age-related health issues, you are in fabulous shape and together we can set a course of treatment that will ensure a much higher quality of life."

She turned toward Libby. "The single greatest problem I see in my practice is patients lacking family support. And it is obvious that's not the case here. I realize this is quite a bit to take in, but are there any questions you have right now that I may be able to answer before we head to the desk to schedule the scan?"

"No immediate questions," Mae said. "I'm sure I will have several in the future."

"You can call the office at any time. If I'm not available, Olivia or one of my nurses will get the message to me and give you an approximate time that I can return the call."

"I'll do that."

"I have a question." Libby said.

"Of course. What would you like to know, Libby?"

"You are going to hate to hear this," Libby hesitated, "but I have been doing some research on the internet and everything I can find on dementia suggests that early intervention is key."

"I agree entirely, and for the record, I think the internet is fantastic when the sources are factual and overseen by licensed physicians. What was your question?"

"I know you need the scan results to confirm your diagnosis, but should we be looking into anything right now, while we wait for the results? Diet changes, supplements, or even housing? I know you think my grandmother likely had symptoms before anyone realized because she lived alone. Obviously my brothers and I see Mom all the time, but we are not doctors. Should Mom be interviewing visiting nurses, or even long-term care facilities now—so that if the time comes, far down the road, she's familiar with the personnel and has the final say in her care?"

"Elizabeth, that's a long way off," Mae said. "I think you are getting ahead of yourself."

"Yes and no," Dr. Rashan responded. "I think taking a proactive approach to your potential medical and supportive needs could be quite helpful. By no means do I see the need being immediate, but I often suggest families have an enjoyable dinner with honest conversation early on in the process. Be straightforward with your children, Mrs. McGinn. Tell them what your wishes are. Any decisions on where you live, what treatments to accept, even the doctor you choose need to be your choice. It's lovely to have a supportive family, but children often will have different views on what their parent wants."

Mae nodded and made a mental note to write her long-term care plan down before anyone else made decisions for her. "I'll make sure my choices are clear *before* I reach the point I can't think for myself anymore."

"Mom, think positive," Libby said. "We'll go ahead and get the CAT scan and see what Dr. Rashan thinks after that. While we wait, I'll have everyone over and burn us a marvelous dinner, and you can tell us your wishes. We'll yell at each other in true McGinn fashion until we reach a solution. No one is making permanent decisions without you. Schedule the scan and we'll start from there."

Chapter Twenty

Two days prior to Thanksgiving, Dr. Rashan called Mae with the scan results; Vascular Dementia confirmed. With stiff upper lip, Mae phoned Libby with the news, and in the same breath offered turkey-basting tips as though the life-altering diagnosis was nothing more than a runny nose.

Libby, rocked to her core, tore into the Cheese Bites.

"Why don't you get out tonight?" Bob suggested on his way out the door for work. "Call Caroline and you wild women go shoe shopping, or something equally girly, and take your mind off everything."

"I think you're onto something," Libby said between bites. "We could both use a break. Caroline's going head-to-head with Trev lately; I know she could use time out." She mentally checked off her to-do list for the rest of the day. "I think I've got Turkey Day covered, we just need a few odds and ends I can grab tomorrow. Can you handle the kids tonight?"

"I wouldn't have suggested otherwise. You need this, Lib, go out and blow off some steam. We have a house full of dysfunctional family descending on us Thursday; take a break while you still can."

"That reminds me, did you confirm what time Shelia's flight lands?"

"Five, I'll blow out of work around three and head

to the airport." Wisely, Bob cleaned and made the guestroom bed in preparation for his mother's arrival. He knew leaving the task to Libby ran the risk of adding more stress to her already overflowing plate. "The guest room is all set, and I'll grab Chinese food for us on the way home from the airport. Go straight from work tonight. Don't come home, the kids won't let you leave. Enjoy. We're covered."

When life handed Libby regrettable news, Bob was the first shoulder she cried on. Caroline was a close second. Her best friend's sympathy was always accompanied by goldfish bowl-sized margaritas and overloaded nachos. Libby needed a mental jailbreak, and Caroline was more than happy to be her partner in crime.

Outside Redwood & Sterling, Libby spotted Caroline waiting by the door. "Hop in," Libby said. Caroline jumped into the front seat.

Her sleek black suit made Libby feel frumpy. "Great. You look like a professional powerhouse, and I'm the sensible-shoe-wearing cute friend."

"Knock it off," Caroline laughed. "I didn't have time to run home and grab a more *get-your-drunk-on* outfit. Anyway, the sensible-shoe friend is always cute, in a frightening androgynous way." She adjusted her coat and settled in. "Did you 'fess up and let Bob know we opted for food and adult beverages in lieu of retail therapy?"

"Yes, he's all in favor."

The friends crossed Rhyme city limits and headed into Norwich for two reasons. First, The Cantina, an authentic Mexican restaurant on the water, served the best guacamole this side of Tijuana. Second, Libby was in no mood for chitchat with the PTO parents destined to be at locally eateries. She needed tequila; it was better outside city limits.

"So, let's get the bad stuff over with on the ride so we can enjoy every wonderful calorie those Nachos Grande pack." Caroline smacked her lips in anticipation. "How's Mae since she spoke with the doctor?"

"She's exactly how you would expect." Libby shook her head. "Firmly avoiding the subject and focusing on anything and everything except what we genuinely need to talk about. Her obsession of the moment is Thanksgiving, and then it will be Christmas."

She pushed her hand through her hair. "The sad part is until we pin her down; she'll just keep going this way. I have to call Sean and Kevin and set up some kind of meeting of the minds."

"Have you three talked yet? Do you *have* a plan?"

"We talked, but as far as a plan—it's got to come from Mom."

Libby took the exit ramp for Norwich. A mile up the road they pulled into the Cantina. The restaurant interior was lit with glowing red candles and hanging lanterns. Bright Mexican blankets hung above a nicked and scratched oak bar.

The host led Caroline and Libby to a booth in back, and within minutes, a young waiter named Rico brought warm homemade tortilla chips and fresh salsa. He took their drink order and disappeared.

"Busy in here tonight." Caroline said, looking to the bar. "Is it just me, or is the crowd over there still in diapers?"

"It's you. We're older than dirt." Libby reviewed the menu. "What are we eating?"

"I need cheese, nothing else really matters." Caroline dipped a chip into the salsa and popped it into her mouth. "I'm not sure why chips and salsa taste so much better when we go out, it's the same stuff I have at home."

"It's the taste of freedom that comes with them." Libby closed the menu. "Let's get the big nachos and fajitas. I'm hungry; forks will only slow me down."

"Works for me," Caroline agreed.

The waiter came back with their drink order. "God bless you, Rico." Libby snatched the margarita directly out of his hand. With the first sip, her tension eased.

"Rough day?" Rico asked.

"Rough month."

"Well, let's take care of that for you." His give-the-handsome-kid-a-big-tip smile was perfection. "What can I get for you ladies?"

"We're going to have the Grande Nachos with extra guacamole and an order of chicken fajitas, extra tortillas, *por favor*."

Rico grinned and turned on his innate Latino charm. "Ah, *se habla español, señora*?"

"Um..."—Libby *no habla*—"Sorry, I can only ask for the library, bathroom, or beer."

Rico laughed. "Well, in the part of Mexico I'm from, that's all you need to know." He picked up their menus. "You ladies just wave if you need anything else."

Caroline sipped her margarita. "No worries Rico, we'll wave until we can't feel our arms."

Chuckling, Rico walked away.

Caroline took in the sight of his backside. "Okay, I think my men sabbatical is taking its toll. I blatantly checked his twenty-something ass without a shred of shame. I'm a horny old woman."

"And I'm proud to call you my friend." Libby grinned.

After half a margarita and power chip-grazing, Libby felt her stress level subside. "I so needed this. Thanks."

"Hey, no thanks needed. You never have to twist my arm for a night out."

Rico returned with two shots of tequila. "Ladies, the gentleman at the end of the bar wishes you to have these. Enjoy." He placed the drinks down and walked away.

Stunned, the women looked to the bar. A heavyset bald man raised his glass. His size-too-small navy suit pulled across his thick waist.

"Help me out here," Libby asked Caroline, "Are we flattered by this, or devastated at the caliber of guy we're attracting these days?"

"Neither." Caroline smiled and mouthed a big *thank you* to their alcohol fairy. "We're thirsty. Just smile at the nice man like he stands a chance. Bottoms up, O'Rourke."

Tequila is addicting, Libby discovered, and when consumed to excess, no amount of food will counter the mind-altering effects.

Alan, the stalker from the bar, joined them with a second shot after dinner. He was a copy paper salesperson from Ohio in town on business. He concluded the polite conversation after he discovered Libby was married and Caroline bragged about her mythical six children.

When the room took on a blurry glow, Libby called home. "Hi honey, I love you so, so much."

Bob could hear the tequila in her voice and smiled into the phone. "How loaded are you?"

"I'm not loaded, I'm just happy. And I love you. You should be happy I love you. I am." Libby rambled while intermittently humming along with the mariachi band. "Don't you love me?"

"Yes sweetheart, I love you, even in your drunken state. I'm assuming you need a ride home. Did your accomplice tie one on, too?"

Libby turned to Caroline. "He wants to know if you're as happy as I am."

Caroline grabbed the phone. "I love you Bob—but not in a sexual way. To me, you will never have a penis. Lib owns your penis."

"Crap." He shook his head. "You are a bad influence. Put Lib back on."

She handed the phone back. "He loves me, too...but he wants to talk to you."

Libby got back on the line. "We both love you. Isn't that great?" A small burp escaped. "Alan does not love either of us. He was nice, but we couldn't love him."

"Alan?" Bob questioned.

"He sells copy paper in Ohio and smells like cabbage. Caroline does not like cabbage or copy paper, so there was no way she was going to end her men sabbatical and head back to the Marriott with him. Poor Alan, no one to love."

She paused only long enough to take a breath. "And then there's Rico, he's young and cute, and his name's not actually Rico, it's Dave—he's a grad student in philosophy at UConn. Caroline may go all cougar and pounce on him. She gets a little scary when she hasn't gotten any in a while."

"You are going to be loads of fun tomorrow," Bob said. He needed a plan to retrieve the duo. "The kids are asleep, and Dom's at poker night, so he can't stay with them." He thought for a second. "I'll ask Sean to come pick up your sorry butts. Stay put. If Alan comes back, tell him you have a big, mean husband who will kick his copy-paper-ass right back to the Buckeyes. And for Christ's sake, put Caroline on a leash."

"That sounds like a great idea," Libby answered. "You have the best ideas. Have I ever told you that? I love your ideas. I love *you,* Bob."

"I got that. Sit tight. The cavalry is coming." Hanging up, he dialed Sean.

"Hey Bob," Sean said. "Everything okay?"

Bob laughed. "Oh yeah, everything is just great, but I need a favor."

"Roof shingles come loose again?"

"I wish." It dawned on him that Sean mighty have a date over. "Sorry, I should have asked right away if you are alone."

"Unfortunately."

"Bad for you, good for me. Your little sister and her evil sidekick managed to get toasted out at The Cantina and need a ride home."

"Nice."

"I know. I'm tremendously proud."

"I'll get them." Climbing off the sofa, Sean slid into his shoes and coat. "How bad are they? Should I put towels down in the truck?"

"They've been drinking since six o'clock with an Ohio paper salesman that smells funny and a young stud named Rico-slash-Dave. Oh, and apparently they both love me."

"Shit. I'll grab the towels."

At The Cantina Sean parked alongside Libby's minivan.

Inside he spotted the pair at the bar with a group of men and women in mud-caked softball uniforms. Empty shot glasses and acres of beer bottles lined the bar. A Goliath of a shortstop, complete with eye black and muscle shirt, cozied up to Caroline with a predatory gleam in his eye. Sean growled under his breath and made his way to the bar.

Libby saw him first. "Yay, it's my big brother!" she slurred. Everybody, this is Sean!"

Shouts of welcome sprang from the crowd. Sean hoped they *all* had a ride home—there was only room in the truck for three.

"Hey." He wedged between Caroline and the cave man. "Big win tonight?" he asked with a *keep off* glare. The crowd erupted before the ball player could answer. Sean turned to face the mob. "I take that as a yes."

A lanky brunette sidled up alongside him. "Have a beer with us, Sean," she purred. "We never win, it's time to celebrate, and you look like you need a good time."

"Wish I could stay, but I can't tonight." He pointed to Libby and Caroline. "I'm just here to shuttle these two trouble makers back to sobriety."

"Come on, just one little bitty drink?" Her mascara-drenched eyes batted.

He sighed. Libido won out. "Okay, one drink."

Bob's phone rang an hour later. He bolted awake and noticed Libby was still missing from their bed. He answered. "Hello?" Dead pause. "Hello?"

Sean spoke. "I love you, Bob."

"Shit."

Kevin pulled his sensible SUV into the lot next to Sean's truck. Rumpled and sleep-deprived, he walked into the restaurant and located his siblings by their loud, pitch-less singing voices. Gathered around the bar, his target trio belted out the best of the '80's with a crowd of ball players, several off-duty wait staff, and three questionable-looking bikers.

Standing apart from the singing, Caroline saw Kevin first. "Hey look, it's Kevin!" she said.

Shouts of "Kevin" rang throughout the bar.

"He was my prom date everybody. Isn't he cute?" Her alcohol-soaked babble continued. "Kev is such a sweetheart, but his wife has implants. He's such a nice guy, he deserves real boobs." She turned to the bikers. "Don't you think nice guys are entitled to real boobs?"

They nodded in agreement.

Mouth open, Kevin put his arm around Caroline's shoulder. "Um, I'm just going to say, *thank you* and suggest it's time for us to all get going. That sound okay to you Caroline?"

She planted a sloppy kiss on his cheek. "You are so sweet, Kev. I love you."

"Yes, I hear there's a lot of love going around tonight." Kevin smiled in spite of himself.

He turned to Libby and Sean, both siblings leaning on the bar for support. "You've managed to drink the place dry, kids. Mae's going to break out the rosary beads after she hears about this one. Get in the car and

I'll take everyone home. Some of us have to go to work tomorrow and, although this is extremely gratifying for me on so many levels, I need sleep."

Sean grabbed Kevin in a bear hug and lifted him off the ground. "Thanks for coming to get us, Squirt. I promise not to puke in the dad-mobile." He motioned to Libby and Caroline. "I'm not too sure about these two, though."

"Great, I'm sure salsa vomit in the car will thrill Suzanne to pieces."

Kevin paid the group's tab. "Let's go troops."

A blast of cold November air hit them as they left the bar.

Libby ran for the car. "Hurry up, open the door," she begged. Kevin popped the lock, and she tumbled into the passenger seat.

Sean slid in back and bumped into something hard. "You got a baby seat back here?"

"Hey genius," Kevin snapped, "I have a baby. I can't strap her to the roof rack."

"How do I get it out?" Sean asked.

"For Christ's sake, don't touch it. It took me a freaking day to get that thing in there right. Just squish in, one of you sit on the hump between the seats. It's a ten-minute ride."

Caroline pulled Sean out of the car. "I'm smaller, I'll ride the hump."

Libby burst out laughing. "Drive over a lot of bumps for her Kev. It will be the most action she's seen in months."

Sean followed Caroline into the car. "Fine, Captain Horny, ride the hump, but if you puke, aim for the kid's seat and away from me."

Within two minutes of leaving the parking lot, all three inebriated passengers were asleep. Libby's head was pressed up against the front passenger window, mouth open, nose pushed up on the glass. A faint trail of saliva dripped down her chin. Seizing the opportunity, Kevin snapped a picture with his phone.

In the rearview mirror, Kevin looked at Sean and Caroline and had an odd thought—*the pair seemed to fit naturally together*. Caroline's head rested on Sean's chest, his arm wrapped snuggly around her. A familiar intimacy existed between the couple, an intimacy Kevin failed to notice before now. He grinned to himself and planned a chat with his older brother on Thanksgiving about his revelation.

The O'Rourke's front porch light came on as Kevin's headlights cut across the front yard. Bob stepped out and walked toward the car. "Thanks, Kev." He lifted Libby from the front seat. She was out cold. "I owe you."

Kevin shut the passenger door. "You owe me nothing." He showed Bob the picture on his cell phone. "This amount of blackmail ammo is worth more than you can ever pay me."

Bob looked at the photo, then down at his wife. "Yeah, I'd hold onto that one. You never know when you may need it." Bob peered into the back seat. "You need help getting those two home?"

"No, I'm good. I'll make sure Caroline gets inside." Kevin pointed to Sean. "I'll drive by his condo and push him out onto the lawn." He got back in the car and rolled down the window. "See you Thursday; we'll pick up Mom on the way over."

"Thanks, I appreciate it."

As Kevin pulled away, Libby regained a small bit of consciousness. "Bob?"

"Yep, it's me." He smiled. "You're home, wild woman, time for bed."

She rolled her head to one side, groaning. "I love you."

"I know." He gave her a small kiss and drew back. His face contorted into an awful expression. "Did you throw up tonight?"

"A little," she grimaced. "Rico's shoes are ruined."

Chapter Twenty-One

"Dad, why are you whispering?" Charlie asked between cereal bites.

"We need to be quiet and let Mom sleep this morning." Bob sat down at the table with Charlie and Shannon. "She had a little too much fun with Aunt Caroline last night and needs to rest. Eat your breakfast and I'll drop you both off at school on my way to work."

Shannon gulped down orange juice. "I'll take the bus."

Of course, Bob thought to himself. God forbid she be seen with me. "Okay, get a move on, bus should be here in five."

Quickly finishing her breakfast, Shannon grabbed her coat and ran out to the bus stop.

"Charlie, what do you want to bring to school for snack today?" Bob searched the pantry, "We've got pretzels, chips, or granola bars. You pick."

"Pretzels please." He finished breakfast and put the dishes in the sink. "Can you pack extra for Sam? His mom keeps giving him celery; he hates it."

"I'll give you a few extra today, but Sam's got to eat what his mom packs." Celery? No wonder Charlie and Sam concocted the snack-stealing plan. "Are we ready? Coats? Check. Backpack? Check."

He brewed a second, stronger pot of coffee before

leaving a note for Libby on the counter.

An hour later, a slow-moving Libby awoke. Her hair, a split mess of sleep-matted grease and Easter grass tangles, clumped in random bunches. Eye-to-ear mascara smudges crisscrossed her face like railroad tracks. Revisited tequila crusted the corners of her mouth, accentuated by specks of what might have been guacamole. She passed the hallway mirror and froze.

"Oh God," she moaned. "This is what shame looks like."

The scent of coffee hit her nose the minute she set foot in the kitchen. Bob's note caught her attention.

"Hello Sunshine:

I put on a fresh pot before I left, thought you could use it. Remember, I'm picking up my mom at the airport at five o'clock—be home around six with Chinese, if you're on solid food by then.

Love you."

She set the note aside and filled a mug. "Ah, gut-burning strength, just the way Momma needs it. You are a god, Bob O'Rourke."

Stump bounded over to greet her. "Hey big guy, no sudden moves this morning." The dog cocked to one side and whimpered. "Yeah, I know Mommy is not looking her best today; she's not feeling so steady either. How about we pop onto the computer and start slow?" Stump, sneaker in his mouth, followed her to the laptop.

With the library closed for the long holiday weekend and family all out of the house, Libby had the day to recover from a night of overindulgence. After returning a few email messages, she clicked into her browser to look for more information on Mae's condition.

Two cups of strong coffee later, she switched off the system and headed to the shower. Spending extra time under the hot spray helped clear out the thirty overweight clog dancers pounding on her brain. Resting her forehead against the cool shower tile, Libby swore off tequila for eternity.

Dry, dressed, and slightly more coherent, she started prepping the house for Thanksgiving. Bob and the kids had done the lion's share of the cleaning while she was out drowning her sorrows, but there were still several little details that needed attention.

Mae was bringing the McGinn heirloom Irish lace tablecloth over in the morning. Libby needed to insert the extra leaves in the dining room table and wash the wineglasses and Grandma Shannon's china that was stored in the cottage.

After a quick polish to the table, she was ready to tackle the dish hunt. "Stump," she looked down at his droopy face. "I'm going out to the cottage. If I don't come back in an hour, go for help." His expression remained blank. She grabbed her cell phone off the counter and left.

She pushed open the creaky door and switched on the light. Twenty years of mostly unused, dusty miscellaneous items of family life stared back at her.

The two- room cottage was structurally sound once you looked beyond the refugee-camp decorating style. It had potential charm. Under the piles of junk were wide-peg hardwood floors. In the living room, a small stone hearth sat waiting for use.

In the corner of the room closest to the front door

was a onetime kitchen, now smothered under Bob's collection of baseball memorabilia. The nook contained two leaded glass front cabinets with tarnished brass knobs, a tiny counter with a large porcelain sink, and an arched window overlooking the yard. Bob had shut the main water supply off, but the faucet still mysteriously dripped from time to time.

In the rear of the cottage a quaint bedroom, spacious enough for two, completed the domicile.

As Libby moved into the room, she saw the china box between the two oversized windows. Digging her way in, she tripped over a pair of hiking boots Bob had supposedly donated to charity. "What else is he holding onto out here?" She picked up the boots and started to move them aside when something fell from inside the lining. Evidence of mice spilled out like nasty counterfeit chocolate ice cream sprinkles.

Reaching the china box, Libby lifted and maneuvered her way back to the door. Beside the exit, beneath a plastic bin of Christmas decorations was a glossy pink box Libby had never noticed before. She set the china down and pushed the decorations aside for a better look. Mae's handwriting scrawled across the top—Mom's Dance Costumes.

"No way," Libby whispered. "She said she threw these away."

Resigned to the fact that she would never fully understand her mother's thought process, Libby promised herself a walk down Memory Lane later that afternoon. Hefting one box at a time into the house, she set out on Thanksgiving prep work.

By one o'clock, all the dishes and stemware were sparkling and the twenty-two pound turkey was thawing in the outside refrigerator. Two frozen pies Libby planned to bake and pass off as her own rested on the counter.

In true New England fashion, she took advantage of the winter cold and chilled several bottles of white wine, soda, and beer on the back porch. No need to take up fridge space when nature could lend a hand.

Taking a minute to relish in her superior homemaking skills, she poured herself a deserved third cup of coffee before settling into the couch with Stump tucked in beside her. The dress box sat on the coffee table.

"What do you say, Stump? Should we see what kind of shape these are in?" She paused and recalled the boots' mouse droppings. "I hope the mini-critters didn't find their way in here, too."

She opened the box and set the lid aside. Reverently, she removed the top layer of tissue paper and revealed the first gown, emerald green chiffon with thousands of crystal sequins. Layers of loose, flowing panels made up the tea-length skirt. Libby's mind traveled back to the way her grandmother carried the dress, as if floating, from room to room. There was no choreography in her movements, simply an effortless grace.

"I loved this one." Libby stroked the sheer fabric. "Gram looked like a princess."

She pulled a champagne satin dress from the box. Although the design was simple, a scoop neck with cap sleeves and sea pearls trim, she knew the sentimentality of this garment outweighed all the others.

"I know this means nothing to you, Stump," she said to the dog, "but this dress is irreplaceable. When

Gram and Gramp eloped, she wore this."

She rubbed his warm fur and continued. "Gramp was shipping out for his first tour of duty, there wasn't time for a big ceremony. The night before his scheduled departure, after Gram's final performance, they ran off and got hitched. Very romantic don't you think?"

Stump yawned and rolled over.

Libby ran a hand down the gown's silky sleeve. "Gramp ran back into the dance hall when they were about to leave and grabbed one of the centerpieces from a table so she would have a bouquet." She smiled. "Wish I'd met him, he sounds like my kind of guy."

Glancing at the clock, Libby put away the dresses for the time being and stored them on the top shelf of her closet.

On her way downstairs, the back door opened. "Mom," Charlie called. "Are you home?"

"Right here buddy," Libby stepped into the kitchen. "How was school?"

"Good." He put his backpack down next to the door and tossed his coat on top of it. "We made cornbread and mushed-up cranberries. I didn't eat any 'cause Nathan kept sneezing all over our table."

"Wise choice," she said.

Shannon came into the house, mail in hand.

"Hey there, how was school for you?"

"Fine." Shannon put the bills and magazines down on the counter. "Ms. Gibbons gave us a book report to do over the break; she is such a witch."

In addition to being a witch, Ms. Gibbons was a member of the Historical Society, and thus one of Libby's least favorite people, but she had to set the right example. "Shannon, she's your teacher, show a little respect."

"I guess." Grabbing the pretzels from the pantry, Shannon headed to the computer. "What time is Dad picking up Nana?"

Shelia. Libby had blocked her mother-in-law's impending arrival from her memory. Her headache started to creep back. "Five; they will probably be here around six o'clock."

The kids adored their grandmother, and with good reason. In addition to buckets of love, Shelia came bearing pricey gifts, and also catered to their every whim.

During her last visit, Shelia got Shannon's ears pierced, conveniently forgetting to ask Libby's permission. In truth, the piercing was not the problem. It was the fact that Libby had planned to take Shannon for her birthday and turn it into a mother-daughter bonding experience, but Super Nana robbed her of the opportunity. Not that she was bitter.

"I'm going to go up to my room and start reading the stupid book for English." Shannon trudged upstairs.

As her daughter went off to do homework, Libby had a momentary flashback to another of Shelia's visits. "Charlie," she said, "Sam cannot, under any circumstances, come over while Nana is here."

"But Mom..." Charlie tried to plead his friend's case one final time. "He promised not to do anything bad this time. We'll stay outside. Please!"

"Absolutely not! Nana was extremely upset when the two of you hid in the bathroom and scared her like that. She specifically asked Daddy to keep Sam away when she visits, and we want her to feel comfortable. We're used to Sam's crazy stunts, but he makes Nana nervous."

Libby was not sure who was more traumatized; Shelia, after the boys jumped out from behind the shower curtain, or Charlie and Sam, unwillingly exposed to a naked seventy-year-old. "Do I make myself clear?"

"Okay, no Sam." Defeated, Charlie snatched his coat. "Can I go over to Dom's? He's making sauce and he said I could help smash the tomatoes."

"Sure, but come back in an hour so you can clean up before Nana gets here."

At five, Libby was dragging. Shelia and Bob would not be home for an hour, and everything was as ready as it could be for Thanksgiving. Kids accounted for, she decided the best way to shake off the remnant hangover was a quick nap. She climbed the stairs to the bedroom, Stump fast on her heels.

The duo curled up under the cool, cotton sheets and puffy down comforter. Stump spooned into the small of her back. The faint smell of last night's nachos hit as her face melted into the pillow. Something crunched beneath her head, and her nose crinkled. "Stump, remind me to change the sheets when we get up. There are bits of hangover lingering in here." Within minutes, the dual snores began.

Sounds of laughter and squeals of "Nana" emanating from downstairs jarred Libby from deep sleep.

"Shit!" She sprang out of bed and frantically rubbed the sleep lines away on her rush downstairs. At the bottom of the staircase, she plastered on a happy-to-see-you smile. Shelia's back was to her.

Bob took one look at Libby and silently mouthed

something she could not decipher.

After hugging the kids, Shelia turned to Libby. Her well-maintained platinum blonde hair and electric pink lipstick complimented the faux white fur coat.

"Hello Libby, darling!" Shelia beamed. "How are you? It's been far too long." They hugged.

"We're so glad you are here," Libby said. "How was your flight? You look fantastic, as usual."

"Thank you, dear, that's sweet of you to say." Shelia frowned and cocked a manicured brow. "Libby, by any chance, have you had Mexican food lately?"

Libby eyed Bob. She was going to smother him with his pillow if he breathed a single word of her tequila binge.

"As a matter of fact I had Mexican food last night. How did you know?"

Very delicately, Shelia withdrew a broken tortilla chip from Libby's hair. "Lucky guess."

Chapter Twenty-Two

Thanksgiving morning Libby was, as Bernie would say, up with the chickens. At five-thirty, she started the coffee pot, stumbled out to the garage, and retrieved the mammoth bird from the fridge. After an hour at room temperature, it was thawed and ready to roast. A few warm-up stretches later, she heaved the turkey into the sink for a proper rinse and reached in proctologist-style for the bag of organs.

Stump sniffed out the early morning commotion and settled in beside Libby for moral support.

Small footsteps behind her made her turn. "Happy Thanksgiving, Mom," Charlie said as she rubbed the sleep from his eyes.

"Hi Charlie, Happy Thanksgiving." Libby washed her hands and gave him a quick hug. "What are you doing up so early?"

"I couldn't sleep." His button mouth stretched into an enormous yawn as he sat at the kitchen table. "Nana snores; I can hear her in my room."

Libby restrained a giggle. "Don't tell her, it may hurt her feelings."

"Okay. Can I help you cook? Like the chefs on TV?"

"Sure." She placed two loaves of French bread in front of him. "Want to rip this up for the stuffing?"

"Okay."

She brought over a large plastic bowl. "Break it into penny-sized pieces and put them in here. Then wait for Gram for further instructions."

"Why?"

"Gram only lets me chop stuff up and get the bird ready. I'm not allowed to cook, that's her job." Libby wrestled the bird into the roasting pan. "She likes to make a lot of the stuff we ate as kids, and I like to let her. I guess it's one of our traditions. You can help me sprinkle salt and pepper on the turkey, Gram lets me do that part. Then we shove it in the oven."

Bob came in while Charlie shredded bread chunks. "Hi gang." He gave Libby a quick kiss and reached for the coffee. "Anything I can do?"

"Nothing food-wise," Libby answered. "But after you wake up a little, can you start the fire and bring in the folding chairs from the garage?"

"Sure." He sat next to Charlie. "What are you up to, buddy?"

"I'm doing the bread for the stuffing. Gram has to do the rest 'cause Mom's not allowed." Libby and Bob exchanged grins. Bread torn, he dragged his chair next to Libby to help season the bird. "Eww gross! What's that?" He pointed to the bag of organs.

"Oh, that's just the extra parts of the turkey." Libby explained. "Some people like to cook them and use some of it in the gravy or stuffing."

Charlie picked up the neck. "They eat the penis? That's disgusting!"

Libby spat coffee.

Bob stepped in to view the offending object. "I bet he was a popular guy in the henhouse."

Libby pushed him away.

"No way, Mom!" Charlie tossed the neck in the sink. "I am *not* eating turkey penis!"

"That's the neck, Charlie," she explained. "No one cooks the penis. I'm pretty sure the farmers just throw that part away."

"Well, that's good." Charlie sighed. Without missing a beat, he asked, "Can I eat my cereal in front of the TV? I'll be careful, I promise."

His puppy-dog eyes were hard to refuse. Libby loaded his favorite bowl and sent him to watch cartoons.

Bob refilled her coffee mug. "Kevin told me he'd bring Mae over around nine o'clock. What do we need before she gets here? Is there some type of anxiety medication I can get you?"

"I'm good for now." Libby sprinkled a little more salt and pepper on the bird. "We need to set up the ironing board so Mom can press out the table cloth, but that's it."

Putting down his coffee mug, Bob motioned to the turkey. "Is that monster ready to meet his maker?"

Libby nodded and opened the oven.

"Don't lift that, you'll hurt your back. I'll put it in." Bob hefted the pan into the oven.

"I was in the market with Mom on Monday, and she insisted on the buying the biggest one they had. For some reason, she thinks everyone needs a pound of leftovers."

Stump dropped his bowl at Libby's feet and broke out the sad, feed-me eyes.

"Trying to tell me something, Stump?"

"I got it." Bob was closer to the pantry and scooped out a helping of dog food. "I'll go a little light on his chow; God knows he's going to scarf up anything that hits the floor today."

Libby grabbed Stump's gas medication. "Don't forget the pill. His digestive system will be in overdrive by the end of appetizers."

While Bob fed the dog, Libby looked around the kitchen. "There's nothing else I can do until Mom gets here. I'll go shower during the lull."

Bob made sure Charlie was engrossed in his cartoons before he spoke seductively, "Want some company in that shower?"

Libby rolled her eyes. "Bob, what's the rule?"

He sighed. "No daytime sex when my mother is here. And if you see fit to grant me a conjugal visit at night, I must be exceptionally quiet and equally quick."

"Good boy."

"I hate *the rule*."

"I hate your mother's Jell-O salad, but the holidays make us all suffer in one way or another. Suck it up."

After a steamy shower, Libby dug out her most comfortable jeans and a festive sweater. Mae, no doubt, would give her an earful for dressing down, but hosting a holiday full of cranberry sauce and red wine screamed for wash-and-wear.

In the living room, Bob set the ironing board up for Mae before shuttling folding chairs from the garage. Shelia, perfectly coiffed, sat with Charlie and Shannon on the sofa, watching the Thanksgiving parade.

A quick peek at the turkey assured Libby all was running according to schedule.

Kevin pulled into the drive ten minutes later and dropped Mae off. The back door swung open.

"Hello everyone!" Mae breezed in on a current

scented with pumpkin pie and cinnamon. "Happy Thanksgiving!"

"Gram!" The kids swooped in for hugs and kisses.

"Guess what?" Charlie said.

"What?" Mae answered.

"I helped rip up the bread for the stuffing."

"Marvelous!"

"Guess what else?"

"I have no idea." She grinned at his effervescence.

"We don't eat the turkey's penis, we eat his neck. But they look the same so you could get confused. I didn't want you to worry if you end up with the neck piece."

"Well...uh...well..." Mae stammered. "Good to know, and thank you for sharing, Charlie. You are a surprisingly well-informed young man."

She shifted gears and greeted Bob's mother. "Wonderful to see you Shelia, how was the flight?"

"Lovely, thank you," Shelia answered. "I sat next to a striking man from Hartford—a doctor on his way back from relief work in Africa. We exchanged emails and made plans to get together after the holidays."

"How delightful." Mae's expression turned stern as she took Shelia's hand and spoke in a hushed tone. "I do hope he didn't contract that nasty disease the news programs talked about last week. Awful really, an odd strain of flesh-eating bacteria. Appendages and such just, plop, fall off without warning." Shelia turned green. Mae continued. "I'm sure that wasn't the case for your doctor friend."

Wisdom shared, Mae turned her attention to Libby. "Is the ironing board set up so I can get started on the tablecloth?"

This is going to be a long, long day, Libby thought. She pointed Mae to the far corner where the board waited for duty. "Shannon, take the cloth over for Gram and plug in the iron. Mom, do you want a cup of coffee before you get started?"

"Yes dear, thank you. Black, please," Mae said.

Libby knew how her mother took her coffee, but it never stopped Mae from telling her.

Shelia, Mae, Libby, and Bob sat at the kitchen table, coffees in hand. Bob spoke first.

"Mom, how did you sleep?" he asked.

"Like a log, sweetheart," Shelia graciously replied. "That bed is very comfortable, it has that nice lived-in quality—soft and squishy."

Lived-in equated to lumpy, but Libby appreciated Shelia's attempt at tact. The homey aroma emanating from the oven reminded her it was time to baste. "Excuse me folks, it's time to check the bird and give it a few coats of juice. Mom, when you're ready, the iron should be hot. I've got all the china and silverware ready to go. Shelia, maybe you could set the table when Mom's finished?"

"Absolutely, I'd love to help." Shelia beamed, happy to be included. "While Mae is hard at work, I'll pop upstairs and put on my face." She left the table and went upstairs to beautify.

Bob returned to the garage for the final batch of folding chairs, leaving Mae and Libby alone.

"Put on her face?" Mae scoffed. "My ceiling has less spackle."

"It's Thanksgiving," Libby begged. "Don't make me put you in time-out."

"Fine, fine. I'll be on my best behavior."

Mae ironed and Libby basted. The big meal was officially underway.

For years, mother and daughter followed the same holiday routine without deviation. There had been bumps in the road, and one sizeable pothole when Suzanne tried to introduce her Broccoli Surprise casserole into the mix, but for the most part *tradition was tradition* and nothing messed with it.

Shannon and Charlie abandoned the television and took Stump to the yard to run off excess energy before the rest of the family arrived.

Basting complete, Libby joined Mae in the living room. "The cloth looks nice, Mom, take a break."

"I'm almost through." Mae pressed the few remaining imperfections. "Do we have enough plates?"

"Yes, I took out the rest of Grandma's china and washed it yesterday."

She remembered the ballroom dresses. "And speaking of Grandma, I thought you told me you gave away her old dance costumes. I found a box of them under a bunch of stuff out in the cottage. Did you put them there when you moved and forget to tell me?"

Mae took a momentary pause from ironing, just long enough to collect her thoughts. "I was so frazzled back then, Lib. Daddy was gone, and I was moving forty years' worth of junk from a big house into my tiny condominium. Honestly, I thought I did toss them away, but maybe I brought them over here for Shannon to play dress-up in. They are just old dresses. What's this fuss about?"

"They were a part of my childhood, and my memories with Gram. I was shocked when you said you tossed them away. It was nice to stumble upon them, that's all."

With a sigh, Mae switched off the iron and faced Libby. "Sweetheart, those dresses do not bring me the same joy they do you. For you it was a fanciful time with your grandmother. I'm so glad you have those memories that you'll treasure always."

She took a long, soothing breath, collected her thoughts and continued. "I know this will be hard to understand, but when I look at those spectacular gowns and recall how vital my mother once was, I can't help but remember the end of her life. How she went from one of the most exuberant and dazzling women I have ever known to a hollow shell."

Mae wiped away tears. "Listen to me, Libby; I never want you three kids to go through that with me. If I ever get to that point, you just take me out back and shoot me. Let Suzanne do it, she's been itching to have a shot at me for years."

"Oh Mom, I'm sorry," Libby said and hugged her close. "I didn't want to upset you, especially today."

Mae pulled away and ran her hand over Libby's curly hair. "Enough. I've had my weepy moment, now let's get back to making dinner. We have hoards of hungry people waiting."

She held up the cloth and inspected for wrinkles. "This looks perfect. Grab the other end and let's get this on the table." They took the lace tablecloth to the dining room and lay it over the white linen under-cloth Libby had previously set in place.

The delicate lace cascaded over the table like a bridal veil. "Beautiful." Mae smoothed out the cloth, lingering a small while, remembering holidays long past. The intricate Celtic heirloom had been handed down from Bernie's parents, and their parents before them.

"I want you to have this, Libby. It belongs with a family, not on the top shelf of my closet collecting dust. Daddy would be happy to know it's with you."

Mae reverently stroked the cloth. "On her one trip visiting from Ireland, Daddy's mother served us Easter brunch on this lace; I still remember that meal. God she could cook. After the meal, she took me aside in the kitchen and told me, she was leaving the cloth behind because her mother would have wanted me to have it. I cried for days. Of course, I found out later I was pregnant, and that explained the tears more than anything else."

Moved by her mother's gift, Libby answered. "I'll take good care of it, Mom. Thanks for trusting me to carry on the tradition."

"Just don't let Suzanne near it." Mae warned. "That insufferable woman will add glitter and beads and ruin it in less than ten seconds. My hand to God, she probably glues sparkles on Kevin's underwear when he's not paying attention."

Shelia came into the room freshly made up. "I'm all yours, Libby. Ready to help. Where is everything for the table?"

Libby heard Caroline's voice in the living room and left Shelia and Mae with the task of table setting.

"I know you said not to bring anything," Caroline said. "But no one can refuse chocolate chip cookies."

"Charlie will love you," Libby said, "and so do I." She put the cookies on the counter and turned to Trevor. "Hey Trev, Happy Thanksgiving."

"Thanks. You too, Aunt Lib." He took off his coat

and hung it on the same peg he used ever since he could reach the doorknob. "Where are Shannon and Charlie?"

"Out back. Can you please go call them in for me?"

"Sure." Trevor opened the back door and Stump jumped up to greet him. A massive paw on each of the boy's shoulders, the pooch licked him until he begged for mercy. "Geez Stump, you need a girlfriend. Enough with the doggie love."

Libby ran over and yanked the giant mutt off him. "Down Stump! Sorry, Trev."

"No prob."

"Out of curiosity, what did you have for breakfast?"

"Bacon and eggs, why?"

"Bacon, he can smell it hours after you digest. It's a gift."

"Nice. I'll remember that from now on."

Charlie and Shannon came in, and the younger generation vanished to the basement for the annual table tennis tournament.

Upstairs, the adults gathered in the kitchen. No matter how many seats Bob lugged, everyone stood in the kitchen.

The doorbell rang. Libby knew it must be Dolores since everyone else barged right in. Her boss was proper to the core.

"Happy Thanksgiving, Dolores," Libby ushered her inside the house. "Please come in."

"Thank you for inviting me, Libby." She handed Libby a covered dish. "I hope it's not too much trouble to have an extra person. I made my mother's sweet potato casserole. It's a crowd pleaser."

"That sounds great, why don't you pop your coat in

the closet and follow me into the kitchen. We'll put this in to warm up." Libby took the dish and led the way to the stove.

Alone in the kitchen, she took the opportunity to question her friend. "Can I get you a glass of wine, Dolores?" Libby asked.

"That would be lovely. White please," Dolores answered.

Libby generously filled the glasses. "So, before Dom comes over, tell me about your date. We haven't had a chance to talk, and I want *all* the juicy details."

Blushing like a schoolgirl, Dolores took a respectable sip of wine. "Dominic was a perfect gentleman. And as hard as this is to admit, his lasagna was top-notch."

"Dom's a fabulous cook, he's bringing his famous stuffed shells today; they're to-die-for delicious. How did he like your pineapple upside-down cake?"

"He ate two very large slices and was very complimentary."

"I knew he'd like it. The man appreciates something special when he sees it. I'm glad you went. It's nice to see two of my favorite people enjoying each other. I know Dom was happy to have your company."

"Did he say anything about our evening?"

One of the joys in life, Libby thought, *was witnessing a new love develop, no matter what age it bloomed.* "He and Bob hit the hardware store last night to pick up a few more Christmas lights—like we don't have enough, right? Anyway, Dom told him how nice it was to spend time with you, and that his friends thought you were terrific. Let me tell you, it's no easy task to pass muster with that bunch, so you know you must have made a great impression."

Dolores stood straighter. "They were a delightful bunch of people, a little rough around the edges at times, but overall enjoyable to spend time with. I can see why Dominic holds them in such high regard."

Libby loved that she referred to Dom by his full name—no nicknames for Dolores. "Do you think you will be doing it again?"

Before she could get an answer, the back door swung in. An oversized Poinsettia balanced on an army-sized tray of stuffed shells blocked the newly arrived guest's face.

"Happy Thanksgiving, bella!" Dom boomed.

"God, Dom. Make two trips next time—you live fifteen feet away." Libby grabbed the plant and revealed a cheerful Dom. "Ah, there you are. Happy Thanksgiving." She gave him a peck on the cheek and took the tray.

"Hello Dominic," Dolores said with a blush. "Happy Thanksgiving. Libby tells me you brought another Italian delicacy to share with us today. If it's anything like your fabulous lasagna, I'm sure it will be delicious."

"Thank you, Dolores. And may I say you look lovely today?" Dom gushed.

Libby hid a grin as he continued. "The secret to Italian cooking is in the sauce. Charlie is doing well as my apprentice this year, Lib. He's got the knack for mashing. Not everyone can mash with his enthusiasm."

"That's my boy, expert masher," Libby said. "Why don't you grab a glass of wine, Dom, and take Dolores into the living room? Mom's entertaining the crowd with tales of her colonoscopy. They seem riveted. Word of warning though, Shelia's visiting."

Once upon a time Shelia had romantic designs on Dom, the feeling was not mutual.

"Thanks for the warning. Bob let me know she was in town at the store last night. By the way, you owe me—your landscape-challenged husband wanted to buy a chainsaw, but I talked him out of it. The man can't master a weed trimmer; I can't imagine the hospital bills with a chainsaw."

"Oh God," Libby put her hand to her heart. "I do not have enough life insurance on that man."

Kevin and Suzanne arrived shortly after Dom, pink cupcakes in hand. Saratoga, dressed in what Libby guessed was an extraordinarily expensive baby turkey costume, sported brown fleece jumpsuit, red feather headband, and strategically placed zipper-waddle. Displeased with her ensemble, the baby wailed her way through the cheese and crackers. Kevin took her into the kitchen for a few laps of bounce-and-walk in hopes his little nugget would pass out before dinner.

Sean, always last to arrive, crept into the kitchen while everyone was in the living room gorging on appetizers.

Kevin and the somewhat-calm Saratoga rounded the corner. "Nice of you to join us," he said to Sean. "At least tell me you had some incredible woman holding you as her sex hostage and you couldn't escape until now?"

Sean patted his brother's shoulder. "Still not getting any, huh?"

"No, damn it. Suzanne said no nooky until the baby's six weeks old. Right now we're at five weeks, four days; not that I'm counting."

Sean kissed the drowsy baby; her chubby cheeks tear-stained and extra rosy. "Hi princess." He looked at Kevin and whispered. "Why is she dressed like a chicken?"

"Hell if I know."

"Is everybody in the living room?"

"Yeah, but don't go there. Mom's talking about her anal cleanliness, in detail. That woman is obsessed with her digestive tract. Want to take my chicken nugget while I get a drink?"

Sean took the baby-handoff and began pacing. "I'll walk Sara for a while," he said in a whisper. "Grab me a beer and leave it open on the counter. I'll grab some on our laps around the kitchen."

Kevin looked at Saratoga, instantly asleep in Sean's embrace, and wondered how his brother, the childless family member, had such a gift with kids. "You've got the touch, big brother. I'll never know how you do it; but at the moment, I don't care."

Sean patted Saratoga's back. "Where do you want me to put her once I'm sure she's out?"

"Lib's got the portable crib set up in her bedroom." Kevin grabbed two beers out of the fridge, popped the caps, and left one on the counter for Sean before joining the others in the living room.

Suzanne frowned. "Where's Saratoga?"

"Sean's here. He's working his magic." Kevin sipped and continued. "Seriously babe, we need to have him over more often, the man is a baby genius." Murmurs of agreement sounded.

Sean, out of sight in the dining room walked the baby and overheard the conversation.

Bob walked over to the fireplace and added a log to

the dwindling flames. "Lib, remember when we were down in Florida visiting Will with the whole family and Shannon? She was two and refused to go near the ocean no matter how much we begged. Sean scooped her up, and five minutes later she was splashing around like a dolphin. The man does have a gift."

Sean smiled at the memory and continued to pace with Sara.

Mae chimed in. "He needs to find a nice girl and settle down *with his gift*. Sean deserves a family."

"Mom," Libby said, "he's a grown man. Leave him alone."

Whispering low to himself, Sean said, "Thanks for sticking up for me, Lib."

"I *am* leaving him alone, but *alone* is what he'll be if he keeps on like this," Mae insisted.

"Appreciate the vote of confidence, Mom," he confided to sleeping baby Sara.

"All I'm saying," Mae continued, "is that he has a lot to offer and he's been by himself too long. Last Sunday, after church, I introduced him to Lana Brown. She's a lovely young widow who bakes a fabulous bundt cake and sings in the choir. She's not perfect, and the tooth gap is a bit distracting, but in certain lights she's pretty. The entire time we chatted Sean didn't say more than two words to her. Honestly, what is wrong with that man? It's like his heart's been bruised or something."

He continued his dining room laps. "I'm not a melon."

"Maybe he's gay?" Mae pondered. "William didn't realize he loved men until later in life. Maybe Sean is a late bloomer also?"

Sean's jaw hit the floor.

Caroline gagged on her wine. "He's not gay," she sputtered.

Kevin took note of her reaction, and recalled how cozy she and Sean looked in the backseat of his car. There was something there. "Leave Sean alone, Mom," he said. "He's got to find the right girl. Maybe he already has, and we just don't know it yet."

He grinned at Caroline. She paled. "After all," he continued, "we're a lot to take in, and McGinns scare the crap out of most women. It takes guts to join this family."

"No argument there," Suzanne said. The crowd laughed.

"We are an exceptionally loving and supportive family, and Sean is a true catch," Mae scoffed. "A single woman searching for a handsome and devoted man would be blessed to have him." Her gaze bore into Caroline. "Isn't that right, Caroline?"

Caroline's mouth gaped. "I, um, well..."

Sean peeked from behind the dining room door and watched her squirm. "Priceless," he whispered.

Kevin jumped to the rescue. "Don't rope Car into this," he said. "Just because she's a single cougar on the prowl for young meat doesn't mean she can speak for the entire herd."

Caroline smiled and offered up a silent "thank you."

Dom, ever the diplomat, said, "Mae, I think Sean can handle his love life and I'm sure he's going to end up right where he belongs. Give him time. Everything great in life is worth waiting for."

Dolores rarely spoke in crowds, but when she did,

the words carried a lifetime of insight. "I agree, Dominic," she said. "Although I don't know Sean well, he seems like a charming young man, and always returns his library books in the allotted time."

Bob and Libby exchanged a grin.

"What I do know is opening up to someone, anyone, is an extreme risk. Perhaps Sean took the risk before and was hurt badly enough to keep his distance from the possibility of history repeating itself. A heart, once broken, is not easily mended."

Family and friends stared into their drinks in silence. Dolores's theory made perfect sense. None realized it more than Caroline did.

In the next room, Sean's mind raced as Saratoga began to squirm. He had to get away before the baby started to cry, alerting everyone to his proximity, and revealing he'd heard their entire assessment of his love life. Gently, he rubbed the baby's back and inched away, but he was not fast enough. The gas bubble Saratoga had been fighting all morning let loose in one enormous burst.

"What the hell was that?" Bob said, shooting out of his seat. "Where's Stump?"

"That was no dog," Kevin said and beamed with paternal pride. "That was my delicate baby girl's mighty wind. I'd recognize those toots anywhere." Suzanne hit him in the ribs.

Sean gave up the charade and strolled into the room with a contented baby in his arms. "In case anyone was wondering, Sara shares her father's knack for clearing a room."

He spoke to Kevin. "She makes the same butt music you did when we were kids; those bunk beds were murder."

"I was *very* talented." Kevin boasted.

"Was?" Suzanne raised a brow.

The flatulence debate continued as guests gathered stray napkins and wineglasses and moved to the kitchen to lend hands getting the meal on the table.

Sean, grateful the group moved off the subject of his bachelorhood, took the now sleeping baby upstairs, laid her down in the crib, and closed the door behind him.

A victory cry rang out from the basement and three children barreled up the stairs into the kitchen.

"I am the man!" Trevor proclaimed. "Three years running table tennis champion!"

"Humble aren't you?" Caroline ruffled her son's hair.

"Hard to be humble when you rock the paddle as great as me." He snagged a dinner roll and took off running for the backyard; Shannon, Charlie, and Stump right behind. Caroline put on a coat and followed along for some fresh air. Libby and Mae removed trays of food from the oven as Sean came downstairs.

"Smells good Mom," Sean said. "Need anything?"

"*Mom?*" Libby questioned. "This is *my* kitchen, you know? I did have some input with this meal."

"Sorry, Lib," he chuckled. "I temporarily forgot the essential salt and pepper you are entrusted to add to the bird. Whatever would we do without your culinary skills?"

"Wise ass."

"Go relax, Sean," Mae said. "I'll have it on the table in about fifteen minutes." She caught sight of Caroline alone on the back porch. "On second thought, dear, can you get some more firewood from out back? I would ask Bob, but he, Dom, and the kids are busy stringing more obnoxious Christmas lights."

"They're not obnoxious," Libby snapped. "They're authentically festive."

"Really? Tell me Elizabeth, when the Virgin Mary gave birth to our Lord, Jesus, did it look like Las Vegas in the manger?"

"I give up." Libby brought the first side dishes to the table.

Sean picked up the log carrier and left to fetch the firewood. Outside, he asked Caroline, "What are you doing out here all by yourself? Did the fart talk drive you away?"

She laughed and said, "After thirty years of McGinn humor, they go right over my head. I only wanted some fresh air. What drove you out?"

"Wood."—he held up the carrier—"and a little escape from the pity glances. *Poor sexually-confused Sean, how will he ever survive without children of his own to care for him when he's old and toothless?*"

"Heard that, huh?"

"Hard not to." He shrugged. "Thanks for defending my heterosexuality."

"My pleasure," she chuckled. "For what it's worth, they're wrong about you ending up alone. Sean McGinn without a wife and brood of kids? Get real. There's a better chance of Kev growing hair than you staying single in today's market. Now toothless, that I could see. You do work with power tools, accidents happen on the job site every day."

He smiled and sat down on the step beside her. "Yeah, what does your crystal ball say about my future?

I'd love to hear it."

"Kids, dog, house, the whole package. You're born for it McGinn, It's in your blood." She slapped his knee. "Better get cracking, find a girl and get her preggo quick. You're not getting any younger, and you sure as hell aren't getting any better looking. Might want to borrow some of Kevin's spray-on hair." She ran a hand over the crown of his head. "Looks a little thin on top."

"Funny, funny woman," he said. "And you should talk, Mother-Of-Teenager. Who's the old one now? At least I'm still dating women closer to our age. I saw the last guy you went out with. Tell me, does the shrimp taste better at the early bird special, or do you just eat at three o'clock in the afternoon so he can use his senior discount?"

"Low blow!" She laughed in spite of herself, and it felt fantastic. It was years since she and Sean were able to sit together without the awkwardness of their past coming between them. She missed him.

"But true." He wiggled a brow. "If you're into that particular age group I'm sure Dom has some buddies he can fix you up with. Of course you'll have to date during the day; none of them can drive at night anymore."

"Be nice! Dom is a sweetheart, and I'm sure his friends are very sexy." She tried to keep a straight face. It did not last. "Okay, *sexy* may be a reach...and you have some nerve commenting on my dates, at least they're *old enough* to drive. When I date we go out to elegant restaurants, not the senior prom."

Although physically on Libby's porch, Caroline's comment rocketed them back in time, to the

Immaculate Conception parking lot all those years ago, the moment their friendship changed into something more.

"I can't believe our prom was over twenty-five years ago." Sean picked at a stray leaf, unable to meet Caroline's eye. "Do you regret it? You and me? We were so young."

"Look at me Sean." Caroline took the leaf from his grasp and replaced it with her own trembling fingers. "I have a lot of regrets, more than I'll ever admit to, but there has never been a single minute I regretted falling in love with you."

Her eyes misted. "In my life, I've made some horrid choices, trusted people I shouldn't, and wasted a lot of time trying to make a perfect life in an imperfect marriage." She let the tears fall. "But one of the best things I ever did was take a chance with you; I have absolutely no regrets in that regard."

"I broke your heart, Car." Sean hung his head. "I know I sound like a self-centered jerk, but I did, and I'm sorry, sorrier than any half-assed apology I can give. For what it's worth, I thought I was doing the right thing back then. Now,"—he watched Trevor chasing Stump across the yard—"I'm not so sure. The *what ifs* are killing me."

"Take it from me, life isn't about the what ifs, it's about what is, and appreciating what you have every day," she said. "There is nothing to forgive. You were right, we were too young, and we needed to grow up, live a little away from each other and see what life was about, outside Rhyme."

He looked down into the eyes of the seventeen-year-old girl he had fallen so deeply in love with all those years ago; the lines around them were new, but the girl was still there. "You are a wise woman Caroline Duffy. Do you know that?"

"I do, but it's always nice to hear." She placed a hand on his gruff cheek. "I need to know something, Sean."

"Ask away."

"Did I do that to you? What Dolores said in there. Did I hurt you without knowing it? When Trev and I came back to town, after the divorce, you seemed distant. You never look me in the eye or say more than 'hello.' I've been here three years, and you still leave the room every time I come in."

Sean took her hand from his face, interlinked it with his, and held tight.

She continued, "This is the first time you've spoken to me for more than three seconds. Unless you count weather or sports."

He grinned.

"What happened to us Sean? Why did you keep me at arm's length? We were friends before anything else. I miss you so much I ache."

"I've missed you too, Car, more than I probably should," he confessed. "I'm sorry if I've been keeping my distance. It's not because of anything you did. I probably should explain."

He fidgeted, uncomfortable with how to proceed. "There's something I need to tell you, something very difficult to share. It's not going to be easy, but there's no sense hanging onto the pride I have left."

"Oh my God," Caroline gasped. "You are gay!"

"I am *not* gay!" he shouted. "Why does everyone think that all of a sudden?"

His voice dropped to a deep whisper. "Let me ask you something, Duffy. Did you ever question my sexuality those nights on the beach? We made more runs to the drug store for condoms than I can count. Or how about the old house on Morgan Street that Dad was renovating? If those walls could talk—"

"Stop." Her cheeks heated at the memory. "I believe you. You're not gay." She paused. "Bi?"

"For the love of Christ, Caroline, I like women! I am not now, nor have I ever been attracted to men. Okay?"

"Don't yell at me! You made it sound like you had some big secret. Sorry I jumped to conclusions."

"It's not a secret." He shook his head in frustration. "I can't believe I'm actually going to tell you this. Mom is the only one who knows. Lib doesn't have a clue. It happened a long time ago, and you deserve to know the truth."

He swallowed hard. "When Lib told me you were marrying The Schmuck, I went a little nuts. I know, I know...I didn't have the right to. We hadn't even seen each other in years...but something about the guy rubbed me the wrong way. He seemed like trouble from the start."

"Very perceptive of you."

"Sorry," he winced. "Don't mean to rub salt in the wound. Anyway, you got engaged, and I went bonkers. And here's the best part...not only was I going to steal you away from Steve, but I was going to get down on one knee, tell you what an idiot I was to let you get away and beg you to marry *me* instead."

Caroline clasped his hand tighter as the breath rushed from her lungs.

Sean continued, "I went over to Mom and Dad's and told them my plan. Mom started crying like a fool and gave me Grandma Shannon's wedding ring. Dad tried to reason with me, told me to slow down and start by talking with you, but I wasn't having any of it. I shoved past him and jumped in my truck, hellbent on getting to Boston...to you."

He forced a laugh. "I was halfway there before I realized I had no freaking clue where you lived. Good plan, right? Steal the girl, worry about her address later. Obviously, I wasn't clearheaded, so I pulled over in Sturbridge and called Lib. I gave her some bullshit story about going to Boston to visit friends and how I wanted to stop by and say hello to you and The Schmuck—you know, congratulate you on the big news. I wasn't about to tell her I was on some crazy mission, chasing after the woman I loved."

Sean paused and his expression fell. "I never got any further than Sturbridge. When I finally stopped talking long enough for Lib to get a word in, she was crying, screaming that I needed to come home right away."

Caroline replayed the timeline in her head. "Oh God...Bernie."

"Yeah," Sean confirmed her suspicion. "Dad had his first heart attack that day. Things looked bad, really bad. The doctors said he wasn't going to pull through. Mom alternated between panic and anger. One minute, she was furious at Dad for not taking better care of himself and the next she was on her knees begging God to save him. That man loved his red meat and Irish whiskey; his liver was a marinated brisket."

Sean smiled, remembering. "You would think after

something like that he would have made a few diet changes, but not Dad. Nope, he just kept living the way he wanted, thinking he was invincible. It took another ten years and two more heart attacks, but eventually fate proved him wrong. "

"I remember Lib's phone call to tell me what happened like it was yesterday. She was beside herself," Caroline said. "She must have called me right after she hung up with you. All I wanted to do was race to Connecticut and be with all of you, but Steve convinced me to stay put. He said I couldn't do anything, and it was a family problem. I can't believe I listened to him."

"You *are* family, Car, always." Sean brushed a stray hair off her cheek and went on. "By the time Dad recovered enough to go back to work it was two months later, and you had eloped into being Mrs. Schmuck. I was so wrapped up in keeping the business running and taking care of Mom, I missed my chance to get you back."

He brushed a kiss across her forehead. "Story of my life; I'm the almost guy, *almost* got the girl, *almost* had the life. Almost isn't good enough."

"There you have it," he finished, "my pitiful excuse for keeping away from you these last years, a fragile ego with a healthy dose of stupid. It's hard to be around the one that got away, especially when she's been part of your life since Tooth Fairies and flashlight tag."

"I wish I'd known." There was a resignation in Caroline's voice. "I would have done so many things differently."

Trevor ran past, cradling a football—his father's

image with his mother's heart. Charlie and Shannon chased him into the front yard leaving the couple in private.

Caroline said, "Things happen for a reason, I suppose. Marriage brought me Trevor. And in an odd way, Bernie brought me back here, to the people I love most. I felt like such an outsider at the funeral, and all I wanted to do was belong again. Right then and there I made the decision to file for divorce, not that it wasn't a long time coming, but something Mae said to me after the service struck a chord."

"What'd she say?"

"It was strange and yet poignant at the same time. She said Bernie loved me like the daughter I was meant to be, and he knew I'd come home. My heart just needed to find the way." She snuggled into Sean's side and placed her head on his shoulder. "Can I tell you something?"

He buried his face in her hair. "Anything."

"If you'd made it to Boston that day, tracked me down and gotten down on one knee like you planned,"—she took a deep breath, pulled back, and met him eye to eye—"I would have said yes. I would have run off with you faster than that old truck could drive, and never looked back."

Don't hesitate. Bernie's words echoed in Sean's head as he took her face in his hands and ran the calloused pad of his thumb along her supple lips. His voice, deep and graveled with a dormant need lay claim to her heart. "I wouldn't have taken no for an answer."

From the back window, Mae watched her son take the first step toward the rest of his life. "It's about time," she murmured. "Kiss her you bloody moron!"

A breath apart, Sean's gaze traveled to Caroline's lips, seeking her approval before capturing the forgotten taste of heaven he longed for. Her sly grin gave him all the permission he needed. He closed his eyes and leaned in.

He never saw the dog coming; she did.

"Look out!" Caroline warned, but it was too late. Stump pounced before Sean knew what was happening, and the soft lips he anticipated morphed into eight inches of drooling, flank steak.

"Damned dog," Mae cursed. "I'm glad they fixed you! Just proves a man's brains are in his testicles."

Chapter Twenty-Three

Rhyme's volunteer fire department did not expect gingersnaps and lemonade, but Mae feeds all guests.

Libby sprinted to the smoldering condominium. "Mom, are you hurt?"

"I'm fine, Elizabeth. It was a little cooking accident, nothing more."

The fire chief rolled his eyes as Mae continued. "I put most of it out with some baking soda, but those touchy smoke detectors go off at the smallest thing. And of course Myrna, the busybody, heard the alarm and had to make a big production out of it and call in the cavalry."

The cavalry was two engines and an ambulance. "I only called you because I knew Myrna would tattle on me, and I didn't want you to worry."

Sean's truck screeched to a halt behind them. He and Kevin sprang out and jogged over.

"Everybody okay?" Sean asked.

"Yes dear," Mae answered. "Why are you all making such a fuss? And Kevin, why aren't you at work? There was no need to rush over here; honestly you three are such worry warts."

"Let me make the call on that, okay Mom?" Kevin asked. "I'm going to go see if we can get back inside." He walked over to the officer in charge.

"Tell me what happened," Sean said to his mother.

"Was it a grease fire, or did something catch in the oven? If it's an electrical issue, I need to know so I can get a team back out here and inspect the other units."

"There's nothing wrong with the electrical," Mae explained. "I had water on the stove, and I walked away for a minute, something must have been on the burner, and it got all smoky. That's all, no drama."

Kevin rejoined them. "They said Mom can go in to get some stuff, but she'll need to move out until the repairs are done, and the building inspector comes through."

"That's ridiculous," Mae fumed. "It was a little smoke, I'm not going anywhere."

"Let's check it out first," Libby said. "We'll decide after we see how bad it is."

The four entered the house to the smell of burning metal. Libby walked ahead to the kitchen. "I'm going to open the window and get some air in here." But there was no window. There was no kitchen. A mess of water and charred debris littered the small space, the remains of a saucepot sat beyond recognition in what was left of the sink.

"Kev," she called to the living room, "can you come in here and help me open this window? It's stuck."

Kevin entered. "Holy shit."

"My thoughts exactly."

"How the hell did this happen?" he asked.

Libby pointed to the remains of the saucepot. "Take it from me, I burn plenty of things in the kitchen, and that type of damage didn't happen 'in a minute.' She put the stove on and forgot. It could have been a heck of a lot worse. Thank God she has an end unit and the kitchen faced out. The fire could have spread to the entire development. What do we do?"

"Okay, let's not confront her right now, she'll freak out. Go help her get some clothes and she'll stay with me and Suz for a few days." Libby started to object, and he stopped her. "No, it'll be fine. Sara is an excellent buffer. We can suck it up while we figure this mess out. Send Sean in, we need to know how much time this is going to take to fix. I can't hold Suzanne back forever, more than a couple weeks, and she and Mom will kill each other."

Libby left and sent Sean in. "Holy shit!" he said.

"That's the consensus," Kevin answered.

"This isn't good."

"No kidding."

"Seriously Kev..." He kicked some debris aside and checked the outer wall. "I've got to rip this all out and shore up the whole thing. We're talking months."

"Dear God, no."

"Yes."

"Suzanne will throw a clot."

"Don't worry, we'll think of something."

Kevin paused. "I think we've got a bigger problem than the Suzanne/Mae cage match, don't you?"

Sean sized up the scene. "Yeah, we do."

"She can't live alone, it's not safe. We got lucky this time, but what if it happens again?"

"It can't. She'll kill herself, or somebody else."

Libby came back in. "I got her to pack a bag, and sent her to Myrna's for a minute. What are we going to do? We need a plan."

"Got any suggestions?" Sean asked.

"No," she answered. "Let's talk privately, the three

of us, before we say anything to Mom. I'm open tonight, how about you?" The brothers agreed. "Good, come to the house after work, bring junk food. I need empty calories when I'm stressed."

"What," Kevin joked, "no tequila?"

"You are never going to let me live that down, are you?"

"I have pictures."

"I hate you."

****

At seven, Sean, Kevin, and Suzanne arrived at the O'Rourke's with several pizzas and two large pink bakery boxes from Annie's.

Libby made an exception to the "no food upstairs" rule and let Charlie and Shannon take a pizza up to the master bedroom and watch a movie on TV.

Suzanne put the baby down in the portable crib and came downstairs to join the rest of the adults in the living room.

"White or red?" Bob held up two bottles of wine. "Or is this the kind of conversation we need both?"

"Both," Kevin immediately responded. He reached over and grabbed one of the cups Lib brought in for the soft drinks. "And don't bother with the nice glasses; I'm good with a kiddie cup. Feels like I'm reconnecting with my inner child. Dibs on the race car."

"Leave me the airplane," Sean shouted. "Lib, do you want a big girl glass, or do you want to duke it out with Suzanne for the ballerina?"

"Listen dummy, you're lucky I even have clean cups. It's this, or a juice box, deal with it." Libby reached into the corner cabinet and grabbed two wineglasses. "Suzanne and I are adults. Bob do you want a wineglass, or the tugboat cup?"

He grinned.

"Never mind, I shouldn't have asked," she said.

Bob poured the wine as Libby passed out paper plates and napkins and took a seat. "Okay, first let me make sure we are all on the same page. Kev, I know Mom told Sean what Dr.Rashan said, but did she tell you guys, too?"

Kevin swallowed a bite of pie. "Yeah, but I think we got the sugar-coated version."

"What do you mean?"

Kevin looked at Suzanne. She nodded. "Mom told us the minimum," he said. "She didn't go into details, so I did the same thing as Lib—surfed the net for info. Kind of grim reading."

Suzanne daintily put down her wineglass. "Tell them about dinner the other night."

"I am honey; I'm just not sure where to start." He rubbed his balding head. "Honestly, I'm not sure it's a big deal."

Sean refilled his cup. "Kev, you're probably right, but let's hear it anyway."

"Mom came over for dinner last week," Kevin explained. "She was her usual bowl of compliments; giving Suz advice, lecturing me on going to church more—typical Mom. We finished eating, Sara started to fuss, and Mom offered to take her upstairs and get her down for the night. We jumped on that like a dog on a bone. Our daughter, God love her, is not a sound sleeper. The baby monitor was on in the living room, and we could hear Mom talking to Sara upstairs, but she's not calling her Sara, she calling her Meghan."

"That is so strange," Libby interrupted. "Mom

called me Meghan when we had our big fight a few weeks ago. She claimed it was 'a slip of the tongue.'"

"Huh," Kevin continued. "It wasn't a onetime slip of the tongue at our place. Mom said the name at least three or four times."

"Does she know a Meghan?" Sean asked.

Suzanne spoke up. "That's the worst part, when Mae came downstairs Kevin asked her about it, and she exploded. She told us to mind our own business and made Kev take her home right away. Of course, she blamed me for somehow fabricating the whole thing. I know you all love your Mom, and I'm sorry she's going through this, but she was a little harsher than usual to me this time. It hurt."

Libby hugged her sister-in-law. "I'm so sorry; I know she beats up on you a lot. I appreciate you putting up with her, Suzanne. Mom can be hard to handle sometimes. Okay, most the time."

"It's okay. I'm tougher than I look. But if I snap and punch her in the nose one of these days, I want you all to know I tried to be the bigger person *before* I resorted to violence." All five burst into laughter. For the first time, Libby was seeing Kevin's wife in a new, more human, light.

Sean took over the conversation. "What are we going to do? Anybody got suggestions? Up until now, Mom's been okay living on her own, but after the visit from the fire department, it's not safe. Ninety percent of the time she's fine, it's that other ten percent that's keeping me up at night."

"I'm with Sean," Bob spoke up. "I think it's time to think about a different living arrangement."

Kevin and Suzanne exchanged a brief glance. "I

don't want to put this all on the rest of you," he said. "But Suz and I talked, and we're good with Mom for the short term, a few weeks maybe, but I think her coming to stay with us longer than that is an awful idea. I'm willing to help financially if we think assisted living is an option. I printed out some info on a few of the top places, but they're pricey." He handed out copies.

"These look good, Kev," Sean said. "But I'm not sure Mom is at this stage yet. The problem is, she's somewhere in the middle, she goes days without an issue, then something changes and we run the risk of a visit from the fire department. She doesn't need a babysitter, but she does need consistency. At least that's my take on it."

"I agree," Libby said. "There has to be a middle ground, a way Mom can stay independent *and safe*. She's capable of caring for herself, but knowing someone is nearby if she needs help would give us all peace of mind. And for the love of all that's holy, she has to think it's her idea. If she even suspects we talked about her behind her back like this, someone is going to pay."

"It'll be me," Suzanne moaned. "You know it will be me."

Sean put an arm around her shoulder. "I promise we'll protect you, Suz. Between the three of us, we can take her."

"So, the problem is,"—Kevin put on his boardroom face—"Mom needs to live somewhere between where she is now, and assisted living, but she cannot live with any of us unless we have a death wish. Her place is rented, and if she keeps having visits from the fire department the management company has the right to cancel her lease. Where does that leave us?"

Bob drained the last of the red wine into Libby's glass. "We need more wine. Lib, where's the bottle of red you stashed after Thanksgiving?"

"Top of the pantry," Libby answered.

"I'm on it." Two seconds later, he yelled from the kitchen, "Lib, I don't see it? Are you sure you didn't drink it? Come help me look."

"He can quote law dating back to the Civil War but can't find a bottle of wine." She pushed back from the table and walked into the kitchen. Bob stood behind the counter, the so-called missing bottle of wine on the counter in front of him.

"Let me guess," Libby said. "You found it the moment my foot hit the kitchen floor, right?"

He wrapped her in his arms and kissed the top of her head. "I found it right away, but I wanted to talk to you alone. And before you jump to conclusions, this is not another sneaky ploy for sex. I know you're disappointed, but no matter how hard you beg I won't give you a quickie on the counter."

She laughed. The release felt terrific. "If not to ply me with sex, what did you want me to come in here for?"

"This *isn't* the wine talking, okay?" He sat in a kitchen chair and pulled her into his lap. "After you talked to Will a few weeks back I started thinking about what might be coming down the road for Mae. I'm a lawyer. We plan. Sue me."

She smiled.

Bob continued, "None of us know how or when her symptoms are going to surface, but if the last month is any indication, we need to be proactive."

"I know, that's why we are all here. Did you have an idea?"

"Yes. But I'm ninety-nine percent sure you are going to hate it."

"Try me."

"The cottage." Libby's blank stare forced him to explain. "It's a disaster right now, and I know it would take some serious work, but what if we converted it into an apartment for Mae? I know Sean could design it so she can live independently, maybe not forever, but for the time being. We could use safety shut-offs on the appliances, and a call button to the main house. I'm not sure what her needs are going to be, but Sean did a lot of that type of work for Joe Battaglia's mom, I know he could make it work for Mae. Plus, Dom's right here and you know he'll be an extra set of hands if we ever need him. The hard part will be convincing her to make the move."

He paused. "You aren't saying anything. I hate it when you don't say anything. It means one of two things, you're about to blow, or cry."

Her eyes moistened, and he said, "Crap, the latter."

He wrapped his burly arms around her while she wept.

"How did I get so lucky?" she asked between sobs.

"I'm the lucky one." He held her tight. "Do you think it's a good idea?"

She pulled back and kissed him. "I think it's a good idea. I may need drugs and counseling later, but I think it's a brilliant idea."

"How are we going to sell it to Mae?"

"No clue, let's go run it by the tribunal." They

stood, and Bob grabbed the wine off the counter to follow Libby back into the dining room.

When they reappeared, the group was laughing over the Thanksgiving discussion of Sean's sexual preferences. "Talk about humiliating," Sean said. "When Mom said she thought I was gay, I nearly choked."

"No worries, Caroline defended you," Kevin said and slid Sean a grin.

He knows something, Sean thought.

Kevin took the newly opened wine bottle and topped off everyone's glass. "You two were gone a while," he said to Libby. "Everything okay?"

"That's up for debate," Libby said. "Bob has an idea, a really good idea, but it may involve a little shock therapy for me down the road."

Bob laid out his plan for everyone. Sean was the first to respond. "In theory, it sounds terrific, and this is Mae Day's slow season, so I could get started as early as next week. One question though, how do we broach the subject with Mom in a way that doesn't sound as if we think she's losing it?" He paused. "Do we think she's losing it?"

"No," Libby answered. "According to Dr. Rashan, there is no reason to assume Mom will take the same path as Gram. The more we keep things familiar, the better for Mom in the long run. That's why it's necessary to convince her to move now. If we wait, and she does turn for the worse, moving her to an unfamiliar environment will be a disaster. In fact, I noticed every time she goes for her follow up appointments, Dr. Rashan puts her in the same room, the blue room. After the last visit, I asked her nurse,

Olivia, about the colored doors. She said keeping the patients in the same room each visit helped reduce agitation in the most advanced cases."

"Is there a chance Mom's condition will worsen if we move her now?" Sean asked.

"From what I've read and everything Dr. Rashan told me, now is better than later. I'll take the first step and broach the subject with Mom. I need everyone's help getting the crap out of the cottage ASAP. Sean, can you drop a dumpster by for the junk?"

"I'll ask Deb to order one for later this week. When do you want to talk to Mom, or do you want us to come with you?"

"No, I'll get the ball rolling," Libby said. "Mom will react better if I speak with her alone. Three McGinns would be overwhelming, and I don't want her to feel ambushed. I'll call if I need reinforcements,"

"I have an, idea," Suzanne said. "That is, if you think it's my place."

"Suz, you have the same place in this family as the rest of us. Go ahead."

"Okay, this is just something I noticed. I find Mae's mood is best on Sunday, after church. She actually complimented my outfit last week, and it was the same one she told me looked like something a blind hippie would wear a few weeks earlier."

"She's right," Sean responded. "Not about the outfit, Suz, I mean when I take Mom to mass she's more agreeable after. Kind of like God forgave her the garbage she pulled the week before, and she's trying to keep her nose clean for a few hours. If I were you, Lib, I'd take her this Sunday and have lunch or something after. While you have her tied up—that's a figure of speech Lib, don't get any ideas—the rest of us can start emptying the cottage."

It was a good plan. Mae was entitled to live where she wanted, and not even her well-intentioned children had the right to strip that away from her. The words Libby selected would have to be chosen carefully. One wrong statement could end any chance they had at convincing Mae the move was the best possible solution.

"Whose turn is it in the church rotation anyway?" Libby asked. The children alternated Mae's church shuttle service after Bernie passed away. The holy rotation kept the unsolicited advice distributed equally among siblings.

"I took Mom last week," Sean said. Mae's play-by-play commentary on female parishioners recently widowed, or even separated or divorced kept him on his toes. "Let me tell you, I should get overtime pay for that one. She dragged me downstairs for coffee hour and turned it into crazy Catholic speed dating. I was introduced as her 'bachelor' son to every woman of childbearing age and by the time I got out, not only did I feel like a prize bull on the auction block, but I'd somehow gotten roped into tiling the rectory kitchen for free!"

"Oh, I've got you beat," Bob said. "Lib was sick a few weeks ago, and the kids and I took Mae to church with us. On the way home, she asked if we could swing by the market so she could grab a few things. We got there, and she picked up the staples, bread, milk, and eggs. Then she headed to the produce section and put four heads of cabbage in the cart. I made the mistake of asking her what she was making. She said cabbage leaves reduce muscle swelling and her shoulders and chest hurt after yoga sometimes. As it turns out, instead of taking ibuprofen, Mae stuffs cabbage leaves in her bra. Try getting *that* image out of your head."

"Note to self," Kevin said. "Never eat Mom's coleslaw."

Libby finished her wine in a gulp. "I'll take her to The Old Mill for lunch. She and Daddy loved going there after church."

"Good call," Sean said. "Why don't the rest of us meet here at nine and get started on the cottage? Lib, will you have time to take a look and see if there is anything you want to keep in there before we start tossing stuff?"

"I gave it a once over a few months ago, but I'll use a personal day this week and take another stab at it before Sunday. Caroline needs to get over here, too, we have a bunch of old furniture from her dad's place, and she might want it back." She looked at the time. "I can't call her now; she's out with Joey Battaglia. I'll catch her first thing in the morning."

"Ooo," Suzanne half-growled. "Good for Caroline, Joe is a hottie!" She patted Kevin's hand. "Not as hot as you, honey."

"Nice save," Kevin said, and gave her a quick kiss on the cheek. "When did they start dating?"

"They've only been out a few times," Libby answered. "It was going pretty strong for a while, but Caroline got kind of lukewarm about him after Thanksgiving."

Sean did an inner fist pump.

Libby continued, "Suzanne's right, though...Officer Battaglia has it going on in all the right places, and I'm not just saying that because I let him feel me up in seventh grade."

"Should I be jealous?" Bob smiled.

"In seventh grade my boobs were chick peas." She squeezed his hand. "You got the better post-puberty deal."

Uncomfortable with Libby's boob talk and eager to move the conversation from Caroline's love life, Sean set a plan for the weekend. "I'll bring a container truck on Sunday. That way we can move the furniture back to Caroline's place or haul it off to the Salvation Army. Same goes for the rest of the big stuff. You sure you're okay talking with Mom by yourself, Lib?"

Libby knew the Pope would celebrate Hanukah before Mae changed homes willingly, but she was ready to try.

Chapter Twenty-Four

Friday morning Sean delivered the billboard-sized dumpster, and after an hour of sorting through the cottage, Libby doubted one would be enough. "Where did all this crap come from?" She pushed a frayed wicker table aside and discovered a litter box stuffed with tennis balls. "We don't even *own* a cat!"

"Lib, you in here?" Caroline called from the front door.

"Back here!" Libby shouted. "Hang a left at the Black Hole."

Caroline located Libby and absorbed the chaos. A true friend, she came armed with coffee. "I had no idea it was this bad," she groaned. "What's the preliminary report, Captain? Is it mainly junk or do we need to sift through everything box by box?"

"It's a tough call," Libby explained. "Keep an eye on Bob on Sunday. He's liable to save his JV basketball trophies and toss my grandparents' wedding pictures. His sentimental meter is quirky."

She raised her cup. "Thanks for the caffeine fix, are you on your way to work?"

Caroline nodded. "I got your message and decided to stop on my way in and see what I had stored in here. It's been so long I can't remember." She saw a few odd tables and chairs, nothing she wanted to keep. "Did you say Sean's taking a load to the women's shelter?"

"Yep," Libby tossed a few books into the trash. "Do you want to get rid of anything?"

"Everything," she laughed. "I'd rather give it to someone who could use it. Is there anything you want my help with before I head into the office?"

"Got a match?"

"Arson is *never* the answer."

Libby sipped her latte. "Hey, I forgot. Tell me about your date with Officer Yummy!"

On a purely physical level, Caroline thought Libby's description of Joe was spot on—great-looking, funny, sweet. Overall, he was the whole package.

The more she dated, the more Caroline was convinced the divorce had affected her deeper than she originally thought. "Joe is great, and if all I wanted was sex, there's no doubt he'd be mind-blowing fantastic. For God's sake, look at him, the man's ass is sacred ground."

"Amen." Libby shouted.

"Why don't I jump him, Lib?" Caroline went on. "I'm horny, he's hot, we get along—it's just not…right. I haven't been able to connect with anyone since..." She stopped. The revelation seized her.

"Since what?" Libby asked.

Since Sean. Since Thanksgiving. Since...forever. "Nothing," she backpedaled. "It's the frustration talking. I need to get to work. I've distracted you long enough."

"Are you sure? You look a little flushed."

"I'm fine," *I'm an idiot.* "Probably a hot flash. I'll give you a call tonight, and we can firm up plans for this weekend." She shoved her way through boxes in a desperate attempt to get to the door.

"Hang on," Libby said. "I forgot. Sean called last night. He asked me to tell you he's got a soft bed—"

"What?" Caroline screeched as she spun. "If that man thinks I'm desperate enough to jump into his bed just because I'm in a dry spell he's got another think coming! The nerve of that self-centered, egotistical..." Libby's laughter stopped her rant.

"—Liner," Libby said. "Sean's got a soft bed liner, in the pickup, in case you need to move anything breakable."

"Oh," Caroline said.

"You thought Sean was offering stud services? Through his sister pimp no less? And all you can say is, 'oh'? Thanks for making my day, Duffy. I haven't laughed that hard in months."

"Glad to help." Caroline opened the door and waved goodbye, eager for escape. "I'll see you Sunday. In case you don't recognize me with all the egg on my face, I'll be the one in the Stay Away From Crazy T-Shirt. Warn the others."

Outside, she exhaled and muttered, "Smooth, Caroline. Very smooth."

****

After a turkey-and-tomato lunch break with a laundry chaser, Libby put her feet up on the couch and buoyed the courage to call Mae.

"Hello?" Mae was breathless.

"Mom?" Libby frowned. "Are you all right?

"Oh, hello dear. I just came in from outside." Libby heard the door close as Mae went on. "Kevin drove me home so I could pick up the Nativity set to use on their front lawn. It wouldn't be Christmas without it."

The two-foot plastic figurines were a McGinn family tradition. As a child, Libby helped Bernie display the manger scene on the front lawn the day after Thanksgiving. Considerably smaller than her former home, the front step of Mae's condominium only had room for Mary, Joseph and Baby Jesus—Sean, Kevin, and Libby divided the remaining figures.

Libby inherited two of the Wise Men—one in flowing gold and red robes, the other, the kneeling king, sported a full mustache and ankle-length navy coat. Feeling nostalgic the first Christmas without Bernie, Libby arranged her pair of kings on the front lawn, regrettably, minus the rest of the Bethlehem crew. The pair looked more like an illuminated 1960's folk band than visiting royalty.

"How did the condo look?" Libby asked. "Sean said the drywall guys can't get in for another two weeks at least."

"It's a mess still," Mae groaned. "Myrna was putting out that hideous, light up Menorah on the front porch when I left. That awful monstrosity is such a mockery to her faith. Cy would never put up with that, God rest his soul." If Myrna's late husband were looking down from the great beyond, Libby was certain the glow-in-the-dark menorah offended less than the plastic Holy Family camped on Mae's porch.

"So," Mae went on, "did you call for a reason, or just to chat?"

"Little of both I guess," Libby answered. "We put the tree up yesterday."

"Oh, that's nice. Did you chop it down or go to one of the lots?"

"We chopped. Dom came with us and supervised

Bob, no missing digits this year."

"What a relief. I love Bob like my own son, but the man should not be permitted to own tools."

Libby recapped the kids' activities, some of the antics at the library, and as much small talk as she could muster before diving into Phase One of the Move-Mom project. "I was thinking we could go to The Old Mill for brunch after church this week," she said. "Would you like to do some Christmas shopping?"

"I suppose," Mae hemmed. "I don't want you to feel obligated, though. I'm sure you have lots going on."

Same old Mae, same old guilt, Libby thought. "Mom, I wouldn't offer if I felt obligated," she continued. "Charlie has an early soccer game and then the kids are going to friends' houses. I thought we could have some time to relax while everyone is accounted for."

"Well then, that would be lovely. Can we go to the mall? I need some new underthings."

Oh God, Libby thought. *Not only do I need to find a way to bring up the cottage, now the day includes senior citizen underwear shopping—this must be what hell is like.* "Sure," Libby feigned excitement. "The mall is great; I can shop anywhere."

"And before I forget, I called Mike Kenny the other day and asked him to come by. I took Dr. Rashan's advice and had Mike bring by my will and a bunch of other things you should have when...well...when I'm not at my best. We made a few changes. He's bringing it by tomorrow."

Mike Kenny, Mae's longtime lawyer, was older than Moses was. "I'm glad you took Dr.Rashan's advice to heart," Libby said. "No offense to Mr. Kenny, but don't you think Bob could handle that for you? Isn't having a lawyer in the family one of life's perks?"

"Well of course Bob could do it Lib, and I'm going to have him look over everything Mike did and make sure the old bird didn't muck it up. Mike is a wonderful friend, but he still thinks Nixon is President; I just want him to feel needed."

"I understand." *No, I don't.* "I'm sure Bob will be happy to go over anything you need." The cottage beckoned. "I better get going. We're on for Sunday?"

"I'll be ready."

Chapter Twenty-Five

"Are we saving cassette tapes?" Bob yelled to Libby from the cardboard box igloo he had constructed in the cottage bedroom. "What in God's name possessed me to buy Steel Drum Hits of the Islands?"

Libby returned a yell from the kitchen. "Rum. It was our honeymoon. Toss cassettes and anything 1980s; it's an era better left in the past. Keep pictures. And bonus points for shots of Kevin with the mullet, he's ticking me off, and I may use it for our Christmas card."

"You're such a loving sister. Remind me not to get on your bad side." Bob left the bedroom and joined Libby in the kitchen. "Besides pictures, is there anything you absolutely want to keep?"

"I trust your judgment. If I didn't know it was out here, I won't miss it. Caroline will supervise the Testosterone Crew for me later. If it were up to Sean and Kevin, we'd bulldoze the place's entire contents into the dumpster."

Bob looked around the room and scratched his head. "It may come to that."

The sound of a diesel motor pulled them outside. Behind the wheel of Mae Day's container truck, Sean maneuvered into the open space nearest the cottage.

Kevin jumped out of the cab and rolled open the truck's rear door. "Let's move some shit!" he said, and clapped with enthusiasm.

"You're chipper today, baby brother."

Sean rounded the truck. "There are two reasons for that," he said. "One, he's a girly man and sits at a desk all day. The last time he did manual labor, it involved a birdhouse and scout camp. And two, Saratoga is officially six weeks old, thus granting him sexual visitation rights with his wife."

"TMI! TMI!" Bob shouted. "What is it with this family? First Mae revisits her colonoscopy over appetizers at Thanksgiving, and now this." His mock expression of horror brought laughter from the others. "I don't know why I put up with this inappropriate behavior. You people disgust me."

Entering with trays of steaming coffee cups, Caroline asked, "Why do they disgust you today?"

"Hey there! Didn't hear you arrive," Libby said, and accepted a cup. "God bless you!"

"Thought we may need it," She passed the remaining cups around to the men. "I parked out front. Now back to why Bob thinks you are all disgusting, not that I disagree. It's just nice to have another supporter once in a while."

"Saratoga is six weeks old." Libby explained with a wink.

Instantly grasping the meaning of her friend's comment, Caroline spun around to Kevin. "Congratulations Kev. Back on the horse, huh?"

"About damned time, too," Kevin agreed. "But enough about my manly ways, we need to get cracking. If Mom warms up to the idea today, this place is going to have to look better than it does right now."

"For once we agree on something," Sean said to his

brother. "Lib, you should get going. We'll get the big stuff onto the truck first. After that the junk will be easier to get into the dumpster, and we can get some sort of system going."

"No worries," Caroline said to Libby. "Go deal with Mae and I'll keep things on schedule here. You know cleaning gets me *hot*. Let me enjoy it."

"If that's the case, you need some serious time in Sean's bathroom." Libby laughed.

"Are you making fun of my housekeeping skills, sister dear?" Sean smiled in spite of himself.

"What housekeeping skills?" Libby teased. "Hey, there's the perfect answer to both your frustration problems. The next time Sean goes out with one of his harem, Caroline can go to his place and scrub the toilets. Bleach for one, loose women for the other. Everybody wins, right?"

Caroline's grin did not quite reach full strength. "Always thinking of my needs, Lib."

"I try. Okay, I'm out of here. Keep an eye on the men, and if I'm not back by three o'clock, call your friend, Officer Yummy, and put out a missing person's report. Mom loves to visit the Community Garden by the bank, that's most likely where she'll stash my body."

After a quick kiss for Bob, Libby snatched her purse from on top of one of the boxes and started out.

The four remaining family members divided the chores. Bob and Kevin tackled the bedroom, dragging out the mismatched chairs and miscellaneous furniture Libby labeled for the shelter.

Sean moved a few of the larger boxes off an old recliner in the living room and lifted the chair out the front door.

Caroline noticed him struggling and stopped boxing up old cups and glasses to help. "Hold on, Captain Muscles," Caroline teased. "I'll hold the door for you."

"Thanks." Sean lugged the chair up the ramp into the truck. "That thing is a beast," he said, and returned down the ramp. "I don't remember seeing it before."

"It belonged to my dad," Caroline explained. "Lib let me keep it here, but I have absolutely no use for it now."

"Ah, free storage, always a good plan." He stopped alongside her at the front door and flashed a devious smile. "Cleaning, huh?"

Caroline blushed. "Don't mock my foreplay, McGinn."

"No judgment here, just reminded me of something I need to do."

"And what would that be?"

"Pick up bleach. My bathroom is very, *very* dirty."

Laughing to himself, Sean went into the house as Caroline stared in disbelief.

Was he flirting? she wondered. *And why am I sweating?*

****

"Look at that altar server," Mae whispered in Libby's ear. "He's wearing sneakers! Can you believe that?"

"Mom, be quiet, people can hear you." Libby answered.

"Sneakers...on the altar...that's disrespectful. You don't see Fr. Rodriguez in flip flops, do you?"

"I'm sure the kid's going to hell. Now zip it and let

me pray." *Patience,* Libby thought, *pray for patience.*

After services, the Old Mill's perky blonde host seated them in a booth overlooking the tumbling waterfall.

"What are you grinning at Lib?" Mae asked.

"Memories." Libby answered. The sights and smells of the restaurant took her back to childhood, and the special lunches she and Mae shared after back-to-school shopping. Shoes, Libby had discovered, were the only true way to express yourself in Catholic school; the starchy gray uniforms sucked the individuality right out of you. "Remember when we came here after our annual back-to-school shopping trips?"

"My, that takes me back," Mae said with a wistful glow. "You were easy to find shoes for, but the boys were a nightmare. Once puberty hit I gave up and made your father take them. I swear the odor from those feet could kill a buffalo."

She put on her glasses and picked up the menu. "So, what shall we order?" Mae's segue from smelly feet to scrambled eggs was well-timed as the waiter came to take their order. Within minutes, piping hot broccoli and cheese omelets and fresh raisin bread toast were set on the table with a carafe of dark roast coffee.

"This cheese is bad for my cholesterol, but sometimes you have to splurge." Mae savored the first bite with pure joy. "How's yours?"

"It's worth every minute in treadmill purgatory," Libby said. Between sips of coffee, she plotted her next move. "Do you still want to go to the mall after we're done here?"

"Actually, since it's a little warmer out today, I thought you could take me over to visit Daddy. I haven't been to the cemetery in a few weeks, and I want to make sure that strange little groundskeeper is keeping up with the weeds."

Mouth full of toast, Mae remembered the legal paperwork in her purse and bent to retrieve it. "Mike dropped these by yesterday. Bob can look them over whenever he gets a free minute, no rush. I'm not planning on going belly-up anytime soon."

"Nice image, Mom." Libby placed the paperwork into her bag and pulled out her credit card. She signaled the waiter. "I'm picking up the check, no arguments."

"Why do you assume I'll argue?" Mae said.

"Are you serious? The last time I tried to take you out to dinner you acted like letting me pay was a criminal offense."

"I've learned to be pampered. All the daytime talk shows say I am entitled."

"Well, we all know daytime talk is law."

****

Saint Luke's Cemetery sat on a sloping hill overlooking the glistening shoreline's tranquil landscape. Contrary to Mae's opinion, it was meticulously maintained. Bernie's gravesite was at the highest point, a secluded spot surrounded by maple trees and perennial flowers.

"Hello sweetheart," Mae spoke softly to the headstone and stroked the smooth marble surface with the palm of her hand. Inconsolable at the time of her husband's death, Mae entrusted Kevin and Sean to select the marker. Engraved with Bernie's date of birth and death, the bottom of the stone was etched with a replica of Yankees Stadium—a final gift from the McGinn boys to their dad.

"We should have picked up a wreath on the way over," Libby said.

Mae shook her head and said, "Pine needles make Daddy itchy."

Libby refrained from pointing out the obvious. "Do you want me to leave you alone for a few minutes so you can talk to Daddy in private?"

"No, stay and visit." Mae brushed a leaf from the stone. "I have long talks with your father every day. He listens much better now than before."

"I bet he does," Libby chuckled. "Listening was never one of Daddy's strong points."

The women stood in silence at the peaceful site, the only sound the distant crashing surf. A cool breeze blew off the ocean as the few remaining autumn leaves crossed the ground at their feet.

Libby felt the weight of the coming conversation bear down on her shoulders like a lead blanket and struggled to find the right words.

"It's all right, Libby," Mae said, interrupting her thoughts. "Say what you need to. We're here for a reason. We both know it."

Shocked by her mother's perception, Libby stared at Mae.

The older woman's eyes were moist but holding back. She continued. "Spit it out, honey. I won't have a public tantrum. It's obvious you have something important to talk to me about, and I think you've delayed long enough."

Libby's shoulders slumped. "How'd you know?"

"Well, let's examine the facts..." Mae grinned despite the gravity of the moment. "You took me to church, plied me with brunch, and now you're standing there biting your bottom lip raw. Daddy used to call that *your tell*. We always knew something was wrong if your bottom lip looked like it had a run-in with a cheese grater."

"Huh?" Libby ran her tongue over her bottom lip. "I never noticed."

"In your teens, we were pretty sure you were going to bite clean through it," Mae joked. "At least your nervous habit isn't offensive; whenever Kevin lies, he grabs his testicles. Since the day he was born that boy treated his penis like an accessory. It's terribly inappropriate, especially at parties."

"And there's an image I'll never shake." Libby shivered. "Dare I ask about the perfect son, does Sean have a tell?"

"Sean was the hardest one to spot," Mae explained. "He's always grabbing at his hair; pushing it out of his eyes and such, especially when he's under stress or wrestling with some type of big decision." Libby knew exactly what Mae described; she had seen her brother do it thousands of times. "But here's the trick with Sean, he's right-handed, and when he's fibbing, he still pulls at his hair, but with his *left hand*. It is the oddest thing. "

"That is strange," Libby said in amazement. "I never noticed that before. Makes me want to play poker with him soon."

"The three of you don't even have to open your mouths; I can tell something's wrong just by looking. Your bottom lip's raw, Kevin's a sexual deviant, and Sean becomes a lefty; simple."

Mae took a deep breath and continued, "In the last week Kevin has stopped by twice to visit, adjusting his privates the entire time. Sean came by after work last night, and might as well have given himself a home permanent with his left hand, and now you, Elizabeth...stop biting that lip, it looks like hamburger. Tell me what's going on."

Be honest, be gentle, be ready to take cover, Libby thought. "We're worried about your living alone, Mom," she said. "None of us—Sean, Kevin, or me—wants to rip your independence out from under you like a cheap throw rug, but after the fire..."

"I burned a pot Libby, not a city block."

"You burned an entire room to ashes." Libby stood firm and went on. "But that's a small piece of the big picture. Please don't lump yourself in the same category as Gram—we don't—and I know what happened to her terrifies you. Remember, you take much better care of yourself. And even if it is the same disease, Dr. Rashan insists your case is dramatically different."

Mae nodded, but said nothing as Libby continued. "There's no easy way to say this, Mom; Sean, Kevin, and I feel it would be best if you had more help around—so nothing like the fire happens again."

"You mean like a visiting aide or something?" Mae asked.

"We have something better in mind," Libby said.

"I am not, under any circumstances, ready for a nursing home, Elizabeth." Mae's tone hardened as she went on. "Do not insult me or my capabilities by suggesting that."

Proceed with caution. "We're, not suggesting that Mom," Libby said. "And for the record, I plan on smothering you well before nursing home time."

"Tone, Elizabeth."

"Fine, but you are going to hear me out on this. We had an idea—all of us, Bob and Suzanne included."

Mae's eyes rolled as Libby's lecture went into overdrive. "Do not roll your eyes at me." *Head slap.* "Crap, now I sound just like you. Next I'll be asking you if you need to 'make pee' before we get in the car!"

Mae held off a grin as Libby went on. "The point is, Mom, the condo won't work. You are in no way nursing home material, but there's a strong chance one of us will go on trial for murder if you move in with any of us. Agreed?"

"Agreed," Mae said. Regrettably she had reached the same conclusion weeks before. "And you three masterminds devised a workable solution?"

"I think so," Libby said. "It was Bob's idea."

"I like it already; he's the sensible one in the lot of you."

"Nice to know you think so highly of him. Me— your own flesh and blood—not so much. But it's good to know I married *into* respectability."

Mae giggled as Libby pressed on. "Here's the deal...for years Bob and I talked about renovating the cottage. Shannon wants it for her bedroom, but there is no way that's going to happen. Structurally, Sean says it is in great shape. It needs cosmetics—plus heat, AC, and some new insulation—but he thinks he can convert it into a private apartment. Mae Day is slow this time of the year, so he could start immediately. As we speak, Sean, Bob, Kev, and Caroline are over there cleaning it out, top to bottom, in hopes you will come back with me, take a look, and see the potential."

Heavy stillness settled over them. Libby was

unsure whether to say more or run for shelter.

Mae's voice was barely a whisper. "May I speak now?"

"Of course."

"Are you saying—my children, the three I birthed and the three I consider equally my own—would like to build me a home I can live in with a sense of privacy, and still be close enough to ask for help if I need it?"

Mae's Wedgewood blues dampened. "I think—no, I know—I would like that very much."

"Really?" Libby beamed. "Don't you want to fight me just a little? I came prepared with a list of arguments—I feel cheated."

Mae laughed and linked arms with Libby. "I do want to fight, sweetheart, but not with you. I want to grab this disease by the throat and strangle the life out of it, but I've come to a point in my life where I know time is a gift, and anger will only squander it. Instead, I've decided to squeeze every bit of joy out of life and focus on the time I'm blessed to have, not the time I may lose."

Mae continued, "I watched my mother disappear. I saw her mind slip away faster than her body. If fate has the same in store for me, no matter how long the trip takes, I'm going to hold on and enjoy each and every minute for as long as I'm given. I'm scared...but of nothing physical. I'm afraid to lose moments—not the big ones, weddings, graduations—it's the small, insignificant moments that change a life. Those are what I'll miss most, the little glimpses of my life I've never shared."

"Tell me one." Libby squeezed her mother's arm tight. "Tell me, and I'll remember every detail and tell you the story over and over."

A genial smile crossed Mae's lips. "The day I met Daddy, that's a favorite."

Libby's heart melted as Mae reminisced. "Bernie was an absolute mess when he walked in. He was just off a job site, filthy with cement dust and mud. He was the new guy on the job, so he got the dirty work. God, he smelled awful. Nevertheless, there was something about him—confidence that pulled me toward him—and when he asked me to dinner, I didn't hesitate for a second. I looked right past the dirt and body odor and fell in love with him, stink and all."

"Daddy always said you were the princess that married the ditch digger."

"He treated me like a princess. Even in our worst times he made me feel like I was the luckiest woman in the world."

Mae looked out to the ocean, her expression melancholy. "Some of the sad times broke my heart to the point that I wasn't sure I could recover. And as strange as it sounds—like the day I met your father—I'm afraid of losing those moments, too."

"Why? Forgive me if this sounds insensitive Mom, but I would imagine one of the few upsides of dementia is losing painful memories."

"Those memories make you who you are; they are the stones you build life's foundation on. The good memories, too, but the bad ones test everything else. They show you how much you can handle and still find happiness. Don't get me wrong, there are a few memories I'd like to forget. But the big ones...those I want to hold onto for as long as I can."

"I understand; you take the good with the bad.

Let's take this a step at a time, starting with where you can live and feel comfortable."

Libby shivered and rubbed her hands together. "It's getting cold. Are you up to coming over to the house for a peek at the cottage? Remember, nothing happens until you say so."

"I'd love to," Mae said. "Go warm up the car. I need a minute to say goodbye to Daddy."

Libby kissed her cheek and left.

Mae turned to the grave marker. "Did you hear that, sweetheart? The kids have it all worked out. You don't need to worry about me, I'll be fine. Of course, if you want to send down a little patience, I won't turn it away. You know my temper." She smiled and ran a hand across the top of the stone. "We did well, Bernie. Very, very well."

Chapter Twenty-Six

"Lift, you skinny wimp!" Sean screamed as Kevin dipped the front end of a couch too low and missed the ramp onto the truck.

"I am!" Kevin yelled back. "You're going too damned fast...slow down!"

"Charlie has more upper body strength than you!"

"Bite me, dumbass! Some of us got brawn, others got the brains."

"You two haven't changed since grade school," Caroline said as she came into the van behind them with cardboard boxes. "Do I need to get the hose and break this up?"

"He started it!" Kevin and Sean answered simultaneously

"Take a break," Caroline said. "It's obvious one of you needs a timeout, and I'm too tired to decide which one."

"Fine," Kevin said, and stormed down the ramp. "I'm taking my timeout in the kitchen, with a beer."

Sean fell onto the sofa, and Caroline joined him. "It's starting to look better in there," she said. "Do you think you can work your magic and turn it into something resembling a home?"

"I know we can make it look great. The real problem is, can we convince Mom to move in?"

Sean laid his head on the back of the sofa, noticing

the box Caroline brought in. "What's in there?"

"Stuff from my dad's house; pots, pans...oh, and *these*." She pulled out a pair of dingy ice skates. "Believe it or not, these were once white. I went through a figure skating phase in eighth grade."

She went on, "Mom used to take me to the rink at dawn, three days a week, for lessons. God bless her. I thank my lucky stars Trev never wanted to play hockey. That's not the kind of schedule I'm willing to keep."

Caroline pulled back the tongue of the left skate. "See these stars?" Sean leaned over for a closer look as she explained, "I drew one every time I landed a double axel. Notice there's only two; thus, my career as a professional skater was short-lived."

"Skating's loss is advertising's gain," Sean teased.

"Thanks." She put the skates back in the box and placed it in the pile with the other donations. "I still remember those early morning practices. Mom sat in the freezing rink without a single complaint. I was so lucky to have her, even for a short time. I miss her, every single day."

"She was one in a million, just like her daughter," Sean said.

Caroline smiled. "Speaking of mother-daughters...Do you think Lib is okay?"

"I checked my phone a few minutes ago, no urgent texts for help, so I assume Mom either entertained the idea, or Lib is bound and gagged somewhere unable to call for help."

He scanned the truck and let out a long whistle. "I can't believe all this stuff was crammed into that little house."

"I know," Caroline said. "Once the junk came out

you can see the size of the place. I think it's perfect for Mae—enough room, and plenty of privacy."

"I had a job over in New Haven a few weeks back, an old Victorian the owners wanted to update," Sean explained. "They were going to toss out the old claw foot tub, so I snagged it. I think it would be perfect in here. And I've picked up some old door knobs and hinges that would look fantastic in the kitchen."

Caroline looked at him and grinned. "You are excited about this, aren't you?"

"I have downtime right now. This should be a good project to keep me busy during the winter."

He looked at Caroline, her head tilted to one side and eyebrows raised. He said, "Okay, *yes,* I'm excited. I actually like restoration work better than new construction, and *yes,* I enjoy a challenge. Happy?"

"Yes. You can try and be blasé all you want, but I know you want to do this for your mom, and that's why you're a good egg, Sean McGinn." She gave him what she intended to be a quick kiss on the lips, but lingered slightly longer than smart.

Sean grabbed onto the back of her neck and deepened the kiss before she could pull back. Her lips parted, and a moan from deep in her dormant sex drive sent his mouth into frenzy. She found the bottom of his soft cotton T-shirt and slipped her hands under the hem. Running her fingers over his chest hair, his nipples snapped to attention, along with his common sense.

"Whoa,"—he reluctantly pulled an inch back—"I have to breathe. Give me a second." His panting was matched only by hers. His low growl warned, "You're opening an old door here, Duffy. Once it's open, I'm coming in, slamming it shut, and putting up the *Do Not*

Disturb sign until neither one of us can move. No one in, no one out. I've waited too long."

She licked her plumped-with-kisses lips.

He groaned. "You play dirty," he said. "I like it."

The sound of a car in the driveway sent them scrambling to their feet and to the truck ramp.

Caroline waved to Libby and Mae as they got out of the car. "I feel like I just got caught making out on the front porch," she said between her smiling teeth.

"You're lucky they came when they did," he said. "If it were up to me we'd be testing the springs on that old couch right now."

Sean mirrored her clenched smile and waved to Mae and Libby as he said, "Forget what I said in the office the other day. This is not over. Not by a long shot. We're just getting started."

Caroline felt heat creep into her cheeks as she walked over to say hello. "Welcome to chaos!" she said to Mae and Libby. "How was brunch? Did you have the omelets, or the French toast? I love The Mill, they have the best food."

Mae hugged Caroline, and said, "You can stop acting like a cruise director, dear. I appreciate it, but there's no need. I'm considering the idea you kids came up with." Mae frowned and put her hand to Caroline's head. "Are you feeling well, Caroline? You look flushed."

"Oh," Caroline stammered. "Well, it must be all the moving and lifting. I'm a little overheated, that's all."

Sean jumped down from the truck and joined the group. "Hi Mom, how was brunch?"

"Sean Bernard?" Mae saw her son's equally rosy

complexion. "Is everything all right?"

Libby took note that he ran his left hand through his hair.

"Sure, why?" he answered, again hand-combing lefty.

"No reason," Mae's lips broke into a sly smile. *Well, well, well, it's about time.* "You both appear a little overheated. Don't they, Libby?"

Libby's stare went from Caroline to Sean and back again. Neither looked her in the eye. "Why yes, they *do* look a little red." *No way, there is no way—Sean and Caroline? That has to border on incest, in a strangely good way.* "Where are Bob and Kevin?" she asked. "Shouldn't they be helping?"

"Kevin's in the house on his beer break. Union rules," Sean said. "I think Bob is in the back room sorting tools—lots of metal banging going on."

He looked at Mae. "So Mom, you're okay with this? Living this close to Lib would drive me to drink. Think you can handle it?"

Libby slapped his arm.

"Darling,"—Mae put her hand on his cheek—"I know you will build me a palace out of a pile of sand. Or in this case, a lovely apartment out of a tool shed."

"Mom," Libby interrupted, "this is far from a tool shed. All you've seen is the piles of junk stored in there, not the real house. It's somewhat nice once you get past the clutter—wood floors and lots of light; private, and still be close enough to drive me 'round the bend. Come in and take a look."

Cleaning efforts were evident when the group walked in. All boxes and dilapidated furniture had been removed from the living room, Caroline gave the floors a quick sweep and damp mop hours earlier, and the small fieldstone hearth was vacuumed clean of cobwebs and waiting for a toasty fire. In the miniature kitchen, the scrubbed-clean lead-glass cabinet doors sparkled over the now-empty-of-old-magazines-and-newspapers porcelain sink.

"I have to admit, this *is* much nicer than I anticipated," Mae said. "It still needs loads of work. Are you sure, there's time for this, Sean? I know the lion's share of the work is on your shoulders."

"I've got time, Mom. And Lib, Caroline and Suzanne are going to help you pick out the fixtures and girly touches."

"Right," Caroline added, "And Sean even has a—"

Before she could tell Mae about the claw foot tub, Sean yanked her into his chest and clamped a hand over her mouth.

"Shh, it's a surprise. Mom has to wait and see." Sean released her mouth but left his arm snugly around her waist.

The earlier crimson returned to Caroline's cheeks, confirming Mae's suspicion the couple's complexions had nothing to do with the day's manual labors.

A loud crash came from the bedroom. "Shit!" Bob yelled.

Libby ran to the room, followed closely by the rest.

Bob, seated on the floor, rubbed his foot. "Dropped a training wheel on my toe," he said. "Those suckers are heavy."

"Poor baby." Libby sat alongside him. "But it looks like you made a ton of progress back here."

"It is amazing how much crap you can accumulate in such a short period of time." He pointed to boxes by the door. "Those are pictures and stuff you probably want to keep; the rest of this can go."

Libby frowned. The top box brimmed with trophies. "Are you sure you want to part with the triumphs of your youth?" she asked.

"Honey, you are the only trophy I need." He planted a dramatic kiss on her lips.

"Aw, he's so sweet." Caroline said.

"Not so fast." Libby wiggled free. "We've been together long enough for me to know you want something in return. What is it?"

Bob stood and dusted off his pants. With a smirk on his face, he said, "You know me so well. As it just so happens I found some of my old Yankees pictures, from back in my apartment, and I got to thinking. You know that blank wall in the living room, the one that screams for some artwork?"

"I'm going to regret this, but yes."

"I was thinking of getting some of these eight-by-tens framed up and hanging them over Old Stink. Great idea, right?"

Sean picked up the pictures, and said, "These are awesome, Bob. You know I could put some direct overhead accent lighting in and really bring attention to them—especially this one." He held up a black-and-white team photo of the 1937 World Series Champion New York Yankees.

Bob's face lit up like a kid on Christmas morning. "Really? That would be perfect!"

"Yes, Sean, *perfect*." Libby sighed. "Maybe while you're at it you can put a urinal in the downstairs bathroom; really make it feel more stadium-like."

The front door closed, and Kevin entered. "Here's

where you all went." He gave Mae a quick kiss. "What do you think of the place, Mom?"

Mae walked around the bedroom and took in the large windows and hardwood floors. "It *does* have a certain charm."

"Did Sean show you the blueprints yet?"

"You had time to draw up blueprints?" Libby asked.

"Preliminary stuff, nothing set in stone. I thought it would help Mom get a better idea what the place would look like after we're done."

"Wow, I'm impressed. When did you have the time to do that?"

"I had a few hours last night and took a shot at it."

"Wait a minute," Kevin said. "I thought you had a hot date with that dental hygienist last night."

Sean cast a glance at Caroline. Their eyes met and held. "Change of plans."

He smiled and switched subject. "I left the blueprints on the kitchen table. How about we head in and all take a look."

****

With everyone seated around Libby and Bob's kitchen table, Sean explained the designs. "I figure we'll need to rough in the heat and AC first. Surprisingly, the electrical is in decent shape. As far as the kitchen goes, Mom, you are going to need to pick out some appliances and a new faucet, but I think it would be great to keep the original sink; it's got a lot of character."

"I agree." Mae answered. "How bad is the plumbing? You know Daddy always said plumbing kills the budget."

"I can't tell until we put the water back on out there, but it looks like one of the previous owners took a stab at bringing it up to code. It shouldn't be too bad, but you are going to want to add a shower. That will be some work. What about a dishwasher?"

"I don't need one; I rarely use mine, as it is. I'd rather you spend time buffing up those floors and double insulating."

Libby tapped her fingers on the table. "Give us a ballpark, big brother," she said. "How long do you think the project will take?"

"I know I sound like a typical contractor, but the truth is it's hard to say. We're not making any significant structural changes. Adding a full bathroom and new roof will take time, and we need permits. That's mostly a matter of getting the town inspectors out here and on schedule. If we start the first of the year, to be safe, I'd say three months."

"Mom," Kevin spoke up. "I know Suzanne is not your favorite person, but we were wondering if you would like to stay with us and help with Saratoga until the place is ready. We can make it work if you're willing to give it a try?"

"I appreciate that, Kevin." She held his hand. "The last weeks have been lovely, but I think we both know that's not a smart idea. And not because of Suzanne, who for the record, I love just as much as the rest of you—but we need to take each other in limited blocks of time. Living together that long would be too difficult."

Bob stood up and went to the fridge. "Mae, you can stay here," he called over his shoulder. "You'll have to cook for your room and board. Someone's got to save us from Lib's gourmet *experiments*."

Libby wanted to kiss and kick him at the same time.

"You are a sweet man to say that, *and* my favorite son-in-law, to boot," Mae said, "but I've made other plans."

The group shared joint confusion.

She explained, "I spoke with William last night, and he invited me to live with him for a while. At the time, it was just a stopgap until I could figure out what to do next, but now we have a plan and I'll enjoy the time away—worry free. I think a warm climate for the next few months is just what the doctor ordered. After all, Will and I are not getting any younger, and we hardly ever see each other."

A quizzical look on her face, she asked, "Do you think if William has dementia, he'll forget he's gay? Good Lord, he'll come out of the closet so many times he'll need a revolving door." No one laughed.

"For the love of Mike, people, lighten up, it's dementia humor. If I can't laugh about it once in a while, what's the point? All of you need to stop looking at me like I'm going to break. I'm okay today. We'll deal with tomorrow when it gets here. Stop borrowing worry. All it will give you is indigestion."

Caroline hugged Mae. "That sounds like fabulous advice. No more worrying tonight. How about we order some Chinese food and finish tossing the garbage out of the cottage.

Kevin slapped the table and stood up to leave. "Good plan. I've got to go get Suzanne and Sara from her parent's place, but we can swing back here after. Place an order at Moon Dynasty and I'll grab it on my way past."

"I love it when Kevin pays." Bob clapped his hands together. "I'm ordering double egg rolls. I deserve them today."

"We all do." Sean dug his keys from his pocket. "I'll run the truck back to the office. José's going to take it to the shelter for me on Monday. Be back in about an hour."

Chapter Twenty-Seven

Thirty minutes later Caroline, Libby, and Mae finished throwing the remaining trash into the dumpster.

With the cottage empty, Sean's blueprints began to take shape in Mae's head. She envisioned the tiny kitchen and new bathroom, mentally selecting fixtures and curtains. With the clutter gone, the little house reminded her of the first apartment she and Bernie shared in Brooklyn. The memory brought her a sense of belonging and contentment.

After giving the floors a final sweep, Caroline left to pick up Trevor from his friend's house, promising to return for dinner.

Alone, Libby and Mae put away the last of the cleaning supplies and sat down on folding chairs for a hard-earned breather.

"You are awfully quiet Mom," Libby said. "What are you thinking about?"

"I was just traveling down memory lane," Mae said. "The apartment Daddy and I had in Brooklyn was about this size. We were so happy there. Imagine if we'd stayed. Three kids in a house this size?"

"That certainly would have been a tight squeeze," Libby said. "I'm glad this place reminds you of a happy time. I want you to feel good here."

She paused, before saying, "Can I ask you

something, Mom?"

"Of course."

"Why don't you ever go back to Brooklyn? I know you still have cousins there. I'd assume you'd want to visit. You've said the city reminds you of the accident—all the traffic and congestion—but it's been years, and no one was permanently hurt. Don't you want to go back and see the places you and Daddy used to go, visit any friends?"

Mae's voice was wistful, "There is somewhere I would like to visit. I haven't been able to for many, many years...but yes, I think it's important to go now. It's one of those memories we spoke of earlier—one of the ones that made me who I am today, and I want to hold onto this particular one as long as I can."

"Great, let's pick a weekend, and we can head in, maybe do some Christmas shopping downtown. Where would you like to go? Your old apartment or maybe Giuseppe's where Dad used to take you for dinner on pay day?"

"Both good thoughts, but I think it's about time I visit St. Patrick's Cemetery."

"Is that where Gram is buried? Of course, we can go. We'll pick up a bouquet of flowers and spend a little time remembering the happy moments."

"Flowers are a sweet thought. My mother loved daises, we always seemed to have them in the house, even during the rough years when money was tight." Mae intertwined Libby's hand with hers. "We'll need a second bouquet, sweetheart. There is someone else at St. Patrick's, someone I should have told you about many, many years ago. But the pain...oh Lib, it was just too much for me."

"Mom, don't get upset. Whatever it is, you can tell me."

"I know I can sweetheart—and it's important that I tell you now in case I get confused later."

Libby nodded, understanding her mother's fears. Dementia patients' pasts and presents often blurred into one.

"When we visit the cemetery, we need to bring a very special bunch of flowers...for your sister, Meghan."

****

"Mae, wake up honey." Shannon Finn held Mae's hand and spoke softly. "Come on honey; open those beautiful baby blues for Mama."

Mae's eyes fluttered opened. The dim hospital room smelled of antiseptic. An IV overhead dripped fluids into her system while oxygen flowed into the mask over her face. Groggy and confused, nothing Mae saw made sense. It felt like a dream until the pain made the situation all too real.

A young nurse hovered nearby and noted her now-conscious patient's vital signs. "Hello, Mrs. McGinn," the nurse said. "My name is Emily, and I'll be taking care of you. You've been in a car accident, and were unconscious for several hours, but you're doing well. I just gave you some medication for the pain, and you will probably feel a little sleepy."

Mae managed a nod as the nurse continued. "Your husband is in surgery, but his prognosis is very good. I'll get the doctor and let him know you're awake, he'll go over everything in more detail." With that, she left the room.

Shannon squeezed Mae's hand. "Hello sweetheart,

don't try to talk. They had to put a tube down your throat to help you breathe. It's gone now, but give yourself a few minutes to wake up before you try to say anything. Let's wait for the doctor to come in and we'll ask if you can have a sip of water."

Mae's world floated around her in wavy lines. *A side effect of the medication,* she thought. The edges of the room swayed and changed shape haphazardly at the slightest movement of her head as she tried to make sense of her surroundings.

She fought off the sedation, and forced herself to stay awake as the memory of the accident began to return—rain, dinner at Giuseppe's, a van out of nowhere barreling straight at them. She heard the sound of breaking glass and smelled a mixture of metallic smoke and burning rubber.

In a blind panic, Mae ran her hands to her stomach. Large bandages and considerable pain met her touch. *The babies, where are babies?* She darted her eyes to her mother.

"Take it easy sweetheart," Shannon soothed. "They took the babies, in order to stop your bleeding. The doctor will be in any minute and he'll let us know how they are. Keep positive thoughts." She stroked her daughter's face, "God has a plan, put this in his hands—it's out of ours."

Tears poured down Mae's face. Shannon took a tissue from the bedside table and dried her daughter's eyes. "I know this isn't how you pictured becoming a mother, it's certainly not how I imagined my first days as a Granny. But I want you to remember one thing—as worried as you are about your children right now, I'm equally worried about you. Be a good girl and stay as calm as you can. Let your body heal, and we'll face what's to come together."

Mae nodded.

"That's my good girl."

An older, slight-of-build man with compassionate pale blue eyes entered the room and came to Mae's bedside. "Hello, Mrs. McGinn," he said. "I'm Dr. Krause. I'm very glad to see you awake and alert. You had a tough go of it when you first arrived." He picked up her chart. "Your latest test results indicate everything is progressing well."

He removed the oxygen mask, took a cup of water from the bedstand, and placed the straw into Mae's mouth. She took a tentative sip. The cold water felt good on her raw throat.

The doctor placed the cup back on the nightstand and pulled a stool close to her bed. He removed his glasses and folded his hands in his lap. His words were crisp and calculated. "Mrs. McGinn, your husband is doing quite well. His condition is still serious, but he's out of surgery and stable. Mr. McGinn's pelvis is fractured, and he'll be off his feet for quite some time."

The doctor moved closer and took a deep breath before saying more. Shannon recognized his body language—it was the same empathic stance the army officer had taken at their front door twenty years earlier. She knew unbearable news was imminent and clasped her daughter's hand.

"When you were brought in you had significant internal bleeding," the doctor explained. "In order to control it, we were forced to do an emergency cesarean section. You delivered a boy and a girl. Did you know you were having twins, Mrs. McGinn?"

Mae answered in a hoarse whisper. "Yes, my doctor confirmed it months ago. Are they okay? Can I see them now?"

"Mrs. McGinn, there were complications," he said. "Your son is holding his own in the neo-natal intensive care unit. There are breathing problems, but overall, he looks quite good for premature delivery. Your daughter, however, was on the side of the womb that sustained the brunt of the impact. I'm very sorry Mrs. McGinn, we did everything we could—she did not survive."

A scream ripped from the bottom of Mae's soul, followed by a complete numbness.

Shannon climbed into bed beside her and cradled her daughter in her arms. "I'm right here, sweetheart," Shannon said. "Hold on to Mommy, I'm right here." Together they wept.

"There are no words I can offer to make this any easier," the doctor continued. "In my practice I deliver terrible news far too often. The loss of a child, however, is by far the most difficult. There is no greater pain for a parent."

He stood to leave. "If you feel up to it, I'll ask the nurse to bring in a wheelchair and take you to visit your son. Do you have a name picked out? I would be happy to let the nursery staff know so they can update his chart."

Mae whispered, "Sean Bernard."

"Nice strong Irish name." The doctor offered a weak smile. "I'm sure he'll be a handsome and healthy young man." He started toward the door.

"Doctor?" Mae called.

"Yes."

"Meghan Rose, my daughter, can I see her?"

"Of course," he said, with a sad, yet somehow understanding expression.

He took a moment to clear his throat. "I've lost a child, Mrs. McGinn, and I can tell you from experience, holding my son as he took his final breath was one of the greatest gifts I've ever been given. That may sound odd, but having the chance to say goodbye to my son helped me heal. I'll have the nurse bring Meghan in. Take your time; I'll make sure you are not disturbed."

"Thank you, for helping my family, doctor." Her voice was barely audible. "And for using my daughter's name. It means a great deal to me and makes her feel real."

"You're quite welcome, Mrs. McGinn," he said. "And I can assure you Meghan is very real, never believe otherwise. A loved child never dies; they simply wait for us in a better place."

Fifteen minutes later, the young nurse returned and placed the small girl, wrapped in a pink receiving blanket, into Mae's waiting arms.

"She's a beautiful girl, Mrs. McGinn," the nurse said. "I'm so sorry for your loss. Sometimes life just makes no sense. I'll give you some privacy, but I'm right outside at the desk if you need me." She checked Mae's IV and walked quietly out the door.

Mae pulled the blanket back and took in every detail. "She's so small; like a china doll. I'm afraid I'll break her. Mom, come see, she looks like you."

"Do you think so?" Shannon peered into the blanket and ran a finger along Meghan's tiny cheek. Her vision blurred with tears. "She has your nose, Mae."

"And your pursed lips." Mae took the baby's hand

and outlined each finger. "Look at these...so long and delicate. I bet she would have played the piano. You could have taught her."

Shannon felt Mae tremble as waves of pain crashed to the surface in one heartbreaking rush.

"Wake up, Meghan," Mae said. "Open your eyes, show Mommy your eyes." She turned to Shannon. "They made a mistake. She needs time to rest. That's all, right Mom? She's just sleeping, but it's time to wake up." Mae began screeching, "Wake up Meghan, come on, wake up."

The nurse burst through the door. "Make her wake up," Mae screamed at her. "Don't just stand there, do something!" Her head spun to Shannon. "Help me!"

The nurse withdrew a syringe from the bedside table and injected Mae's IV with sedative. The effect was immediate. When she tried to remove the infant, Shannon stopped her.

"We need more time, please," Shannon said. The nurse, assured her patient was calm, left again.

Shannon lay with Mae and pulled her close. She knew her words would vanish beneath the volume of Mae's deafening grief, but they were for her as much as her daughter was. "I would give anything, absolutely anything to see this little one grow up into a beautiful young woman like her Mama, but God has another plan, sweetheart. I don't understand it, I'm not sure I ever will, but we need to let her go now."

She ran a hand over Mae's long, smooth hair. "Take a minute, give our precious little girl a kiss and lots of love. You'll see her again, and until then, keep a picture of that sweet face close to your heart."

The room stilled, and the everyday commotion in

the hospital corridors faded away. Street noises from the traffic below ceased and a heavy feeling rested on Mae's heart as she absorbed her baby girl's every detail.

"This isn't how it's supposed to be," Mae whispered tenderly. "You and I were supposed to bake Christmas cookies, jump in leaf piles, share ice cream. I bet you would have liked chocolate best, that's my favorite. It would have been our special little treat on summer afternoons."

She kissed the peach fuzz top of the baby's head and inhaled the perfect smell. "Daddy and I were looking forward to taking you to the beach and seeing your little face light up the first time a wave came over your toes—our little beach bunny, squealing and laughing and loving every minute."

Mae held the baby close. "I'm never going to forget you Meghan Rose, never. No matter what happens, you were my baby girl, in every way that matters. No one can ever change that."

The door to the room opened, the nurse returned, and her solemn expression told Mae without words it was time to say goodbye. On the edge of the bed, Shannon rested her hand on her daughter's leg. "Are you ready, sweetheart, or would you like another few minutes?"

Mae wiped tears from her face. "A few more minutes won't make this hurt any less."

"Time will heal," Shannon said. "It won't bring Meghan back, but after the sorrow begins to fade—and it will fade, I promise—you'll find a way to let go of the hurt and remember her with love."

Mae kissed Meghan's cheek one final time and

handed her to the waiting nurse before collapsing into her mother's arms.

****

"Oh Mom," Libby held Mae close and wept with her. "How could you keep something like that to yourself all these years? You and Daddy must have been devastated. It must have felt like the world was crumbling beneath you. How did you manage?"

"It was long ago." Mae pulled back and wiped her face. "A long time, and a lot of tears."

"It's all starting to make sense now, why you stopped visiting Brooklyn. It didn't just remind you of Grandma; it reminded you of Meghan, too, didn't it?"

"We left for a lot of reasons, sweetheart," Mae explained. "After Daddy finally recovered and we were back at the apartment it felt like something wasn't quite right. Something, someone, was missing. I know Grandma was heartbroken when we left the city, but it was too difficult."

Mae continued, "Our friends and family tried to be happy for us, tried to focus on Sean, but in the end, it was easier to move away and start over where no one knew the sadness we left behind. We visited Mom once a month in the beginning, but after the business took off, and you and Kevin were born, our schedules got harder to balance, and the visits decreased. Somewhere in that window of time, Mom's mind betrayed her."

"I knew something was wrong the minute Grandma Shannon started calling you Meghan. At first it was a few slip-ups, but then she got belligerent, and insisted I was keeping you from her. She began to demand I bring Meghan to visit."

Mae breathed deep and continued. "I wish I were

stronger, Libby, I wish I were more understanding. But losing your sister devastated me, and Grandma's behavior put me right back in that hospital room. I was a coward. I stopped taking you kids to see her and walked away when she needed me most. Thank God for Will. He stepped in and took over while I just turned my back and looked the other way."

"Mom I'm sure that's not true," Libby said. "Grandma loved you with everything she had. She would have understood why you stayed away, if she'd had her full faculties. We were too young to understand what was going on. I'm sure it would have been terribly frightening to see her like that."

"It was one thing to shield you and your brothers from seeing Mom at her worst, but there was no excuse for *me* to stay away. It took me a long time to make my peace with the way I behaved. You kids deserved an explanation, Libby. I know those visits with Mom were dear to your hearts, and I stole them away. I only wish she'd lived long enough to see the incredible mother you've become."

"Thanks Mom. I learned from the master." Libby embraced Mae. Over her mother's shoulder, she looked out the window and saw Sean's car pull up. "Sean's back from dropping off the truck."

"I suppose I should explain things to the boys, too," Mae said, and grabbed at her locket.

"Wait a minute," Libby said. "The letters on your locket, MRM, Meghan Rose McGinn. I've always assumed Daddy messed up your middle name when he had it engraved, but he did it on purpose, didn't he?"

Mae nodded. "To keep our little girl close to my heart, always."

"My father was a wonderful man." Libby sighed and wiped her eyes before opening the front door. "Do you want to talk to Kevin and Sean alone? I can keep everyone else in the kitchen if you want some privacy?"

"No, I think it's time we all sat down as a family. After all, we don't want the food getting cold, and difficult conversations are always better with egg rolls," Mae said with a grin. "Out of curiosity, did you happen to notice the way Sean looked at Caroline earlier?"

"Why yes," Libby smirked, "yes I did. I was going to ask him about it later, as a matter of fact."

"No!" Mae shouted. "Take my advice, Libby. The more you push your brother, the slower he moves. Keep quiet and he might marry her *before* his social security kicks in."

Chapter Twenty-Eight

Loaded with doughnuts and coffee, Libby arrived at Mae Day on Monday to bribe the long-time crew members selected for the cottage project. When Sean had asked for help, the staff, most of whom worked for Bernie from the beginning, volunteered their services free of charge.

"Geez, Lib,"—Deb came from behind the desk and grabbed the top two of six bakery boxes—"when you said you were bringing coffee and doughnuts, I didn't think you meant this many. What gives?"

"The key to working with my mother is a constant influx of sugar and caffeine," Libby placed the boxes on the conference table. "With *this*, all things are possible."

Deb laughed. "I've known your mother as long as you've been alive and I've never had one problem. Besides, Irene's heading the site—she can handle Mae—Sean thought that José had enough drama lately."

"Good call, Irene's crew is great, and she's got the patience of a saint. Mom will test both." Libby motioned to the door. "I've got coffee in the car, got a second to help me bring it in?"

"I got it. Go on in and see Sean. Be warned, though, I just gave him a stack of invoices; he's cranky when it's bill-paying time. Bring pastry to soften him up."

Armed with a Boston Cream, Libby knocked on Sean's office door.

"Come in," Sean muttered. He saw Libby and waved a pink paper in the air. "When did they start making screws out of freaking gold? My truck cost less than this."

She dropped the doughnut on his desk. "We could donate some of Kev's organs to keep the place going. His liver isn't worth a damn, but the kidneys might catch a few grand."

He bit into the chocolate-and-cream goodness like a great white shark. "We're fine. Damned subs try and slip in extra costs in the eleventh hour on every job. Nothing new." He wiped his mouth and continued. "Thanks for breakfast. Did Deb tell you Irene is going to head up the remodel?"

"Yes, and I think she's perfect."

"I figured Mom would be more comfortable with her, and Irene's crew does a lot of restoration work. She'll do the place justice."

He swigged coffee from his I've-Got-A-Big-Hammer mug. "I had to call your favorite people this morning."

Libby frowned.

"Try not to implode, but when I went to town hall for the original plot dimensions for your property, Madame Clerk Sue said the place is listed on the historical register. Now we have to get the construction plans approved through the Historical Society before demo."

"Crap!" Libby pounded her fists into her lap. "Crap, crap, and did I mention, crap? I never even thought of that."

"Yeah, me either. I got the name and number for the Society president, Esther something?"

"Esther Gibbons. And again, crap." Libby's history with The Society was ugly. This called for finesse, and manipulation. A Cheshire cat grin split her face. "I have an idea—flirt. Esther hasn't gotten any since 1962, and if you feed her ego she may be less of a pain in the ass about the plans. If you can't get the job done, send in José, he's a magnet for the cougar-type."

"I am not selling out my best foreman because my hothead sister can't play nice with the big, bad Historical Society. I can't believe you are afraid of a bunch of harmless old women."

"Wait until after you talk to Esther to judge me. You'll see!"

He pushed away the paperwork and leaned back. "How was Mom last night after I left your place?"

"She seemed okay. It's not as if everything is happening tomorrow. She has time to warm up to the idea. I think she's looking forward to seeing Will. As much as they gripe about each other, I think they both need company."

"You're probably right. And when it comes time to pick out paint colors I can email Will the samples, he's good at that stuff. And no, I'm not saying that because he's gay. It's the artist thing—he's just better than the rest of us at it."

"Caroline decorated most of our place." Libby searched his face for a reaction. "I'm pretty sure Bob and I would still be sitting on a futon and eating off milk crates without her help."

"Good to know." Sean ran his left hand through his

hair.

Libby caught the *tell* and grinned.

He said, "Maybe I'll ask her to come with me when I'm picking out the fixtures."

"There's a really great place in Stamford for lights. I can't remember the name, but Caroline knows. She took us there when the Society required 'authentic reproduction' outdoor lights for our porch, and I'm sure we'll have to go the same route with the cottage.

Her inner devil's advocate plotted. "There was a fantastic little deli next door to the lighting place. You can repay Caroline with a big, sloppy Rueben. For a skinny blonde, that girl sure can pack away the pastrami."

He laughed. "And you call yourself her best friend."

"I call them like I see them." Libby stood to leave. "I'll let you get back to your invoices. Call me when you hear back from the Society."

"I will, but don't worry about it too much, I'm sure everything will be fine."

Chapter Twenty-Nine

Tucked into her favorite chair with a juicy romance novel, Libby was interrupted by her ringing cell phone. The faceplate glowed, "Jesus."

"Hey Sean," Libby said.

"Esther Gibbons is a nightmare," Sean said.

"I warned you. The entire group is difficult."

"*Difficult* is an understatement. What did you do to these women to make them hate you so much?"

"I was born."

"Are you sure you didn't accidentally run over one of their cats or something?"

"Just tell me, what do I have to do this time? Match the paint to Ben Franklin's eyes? Plant grass seeds from Betsy Ross's garden? What?"

"Worse, they need to be part of the process. Start to finish, demo to final construction. They want their own pseudo-foreman on the job—at least once a month—and if he or she sees a problem, construction stops until we reach a compromise."

"Are you freaking kidding me? They want someone here? In my house?"

"Sorry, yeah."

"Shoot me now," Libby groaned. *This is for Mom. This will make life simpler.* "Fine, bring it on."

"Bring it on? That's it?"

"What can we do? Is there another option?"

"No."

"Do we know who the Society minion destined to drive me to rehab is going to be?"

"Esther."

"No, not her! Anyone but her. This is *crap* on multiple levels. Not only am I on Esther's shit list, but she's Shannon's English teacher. This will not sit well with my volatile teenager."

"The good news is we can pull permits and start right away."

Libby saw Stump prancing back and forth by the door. "I've got to go. Stump is doing the urine two-step. Call me tomorrow and let me know who to expect and when—I'll stock up on wine."

Stump finished his donation to the petunias and Libby turned off the lights and went upstairs to check on the kids. Contorted like a pretzel in his racing stripe sheets, Charlie was sound asleep. She kissed him softly and moved on to Shannon's room.

"Knock-knock," Libby announced before entering

"Hi Mom," Shannon said.

"You need to go to sleep, kiddo." Libby sat on the bed beside her daughter.

"I will soon," Shannon answered. "I have ten pages left to read in Romeo and Juliet."

"I remember reading that. It's kind of heavy for eighth grade, isn't it?"

"Ms. Gibbons thinks it teaches us 'dating young ends badly.' She's so strange."

Libby kissed Shannon goodnight and refrained from mentioning Ms. Gibbons' impending visits. "Love you. Finish up and get some rest."

"Night, Mom."

"Night, sweetheart." Libby closed the door and crossed to the master bedroom.

Bob sat in bed surrounded by case files. "Who was on the phone?" he asked.

"Sean." Libby met his eyes and slowly began unbuttoning her blouse.

Bob dropped the paperwork. "Am I getting lucky?"

"Yes."

"Hot-damn." He shoved the papers off the bed in one sweep.

She dropped her blouse and exposed a torn gray sports bra. In her best vixen voice, she said, "Does this get you hot, big boy?"

"A stiff breeze gets me hot, Lib." He took a quick sniff of his armpits. "Give me five minutes. I stink."

"No!" she yelled. "There's no time for hygiene. I'll fall asleep. Drop your pants and let's get to it!"

"Your call, but I'm not pretty. Maybe I'll just take a quick rinse." He started to stand.

"Dammit Bob!" She ripped down her jeans as the frustrations of the day caught up with her. "I need sex, right now. Dirty, quick, angry sex. Is that too much to ask?"

"Honey, you're scaring me a little." He waved his hands in the air, palms out. "Don't stop, it's totally getting me aroused. But still...a little scary."

She fell in next to him and pulled a pillow over her face. "Smother me," she groaned. "If I start to kick and flail, press harder. I'll resist at first, but *really*, just do it."

He pulled the pillow off. "Tell me."

She recounted the earlier conversation with Sean. "And to top off my day," she continued. "I'm pretty sure Stump has a stomach bug. It was dark when I took him out, so I didn't have a visual, but the sounds coming from that animal were frightening—like squeezing the last drops from a supersize ketchup bottle."

With a heavy sigh, she covered her face with her hands and continued. "It's not *one problem*, it's a million little things adding up over the course of time. My plate does not runneth over, it spilleth everywhere and maketh another freaking mess for me to clean up. I know I shouldn't complain, we've got a fantastic life. But I waste so much time figuring out how to fix problems, I miss the good stuff. Life keeps going, whether I'm ready or not."

Bob wrapped his arms around her and pulled close. "We've had a long couple of weeks, and it's taking a toll. Between the kids, holidays, Mae, it's been rough. I'm amazed you made it this far without snapping."

He kissed the top of her head. "You've got a right to explode. I'm here to glue you back together. Want me to run downstairs and grab the Cheese Bites? I picked up the jumbo box at the wholesale place. I figured with the demolition starting you might need them."

She snuggled into his chest. "You're a good man, Bob O'Rourke."

He ran a hand down her back and lingered on her butt. "I know what would really help you relax."

She chuckled. "I can't imagine what you're talking about."

"Hey, if memory serves me correctly, five minutes ago you stripped down to your finest lingerie and begged for mattress hockey."

"Yes, yes I did." She pulled up from his embrace and wrinkled her nose. "After consideration and time spent up close and personal, I'd like to revisit the shower option. You smell like pickles."

"I had a little accident with the relish bottle at lunch. Give me five minutes." He sprang up and ran to the bathroom.

Libby lay back and closed her eyes. On the bedside table, her cell phone rang. It was Caroline.

"Hey there." Libby said.

Caroline's voice cracked with laughter. "Hi."

"What's so funny?"

"I just got a call from your husband."

Libby stared at the closed bathroom door. "How? He's in the shower."

"Yeah, I know. He called from his cell and asked me to keep you awake for, and I quote, 'dirty, angry sex.' Do me a favor and stay conscious for the poor guy, he sounds pathetic. You have to throw him a bone occasionally. He also said you're having a bad day and thought you may need to talk, specifically to someone with a vagina. Although mine's been out-of-commission a bit lately, I can still listen."

"My husband knows me too well," Libby said, and settled in for a chat. "Tell me about your day, I want to forget mine."

Chapter Thirty

"You have got to be kidding me!" Libby bellowed. Sean's call did nothing to brighten her Christmas shopping experience.

"I wish I were," Sean said. "Gibbons and her Society cohorts are coming tonight to check the progress. Apparently, they need to be absolutely certain our plans will not diminish any historical elements, including framework."

"What a load of BS! It's two days until Christmas and those girdle-loving cronies have nothing better to do than pester me? Don't they have lives?" Libby gathered her shopping bags and charged out of the mall. "What time are they *gracing me* with their presence?"

"Five. Though she did say after this the plans I provided would suffice until the plumbing is roughed in," Sean explained. "We can start the main construction when Mom leaves next week for Will's place, and if all goes as planned, finish ahead of schedule. It's four-thirty now. Are you going to make it?"

"Do I have a choice?" Libby ripped open the car door and tossed the bags into the back seat.

In the driver's seat, she fired up the engine and set the heat to full blast. "Bob took the kids to Kevin's to help hang Christmas lights on the house. That's a case of the blind leading the blind. So at least I will be able to get there without having to drop anyone off anywhere. God knows I'm only a taxi."

Her temper seethed. "Are you meeting me at the house, or do I have to deal with these women alone?"

"Don't yell *at me*. I'll be there. I'll stop home first and get a helmet, in case I have to pull you off Esther, but I'll be there."

His stab at humor did nothing to cool Libby's temper.

"Mom wants to be there, too. I'm picking her up on my way over."

"Marvelous. This gets better and better," Libby groaned. "Are you all staying for dinner? I've got nothing in the house, so it's take out or PB&J."

"Mom made pot roast. She's bringing it with her."

"Well, that's a bonus. I don't have to cook."

"Lib, it's a bonus for *all of us* when you don't cook."

"Shut up." Libby snapped like a dry twig. Unable to keep her emotions in check she let loose and blasted Sean with a mega-decibel rant. "I suck in the kitchen, I piss off old ladies...anything else you want to add to my shortcomings? Christ knows I have enough to deal with. We can't *all* be as perfect as you, so keep your shitty comments to yourself!" She jabbed the *off* button and hurled the phone into the backseat.

Twinkling lights and festive decorations lined streets, but the beauty of the season was lost on Libby.

At home, she parked behind Sean's truck and caught a glimpse of him through the cottage's kitchen window laying blueprints on the card table. Dark under-eye circles and a five o'clock shadow, well on its way to midnight, framed his face.

"I'm an ass," Libby said to herself. "He's just as exhausted as I am."

She went inside. "I owe you an apology," she said to him, as she took off her coat. "No excuses. I was a bitch, and I had no right to go off on you like that and slam the phone down like a twelve-year-old. Sorry."

"Don't worry about it." Sean yanked her hair the same way he had when they were kids. "We're all on edge. None of this is easy, and you've got the brunt going on in your back yard."

"The construction isn't the problem. We grew up around job sites and the noise doesn't even faze me. I woke up yesterday, and the reality of what is coming down the road hit me like a ton of bricks. I may complain about Mom, but the truth is I rely on her for answers all the time. I'm not ready to be the parent. I'm not ready to see her as anything less than the force of nature I'm so used to going head-to-head with. The thought of her fading away, losing that spark—it's impossible to wrap my brain around."

Sean crossed his arms over his chest. "I know, I was thinking the same thing the other night. Life snuck up and kicked us all in the ass with this one, but at least Mom is being realistic and not fighting the move. It's a step in the right direction. Bob said he reviewed Mom's will, and all the other paperwork, and she was abundantly clear on what she wants as far as medical and financial care. At least she's got a plan. Hopefully we won't need it for a long time to come, but it's something."

"I told Bob I didn't want to know the details, all he said was it looked okay—typical Mae, organized right down to the last detail."

"Was there a doubt?"

Brother and sister shared a smile as Mae opened the front door. "What are you two grinning about?" she asked.

"Libby's cooking," Sean fibbed. "And how grateful I am for your pot roast tonight in lieu of one of her more *creative* dishes. That stuffed pepper trauma still makes me queasy."

Libby slapped his ribs. "Wise ass."

"Watch the toilet mouth, Elizabeth." Mae reprimanded. "The ladies from the society have no patience for cursing."

"Well then I better get it all out of my system before they get here. After all, we wouldn't want to offend Ms. Gibbons."

"Esther Gibbons?" Mae questioned, her brow arched.

"Yes," Libby answered. "Do you know her?"

The sound of a car engine halted the conversation. Four gray-haired women piled out of the garbage-barge-sized sedan and approached the door.

"Okay, best behavior everyone," Sean said while eying Libby. "I'm talking to you."

He greeted the women with his trademark sexy grin. "Hello ladies, please come in. I can't wait to show you what we have planned."

Esther made the introductions. "Hello Sean, these are my colleagues, Mary Watson, June Gunn, and Victoria Simmons."

He shook each hand and motioned them into the room. "A pleasure to meet all of you." He pointed out Mae and Libby. "I believe you all know my sister, Libby, and this is my mother, Mae."

"Hello Esther," Mae said with a sly smile, hinting at a history between the two women. "I haven't seen you since our days together on the Parish Council. Those were fascinating times. Seems like yesterday, doesn't it?"

"Why yes, it does." Esther paled and ended the discussion faster than a celebrity marriage. She directed her attention toward Sean. "You have made a great deal of progress in here since the last time we met, Sean." She motioned to the blueprints. "Are these the changes to the original design we discussed earlier?"

"Yes," Sean answered. "These are a copy, and yours to keep."

"That was very thoughtful of you. Thank you."

"My pleasure," he said while extending the crook of his elbow to Esther. "Can I give you ladies the nickel tour?"

Happy for his attention, Esther linked her arm in his and led the other women.

Once they were of earshot, Libby yanked Mae aside for an explanation. "Okay Mom, give it up. What was *all that* about between you and Esther?"

Mae feigned ignorance. "What are you talking about, dear?"

"Don't give me that. You know darn well what I'm talking about. Esther looked like you hit her with a two-by-four the moment you brought up Parish Council. What's the story?"

Mae grinned, and dropped her voice to a low whisper. "Let's just say I have a little something to hold over Esther. If she wishes the history between the two of us to remain in the past, then she'll know it's in everyone's best interest for our plans to receive the

Society's approval and move forward without delay."

She went on, "After all, I'm sure Esther, a respectable teacher and upstanding member of society, would be devastated if one of her youthful transgressions resurfaced and stirred up scandal."

"Scandal?" Libby's eyes bulged. "I need to hear this. Spill it!"

Mae peered over her shoulder and made sure Sean had the women occupied before saying more. "You must never breathe a word of this," Mae said.

Libby nodded, her eyes bulging in anticipation.

Mae explained, "Esther's tenure on the Parish Council was short-lived, and for good reason. After a bit too much to drink at the Holy Mother Casino Night and Silent Auction, she and a visiting seminary student from Brazil had a little romantic interlude in the bingo room. I walked in and caught them in the act. And let me tell you, it was not an experience I want to relive."

Libby's bawdy laughter cracked the silence. "Oh my God! Esther's a slut!"

"Shh!" Mae warned. "Keep your voice down, or they'll hear you."

"Mom, how could you *not* tell me this sooner?" Libby said. "You know how many run-ins I've had with that woman? She lives to make my life miserable. I could have used this ammo years ago!"

"It's not Christian to gossip, Libby."

"Oh, but blackmail is okay?"

"Blackmail is an ugly word, Libby. All I did was nudge Esther's memory. How she proceeds is up to her."

"You are a piece of work."

"Quiet, they're coming."

Sean returned the group to the main room. "I think those are all the structural changes we need to review," he said. "Does anyone have questions I can answer?"

Victoria spoke. "Sean, you seem to have things well in hand and have been very mindful of the integrity of a home this age...but I have a question about the plaster walls."

"Of course, go ahead."

"It is *always* important to use a contractor respectful of historical homes," Victoria stated. "Do you have someone who specializes in that type of work? Plaster is delicate, and good masons are hard to come by."

Before Sean could answer, Mae offered a solution. "Sean, dear, I believe Tomás would be an excellent choice. He did all the work over at that lovely 1790's bed-and-breakfast in Groton."

Sean nodded. "You're right Mom. Tomás does a lot of our restoration work, and he's local. We always make an effort to use contractors from the area and support our economy."

"The bathroom needs more than repairs, it will require extensive work and two additional walls," Victoria continued. "Do you feel this Tomás-person's experience is capable of that level of craftsmanship?"

"Oh Tomás is wonderful," Mae protested. "He is a real gentleman and intensely hardworking, but I'm not surprised. I believe his marvelous work ethic has a great deal to do with his Latin heritage." She took a long look at Esther and went in for the kill. "Sean dear, where is Tomás from again?"

"Brazil." Sean said. "His whole family came over in the 1980s. The father was a master plasterer and taught all four of his sons the trade. Well, all except the youngest brother, Juan; he's a priest in Boston."

Esther gripped the card table for dear life. She stammered, "Ladies, we've taken up quite enough of the McGinns' time."

She backed toward the door with the blueprints clutched to her chest like a shield. "Everything looks in order Sean. You may proceed as planned. Please call before you select paint colors and I'll assign one of my colleagues here to do the final inspection. I trust their judgment. No need for me to return, ever."

She ripped open the front door. "Merry Christmas—get in the car, girls," she said, and made a beeline for her sedan. Her orthopedic shoes kicked up gravel as the remaining trio, baffled by their leader's sudden about-face did nothing to oppose Esther's stamp of approval.

Sean closed the door and turned to Mae and Libby. "Someone want to tell me what the hell that was all about?"

Libby collapsed to the floor in a fit of laughter and pointed to Mae.

"Mom?" Sean looked to her for an explanation. "What's going on?"

Mae slipped on her coat and gloves and meandered out the door. "I haven't the slightest idea what you're talking about."

A satisfied grin splintered her face. "Pot roast in twenty minutes. Don't forget to wash your hands."

Chapter Thirty-One

Nothing compared to a McGinn family Christmas Eve; traveling circuses produced less fanfare. With each year the gathering grew. Marriages and babies translated to bigger decorations and more gifts under the tree, and a simple family get-together transformed into a wrapping-paper-and-cookie-free-for-all.

Kevin and Suzanne unwillingly inherited the legendary holiday extravaganza after Mae's condominium became too small to contain the growing family.

The McGinn adults participated in a Secret Santa drawing in September. The process cut down on the holiday chaos and allowed three full months to consider the recipients likes and dislikes.

In the beginning the presents were thoughtful and full of sincere well wishes, but it did not take long for the twisted family humor to enter in. Libby owned eight easy-to-follow cookbooks, Sean was enrolled in a high-price mail order Russian Bride bidding war, and Kevin's medicine cabinet sported a lifetime supply of hair restoration cream. The more ridiculous, the better. No one took offense and laughter filled the house.

Despite the tradition, Mae insisted on buying each of her children a gift each year and they reciprocated. The under-eighteen crowd was spoiled rotten and showered with multiple gifts from aunts and uncles, all of which would be broken or forgotten by February.

Over the years, the group had expanded to include in-laws and close friends. Post-divorce, Caroline and Trevor joined the growing circle, as did Dom. Suzanne's parents, Ed and Elaine closed the Shoe Horn at noon and drove over with Mindy in thinly veiled hopes their youngest daughter would eventually bag Sean and become a McGinn herself. Shelia traveled to her brother's in California for Christmas, but always managed to send the kids the single most noise-inducing gifts available, for which Libby was eternally grateful.

"Is it me," Bob asked as the family pulled into Kevin and Suzanne's driveway, "or does it look a little like a multi-colored air traffic control pattern?"

"It's a little much," Libby agreed. "I'm particularly fond of the inflatable surfing Santa. Nothing says Christmas like Saint Nick hanging ten."

Bob turned to the kids in the backseat. "Okay, listen up. No repeat of last year. Charlie, if someone gives you a car model you already have, you do not hand it back and ask for cash. Say 'thank you,' and we'll deal with it later. Got it?"

"Got it." Charlie nodded.

"Shannon," Bob continued, "your grandmother is not a teenage girl. She does not keep current with fashion trends. Try and muster some enthusiasm when you open her gift."

"But Dad," Shannon whined, "last year she knit a sweater with kittens on it!"

"Gram went out of her way to make you that sweater, and if this year's ensemble has dancing kangaroos, smile and be grateful."

"Fine." She opened the car door. "Can we go in now?"

"Go, but remember what I said." Charlie and Shannon slid out of the car and ran to the front door.

"In her defense," Libby grinned. "That *was* the ugliest sweater known to man. The cats looked a little mange-ridden."

"It *was* hideous." Bob shivered. "But Shann's got to work on her game face. You didn't see me screeching in horror at that yellow- and black-striped golf shirt—I looked like a jaundiced bumble bee."

Libby gave him a quick kiss. "Ready?"

He took her face in his hands. "We could leave and make a run for the border. The kids are already inside; they'd never catch us."

She pulled on her hat and opened the car door. "And miss all the fun? Come on. Be a man. Let's go." They trudged up the snowy walkway with gift-stuffed shopping bags, and rang the bell.

Kevin answered and rushed them inside. "Don't ask questions, I'll explain later." He pulled them into the side hall and closed the door. "For right now, all you need to know is Suzanne's hair *looks fantastic*. Got it? Fantastic! Do not stare directly at it; you won't be able to look away if you do." Footsteps sounded from the hallway. "Shit, here she comes. Remember, *fantastic*."

Libby saw her first. *Dear God in heaven. Did she pay someone to do that to her?* Suzanne's once-blonde flowing hair was sliced and diced into a shag carpet/corn stalk mating.

"Hi Lib, Bob, Merry Christmas." Suzanne kissed them and turned to her husband. "Kev, take their coats."

"Wow." Bob struggled to maintain a look of sincerity. "Great hair, Suz." Awkward pause. "I need a beer." He sprinted to the family room.

Coward. Libby said, "I agree, great cut. I bet it's a lot easier to get ready in the morning now, huh?"

"Cut the crap, Libby." Suzanne's eyes welled up. "I look hideous, and all I wanted was a little trim. Mr. Frank convinced me this would be 'chic and easy to take care of' now that I have Saratoga. When I got home from the salon and went in to pick her up from her nap she screamed. I scared her. My own child is afraid of me."

Libby hugged her. "No, no. I'm sure that's not it." She played with the blonde spikes atop her sister-in-law's head. "I won't blow sunshine up your ass. It's not your best look. But come on, it's hair, and it will grow back."

"Thank you for saying that." Suzanne wiped her eyes. "I appreciate the honesty. Kevin just keeps telling me how fantastic I look. Dumb ass!"

"Men don't understand hair trauma."

"Let's get some wine. Everyone else is here, including your mother. She informed me I look like that successful lesbian girl on the talk show. I know she intended it as a compliment, but I may have to kill her anyway."

"Get in line."

The women entered the living room to a sea of friends and family, all gathered in front of the fireplace with drinks and food in hand. The children ripped through their gifts in record time, and Trevor and Charlie headed to the playroom to assemble an air hockey set.

"I'll take Sara if you want a break, Aunt Suzanne," Shannon volunteered.

"That would be wonderful, Shannon. I could use a break. Just bring her back if she starts to get fussy. She didn't take a good nap today."

"Okay, we'll go watch Christmas specials in the TV room."

"Thanks Shannon, you're a sweetheart." When Shannon was out of earshot, Suzanne continued, "If I have to watch those f-ing puppets sing about Santa one more time I'm going to snap their little felt necks." The group burst into laughter.

Kevin clapped his hands. "So, can I get anybody a drink before we swap our tasteful and lovingly selected gifts?"

"I'll help you." Sean said.

Orders placed, the brothers went to the kitchen. Kevin opened a bottle of white wine and grabbed glasses. "So, has Mindy been cozying up to you tonight?" he teased Sean.

"As always." Sean took the glasses and poured while Kevin went to the fridge for beer. "I thought I was pretty clear last time, but Mindy and her parents only hear what they want to hear."

"Why don't you just come right out and tell her you're not interested. Or better yet, take a chance on someone else, bring a date to the next family function. Really give old Min the message you're *not available*."

"Oh yeah," Sean grinned. "Bring someone into this chaos. No thanks, I'll keep my private life private."

Kevin popped the tops off the beer and put the bottle opener on the counter. He faced Sean, sighed, and shook his head.

"What?" Sean asked.

"I'm not sure who you think you're fooling, but if you wait much longer the opportunity of a lifetime is going to blow right by you, big brother. She's one in a million, and we all know it. You're going to miss your chance unless you step up and do something. This is getting ridiculous."

"Mindy? You are out of your mind. The woman has the IQ of a zucchini?"

"Give it up Sean. You and I both know I'm not talking about Mindy." He glanced into the living room, directly at Caroline laughing at something Bob said. She looked right at home with the McGinn bunch. Kevin smiled and returned his focus on Sean. "You're an idiot if you don't make a move, and soon, Battaglia's a great guy and he's not going to give up easy."

Kevin motioned to the counter. "Do me a favor, grab those napkins on your way back in."

Sean stood stock-still, mouth gaping, glasses of wine in each hand. Did *everyone* suspect how he felt about Caroline? He made his way back to the living room and handed off the first glass of wine to Mindy. "Here you go Min, a little holiday spirit." He forced a polite smile.

"Thank you, Sean," Mindy cooed. She pulled her shoulder blades back in a cleavage-boosting attempt. "You are so sweet to take care of me."

"No problem."

He brought the second glass to Caroline as her lips curled into a knowing grin. "You are enjoying this too much. Knock it off."

"I like watching you squirm."

Caroline's amusement-laced comment made him

chuckle.

"I must say, Mindy's frontage is looking particularly robust tonight, don't you think?"

He grinned and took a seat on the floor to Caroline's right as the gift swap began. "I hadn't noticed."

Bob played Santa and distributed the gifts. Per tradition, no one tore a shred of paper until everyone had something to open.

"Are we ready?" Mae asked.

"I think so," Bob answered. "Does everyone have a gift?" Nods all around. "Okay, have at it."

Elaine was the first to gush. "Oh how beautiful, a bracelet. I love it! Whoever picked this out is a gem, no pun intended!" She slid the new bangle on her wrist and peered into Ed's gift box. "What did you get, dear?"

"A book." Ed's ample caterpillar brows knitted together. "Let me just see what the title is. Oh, look its Dick Cheney's new biography. Great choice. I'll read this on the flight to Houston for the shoe convention."

What's more exciting, Libby wondered, *a shoe convention or a political memoir?*

Kevin spoke. "All right, I have to see what this is. And I swear to God if it's more spray-on hair, someone is getting slapped." He ripped through the paper and found a black jeweler's box containing sterling silver cufflinks. "Wow, whoever had me went over the budget. These are amazing."

Libby spoke up. "I'm breaking the Secret Santa code. I picked your name in the draw. Look close, and hopefully you'll recognize where I got them."

He took the cufflinks in his hand and held them under the light. "They're monogrammed. MF?" Then it hit him. "Holy Cow, these are Grandpa Finn's; the ones in their wedding picture, right?"

Nodding Libby said, "They were in a box I found out in the cottage. I had them polished up for you. Do you like them?"

Kevin walked over and kissed Libby on the cheek. "I love them, thanks. These are great."

"Bring those over here, Kevin," Mae asked. "I want a closer look."

He handed her the box and joined Suzanne on the couch.

"I remember these," Mae said. "Mom kept them in her jewelry box next to her pearls; two memories from her wedding, side-by-side in her little safe spot."

Libby saw the moment the pleasant memory flooded Mae's face. It did her heart good to hear joy in her mother's voice when she spoke of Grandma Shannon.

"What did you get Mom?" Libby asked.

Mae passed the cufflinks to Kevin and opened her gift. She frowned. "Huh, I'm not sure exactly what it is?"

"It's a Yoga suit!" Elaine chimed in. "Suzie said you go to a class every day, so I went to the Sporting Barn. The salesgirl said this is what everyone is wearing. Isn't it super cute?"

Mae managed to keep her world-class manners in place and withdrew the hot pink body suit for all to see. "It's just spectacular, Elaine...a real showstopper." *Dear Lord this is hideous.* "I can't wait to wear it." *Never going to happen.* "I'm sure everyone will want one as soon as they see me."

Bob leaned into Libby and spoke softly. "She's

going to look like a life-sized jelly bean."

Libby gagged on her pig-in-a-blanket. "I need wine." She stood and motioned toward the kitchen. "Anyone else need a drink?"

"I'll help." Caroline followed. They barely made it out of the living room before erupting into a fit of laughter.

"Oh. My. God!" Caroline spoke first. "If Mae ever, ever dares to wear that thing you have to call me! Anywhere, anytime, anything I'm doing will be dropped and I'll be running over to see her in that get-up! I don't care if *Mr. Perfect* is in my bed professing his undying love, you call me the minute she puts that thing on!"

Out of breath, Libby held her stomach and groaned. "Stop, I hurt. I laughed so hard I pulled a muscle."

"Wine," Caroline refilled the glasses. "We need wine, and a moment to get ourselves together."

"Good plan." Libby sipped. "That's got to be my favorite Christmas moment of all time; it's goes down in history right next to Sean's man purse."

"Oh God, remember that? Suzanne was so proud; she thought he could use a pretty briefcase to carry around blueprints." Caroline sipped and went on. "Sean tried so hard not to look mortified, it must have killed him."

"My brother can take one for the team when he needs to." Libby seized the topic shift. "Can I ask you something?"

"Sure."

"I may be way, way off-base here, but is something going on between you and Sean?"

Caroline, lost for words, fidgeted with her wineglass.

Libby noticed her unease, and said, "Well, huh! Maybe I'm not that off-base. Listen, you don't have to say anything, it's none of my business. You two are adults, I won't pry." She couldn't pull it off. "Okay, that's total bull. Tell me everything, tell me now—I have to know!"

"It's not a simple answer, Lib."

"Sure it is, I don't want details, I mean, ick, he's my brother. All I want is a yes or no. Are you two involved? If you think it's going to affect our relationship, don't. With the exception of Bob, you're my best friend, Nothing changes that."

"Thanks. I needed to hear that, and I'm not trying to be evasive, I just don't know what to say, or even how to say it. I can tell you this, though...there's a history, one that we probably should have told you about a long time ago, but it was simpler to keep it between Sean and I. The fewer people who knew, the fewer people disappointed when it went south. But as for now, I honestly don't know what the hell's going on."

Dom walked into the kitchen. "Sorry ladies; am I interrupting something?"

"Not one little bit," Libby answered. "Are you here for wine, Dom?" She squeezed Caroline's hand and mouthed—"talk later."

"Nope, although after seeing that exercise outfit, I could use a stiff shot." They giggled as he continued. "I made some cannoli. Come help me get it out of the fridge."

Caroline watched him slide the tray out of the

fridge and groaned. "Dom, you are killing me. No matter where I am for New Years, I will officially be wearing the largest pants I own, thanks to your cooking."

Dom shook his head in disapproval. "Girls today, you're all too skinny. In my day, women were curvy, like a beautiful Italian country road. You ladies are great just the way you are. No diets! They ruin nature's perfect canvas."

Caroline kissed his cheeks. "Will you marry me?"

"A tall, leggy blonde?" he joked. "I'd be dead in a week."

Libby gently punched Dom in the arm. "He can't marry you, he's got a girlfriend. Don't ya', big guy?"

Dom blushed and waved away Libby's comment. "At my age we do not have *girlfriends*. Dolores and I *enjoy each other's company*. Lucky for her she's off with her sister while I'm stuck here with these crazy people."

"Hey," Libby said. "Those 'crazy people' are my family!"

"I know, bella, and I love them all. Come on ladies, help me bring the pastry in and sit between me and the sparkly tree. I can't look at it anymore, I'll have a seizure. Who uses that much tinsel, and pink nonetheless?" They followed Dom into the crowd and took their seats.

"All right, Caroline and Libby are the only two who still need to open their gifts," Suzanne said, "Libby, you go first."

"Okay," Libby took note of the wrapping paper. Happy woodland creatures, in pink satin bows carrying glittery heart-shaped packages. The gift giver was no mystery. Inside, under layers and layers of colored tissue paper she found a beautiful sterling silver necklace with a deep blue stone at the center.

"Oh this is stunning." A descriptive card from the artesian was attached. Libby read aloud, "'A Native American amulet guaranteed to soothe tension and relieve stress.' This is an absolutely perfect gift for me."

She turned toward Suzanne. "Thank you Secret Santa...whoever you are." Suzanne glowed with pride. Libby tossed the paper into the pile of discarded wrapping. "Okay Caroline, your turn."

Caroline lifted the two-foot square box into her lap and guessed at the contents. "Let's see, earrings?" she joked. She tore gently at the paper and dug through hundreds of packing peanuts until she reached an oddly shaped red velvet bag. She shifted her gaze from person to person. "I'm getting a little nervous; my secret Santa went to a lot of trouble to build suspense." Untying the drawstring at the top of the bag, she reached inside and withdrew a pair of gleaming white ice skates. Puzzled, she spotted a card at the bottom of the bag. "Wait a minute, there's a note."

"Read it." Mae encouraged.

Caroline slid out the card and read. "Some memories, like those we love most, are worth holding onto for a lifetime."

"Lovely, but I don't understand the meaning." Mae said.

In a moment of enlightenment, Caroline spun in search of Sean and found him in the kitchen doorway. Their gazes locked, and the rest of the room faded away.

His graveled voice cracked, "Look inside."

Hand trembling, she picked up the left skate and peered down into the boot; two stars. A sob escaped. Although the room was full of family, Caroline saw only Sean; the sensitive boy she fell in love with—now a man whose sentimentality stole her heart. She placed the skates on the coffee table and walked to him. She took his face in her hands. "You absolutely take my breath away. Do you know that?"

He rubbed his thumb over a stray tear rolling down her cheek. "Don't cry Car, I made you do that once before, and it almost killed me. I can't take it again."

"Happy tears this time, I promise."

She stepped closer and dropped her voice so only he could hear. "Tell me, is everyone staring at us?"

Sean glanced over her shoulder and smiled at his family's anticipatory grins. Mae dabbed her eyes with a tissue and clasped her hands over her heart. "Yes," he chuckled. "I'd say we have a captive audience."

"Good," She took a deep breath. "Let em' watch, cause I'm going to kiss you, in front of them all. And I'm not talking a friendly peck on the cheek. Will that bother you?"

His eyes darkened. "Not in the least."

She wrapped her hands around his neck and fingered the soft hair at the scruff of his neck.

His pulse raced.

"You're sure? It's going to be slow, and long, and very, *very* personal," she purred. "One of those kisses that will make the parents in the room grateful the kids aren't around. Oh, and on a sad note, what I'm about to do to you will send Mindy directly into mourning."

He dug his fingertips into the small of her back and

gripped tight. "Mindy looks great in black."

She drew his head close. "Sean, I'm opening that door."

"Come on in, Duffy," he groaned. "I've been waiting too damned long." Without hesitation, he pulled her the final distance into his arms.

Oblivious to anything but each other, Caroline Duffy kissed Sean McGinn with more passion than should ever be expressed outside the bedroom, let alone in front of family and friends.

Several minutes later, loud applause and whistles from the peanut gallery made Sean reluctantly pull away. With a smile of epic proportion, he looked down into the face of the only woman he ever loved. "Does this mean you *like* the skates?" he asked.

Laughing, Caroline hugged him close and answered. "I *love* the skates."

Chapter Thirty-Two

Mae owned three suitcases, all constructed prior to 1970. The smallest resembled a floral school bus.

"Mom," Libby looked over the luggage eating up every inch of square space in her front hall. "Uncle Will has a washer and dryer. Do you really *need* all this stuff?"

"Elizabeth, I don't criticize those garbage bag-sized purses you carry, do not judge my packing abilities." Mae took her coat off and hung it in the closet. "Now, since Sean was kind enough to bring me over tonight, and Bob is taking me to the airport bright and early, why don't I say *thank you* by making dinner?" Rooting through the kitchen, she dug out frozen chicken and set it in the microwave to defrost. "Where are the kids?"

Libby grabbed the potatoes from the veggie bin and started to peel. "Shannon should be home any minute and Charlie is out in the cottage helping Sean. I'm beginning to hope this will be an ongoing education. My poor son can't learn tool-handling from his father, and Sean loves his new apprentice."

Mae smiled. "He's in his glory showing Charlie how to build. Daddy used to do the same thing with him. Sean loved going on job sites and hammering his little heart out. Maybe Charlie's the future of Mae Day."

"Maybe, or maybe he's destined for law like his father; he certainly knows how to negotiate."

"Tell me about it, the little bugger does have a gift. I still have at least seven boxes of popcorn from last year's scout fundraiser, and I can't even *eat* popcorn with my dentures."

Mother and daughter continued to build the simple dinner, side-by-side. Chicken baking, they took a seat on the couch in front of a crackling fire. The glowing orange and gold flames cast a soothing tone over the room. The warm hearth and smell of burning oak somehow made everything less stressful.

The kitchen door opened, and Bob entered with a covered dish. "Hello ladies. Anyone interested in some Tiramisu?"

"Let me guess," Libby said. "Tony's son-in-law committed yet another random act of stupidity?"

"Yep," Bob grinned. "Not so bad this time. Had a few too many down at the Italian-American Club and tried to walk home. Little mishap with his neighbor. Apparently all condos look alike when you're in the bag, and Mrs. Ramos was none too pleased to find him asleep on her living room couch this morning."

"Why didn't the silly woman lock her front door?" Mae asked.

"Her husband works third shift, and he forgot to lock up on the way out. Thus the uninvited guest." Bob put the dish into the fridge and went to hang up his coat. "Dinner smells good. What are we having?"

"Rosemary chicken and scalloped potatoes," Libby answered. "And before you ask, Mom cooked. I was relegated to peel-and-chop duty."

He leaned down and kissed his wife before taking

his seat in Old Stink. "Nothing is sexier than a woman who can chop."

Mae took in the pair. Her daughter had found a rare gem in Bob. "Do you two realize how truly lucky you are?"

"Because my cooking hasn't killed anyone yet, or because Bob brings home edible legal bribes?" Libby asked.

"No," Mae smiled. "I mean to have each other, to have these simple times to laugh about. The big stuff is important, too, but it's the day-to-day with Daddy I miss most. We used to take a few minutes before bed every night and talk about the funny things that happened. During the tough times, it was hard to come up with even one, but somehow, Daddy always found a way to make me smile."

"Bernie was one of the great ones," Bob said. "He always made the biggest problem seem like a drop in the bucket."

"He did indeed."

Sean and Charlie stormed into the house from the yard, chatting like old drinking buddies. "Can I use the nail gun tomorrow?" Charlie pleaded. "Please?"

"Sorry pal." Sean grinned as he answered his eager-to-learn nephew. "The nail gun has an age requirement, and you have about ten more years to go. Tell you what, I'll let you use the insulation machine and shoot some foam into the walls when we're ready. How does that sound?"

Bob overheard the conversation. "Hey, *I* wanted to use the insulation machine!" He argued, "You said I wasn't allowed."

"That's right," Sean answered. "You *are not*

allowed. Charlie, however, can tell me the difference between a hammer and wrench. When you can do that, we'll revisit the subject."

"No fair," Bob pouted.

Charlie patted his father's shoulder in a loving, yet placating way. "It's okay Dad, I'll teach you."

"Thanks pal. I can always count on you."

Sean jiggled his keys as he looked down at his watch. "I have to run, but I'll be back Sunday to do the last of the framing. Irene will be out tomorrow afternoon with the electrician so we can rough in a few new outlets. She's got the key, Lib—you don't need to stay around to let her in."

"That's fine."

Libby took note of Sean's hurried mannerisms. Earlier in the day, she'd spoken with Caroline and knew Sean was coming to her house for dinner. Libby felt the urgent need to tease. "Do you want to stay for dinner? We're having rosemary chicken, and Bob brought home Tiramisu. After all, it's Mom's last night home, and I'm sure you want to spend time with her, right?"

"Sounds good," he tried to look sincere, all the while checking his watch. "Mom, you know I would stay if I didn't already have plans tonight. But I can't cancel at the last minute." He saw Libby turn giddy and knew the jig was up. "Okay, knock it off Lib. It's obvious you know I'm going over to Car's tonight. Stop grinning like an idiot. It's just dinner."

"But it's so much fun to make you blush. Can't I just mock you *a little*?"

"Libby," Mae interjected. "Stop teasing your brother." She stood and walked Sean to the front door. "Come on dear, I'll walk you out."

Mae zipped into her coat and followed Sean to his truck. As he opened the driver's-side door, she noticed a bouquet of daisies on the passenger seat and remembered the pink carnations Bernie brought her each payday when they were first dating.

"It's nice to see my son still knows how to court a lady," Mae said.

Sean blushed. "Let's not make a big deal out of this, Mom. Caroline and I are taking this slow. Give us some time to figure out what comes next, okay?"

"Do you love her?"

"Mom," Sean shook his head. "That's *not* a 'take it slow' kind of question."

"Do you?"

"What do you want me to say here, Mom?"

"To me, don't say a word, but to Caroline, say what's in your heart...and at every opportunity. She needs to hear it, even if *you* think she knows. The words are important, Sean. The flowers are lovely, but never forget the words. Nothing is more powerful than telling someone how much you love them. Promise me you'll remember that."

He kissed his mother's soft cheek. "I promise."

"Good. Now hop in and get a move on. You should never keep a lady waiting."

He obeyed and jumped into the cab of the truck and started up. Door closed, he rolled down the window. "Have a safe trip. By the time you get back we should be ready for the final inspections. When I spoke with Uncle Will last week, he said he's got lots of plans to help you pick out paint and new furniture."

"God help me." Mae shook her head. "That man believes shopping is an Olympic event. I'm going to need to take extra vitamins and double up on my yoga just to keep up with him."

"You can't fool me, Mom. I know you love it."

"I love my brother, that's all that matters. Spending time with him will be a treat."

"Good. Now I've got to go, but call me tomorrow night when you get in."

Mae put her hand on Sean's cheek, her eyes misty. "Thank you Sean, for all you are doing for me. No mother could be more blessed."

"Mom, you know we love you. Don't go getting all mushy on me."

She shook her head. "I'm allowed to be mushy, I'm your mother, and it's my right." She backed away from the truck. "Now get going. Have a lovely dinner, and give Caroline my love."

"Will do." He started to back out.

"Wait, Sean," Mae said.

He stopped and looked at her expectantly.

"One more thing. If that young lady does not have my mother's ring on her hand by the time I get back from Florida I am going to be extremely disappointed in you. And in this one case, and only this case, I will not frown on a grandchild conceived outside of wedlock." With that, she pivoted and returned to the house.

Sean sat in his truck. Motor running. Speechless.

****

After dinner, Libby and Bob took Stump for his nighttime walk as Mae settled in front of the fire with Shannon and Charlie.

"Gram," Charlie asked, "when you live in the cottage can I come over for sleepovers?"

"Of course Charlie," Mae answered.

"Can Sam come sometimes?"

"We'll have to wait and see on that." The thought of Sam gave her palpitations. "I think it may be nice if it's just the two of us, don't you? We could have a little fire and roast marshmallows; like a campout in the living room. Would you like that?"

"That would be so cool."

Mae knew the days her grandson would think she was cool were numbered, so she relished each minute. "Very cool. Now off to bed with you. Give me a big smooch, I won't see you in the morning before Daddy takes me to the airport. We'll be up with the chickens."

"What chickens?" Expressions were lost on Charlie.

"Never mind dear, just give me kiss goodnight and run up to bed."

Charlie went up to bed, leaving Shannon on the couch with Mae.

"Can I ask you a question, Gram?" Shannon stifled a yawn.

"You can ask me anything, dear," Mae continued. "Better make it quick, though, you look sleepier than your brother."

"Do you think thirteen is too young to have a boyfriend?"

"Yes."

"Really?"

"Yes, at thirteen girls are remarkably mature and use their heads. Boys still like to spit and pass gas."

Shannon laughed as her grandmother continued. "That never completely goes away. Grandpa Bernie used to giggle like a little girl every time he broke wind.

It was awful."

"Gross."

"Yes, Grandpa could be disgusting at times, but I loved him with all my heart." Mae gathered Shannon around the shoulder, and whispered, "I'll tell you a secret. If you wait another couple of years, the boys will stop most of the gross stuff and a few—not all—will develop manners. If you're smart, you'll wait for the manners to kick in before dating. The boys will treat you much nicer *and* they will be far less stinky."

Shannon giggled and hugged Mae. "Goodnight, Gram. Have a nice time with Uncle Will. He's the best!"

"Yes, he is, and I'll tell him you think so, too. Goodnight princess, sweet dreams." As Mae watched Shannon climb the stairs, she savored the moment. Her first grandchild was growing up.

In from the cold, Libby and Bob joined Mae by the fire. Stump stretched belly up in front of the flames and groaned in sheer delight.

"Isn't he going to burn his under parts?" Mae asked.

"He seems to enjoy having them lightly toasted." Bob leaned down to rub the dog's pink stomach. "We'll let him live dangerously."

"Did the kids go to bed?" Libby sat down next to Mae.

"Yes," Mae answered. "And without complaint. I think they were pooped."

"Me too, long day at the office." Bob rose and stretched his hands overhead. "But hey, we got a terrific dessert out of it. I'm going up. Are you ladies coming?"

"I'll be up in a minute," Libby said. "I have a

couple things to do first."

Bob gave her a quick peck on the cheek and looked at Mae. "What time can you be ready to leave tomorrow for the airport? If we hit the road by five-thirty we should be all set. Will that give you enough beauty sleep?"

Mae grinned. "Why, yes, my dashing chauffer. I believe that will be just fine."

"Very well, madam." He executed a royal bow. "I'll have the pumpkin coach loaded and awaiting your arrival." He waved goodnight and went upstairs.

"You got one of the good ones, Lib." Mae patted her daughter's hand. "He's a keeper."

A loud thud came from the top of the stairs, followed by a few choice expletives.

"He's a keeper all right," Libby said, "and a klutz."

"True." Mae smiled. "But a loveable klutz."

Libby bent down to rub Stump. "Are you all packed? Any last minute things you want to borrow? Book for the plane, neck pillow, bikini?"

"Never in my life have I worn a bikini, Elizabeth." Mae's cheeks pinked. "And I can assure you, now is not the time to start. I'd look like rice pudding wrapped in a rubber band."

"Another snack I can no longer enjoy, thanks to your vivid imagery." Libby stood and headed to the kitchen. "I need to turn on the dishwasher. Do you want anything before I turn the lights out?"

"No dear." Mae got to her feet. "I'm going to turn in, I have a busy day tomorrow, and Will has some big welcome dinner planned with his friends for me. I do hope there is none of that dreadful karaoke this time. There are only so many show tunes I can sit through."

"Mom, be nice."

"I am being nice. It was all-musicals, all-the-time. I didn't create the stereotype Lib, but your uncle continues to reinforce it with each new chorus."

"I'll get up in the morning and say goodbye before you leave."

"No, no dear, you sleep in. I'll call you when I get there. I know your early morning personality. If I wanted someone grunting and snarling at me I'd go to the zoo."

"Okay, okay, I'll give you a big hug now and save you from my morning snarls."

The pair shared a long embrace. Mae pulled away first and placed a hand on Libby's cheek. "Thank you, sweetheart, for everything. I know you've been juggling many things lately, and I want you to know I appreciate all you have done for me."

Her eyes glistened. "You've made a very frightening time in my life less isolating, and I don't know what I would do without you and your brothers."

"Oh, no you don't. No crying allowed. Do you hear me?" Libby tried not to well up, but failed. "There will be no tears. We have lots of good things happening right now. No sad stuff. Got it?"

"Got it." Taking a deep breath, Mae brushed tears aside and continued. "I'm going up to bed and count my blessings, and you will be at the top of the list. I love you, Libby."

"I love you, too, Mom."

With one last hug, Mae started up the stairs. At the top, the last picture on the left drew her gaze.

Libby watched her mother, illuminated only by the dim hallway light, caress the worn black and white photo, a gentle smile on her face.

"Goodnight sweetheart," Mae whispered to Bernie. "It's going to be all right now, I'm home. Rest easy my darling."

****

A healthy cry later, Libby climbed into bed next to Bob.

"All locked up?" he asked.

"Yep, and the fire was just about out. As long as Stump contains the flatulence the house won't go up in flames."

"Pretty big risk. Does our insurance cover fire by dog ass?"

"I took out a rider."

"Smart woman."

Snuggled into her husband's waiting embrace, Libby felt her train wreck life jump back on track. "Have I told you how much I love you?"

Bob remained quiet.

Libby asked again, "Bob, did you hear me?"

"You can tell me you love me anytime, I'll never get tired of hearing it." He dropped his voice to his best sexy baritone. "But you know what would really make me believe you?"

Libby chuckled. "I'm going to go out on a limb...does it involve getting naked?"

"Naked is a plus," Bob growled. "But if it's a deal breaker, I'll settle for partially-clothed, marginally-enthusiastic."

"I think I can work with that. But keep the screams of ecstasy to a minimum. Mom's asleep down the hall."

Bob tore his T-shirt over his head. "I know, I know—the house guest rule—quick and quiet."

"Tonight, big boy,"—Libby kissed him—"just quiet."

"Hot damn!"

Epilogue

"Daddy is hung crooked," Mae said, her face pinched in concentration

"Excuse me?" Libby sputtered.

"Over there, in the fishing picture from Lake Womoga." She pointed to the soft ivory wall between the small kitchen area and bedroom. "Put the nail a little more to the left, that'll straighten him up."

Relaxed and freckle-tanned from her time in the Keys, Mae roamed from room to room of her new home inspecting every detail. Pausing beside the fieldstone hearth, she ran a hand along the mantel Sean had fashioned from discarded railroad ties. Family photographs spanning decades of McGinn relatives lined the glossy wood from end to end.

In the living area, a gingham blue sofa and love seat surrounded the oval coffee table Bernie had built as a tenth anniversary gift. Mae smiled at the memory and recalled the late nights he toiled in the garage over the project. He was insistent the piece be sturdy enough to support the weight of Kevin's new fascination with furniture jumping.

In the kitchen, new drapes framed the lead-glass window. A gift from Caroline, the muted rose and sage green print curtains came from a three-day shopping trip with Sean to an antiques market in upstate Vermont. Why it took three days to buy curtains, Mae was unsure, but she had a sinking feeling they did more than shop for window treatments.

By far, the showpiece of the renovation was the new bathroom. Beneath the pristinely restored claw foot tub, black and white subway tile covered the floor in an intricate pattern. A full handicap-accessible shower stood in the corner with original *Hot* and *Cold* faucet handles Sean picked up at a demolition site in Stamford. Plush white towels draped from custom racks designed from discarded copper pipe. Black and white sketches of Rhyme complimented the slate-blue walls.

In the bedroom Mae's breath caught. Upon moving to the condominium she'd replaced the custom cherry headboard Bernie designed for a more utilitarian piece to accommodate the smaller room—the change broke her heart. Here, nestled between the oversized windows sat Bernie's masterpiece—a carved Celtic knot at its center, elaborate scrollwork climbed the surface of the headboard from left to right in a series of intertwined hearts.

Libby approached and noticed tears in Mae's eyes. She placed an arm around her and said, "It was in pretty bad shape when Sean found it during the clean-out, but he knew you'd want it. He and Caroline spent weekends stripping and sanding the damage. I tried to help, but the lovebirds were better off alone. Shannon and Charlie helped with the stain and Trevor did the finishing coat of polyurethane. It was a group project, a *welcome home* gift to you. What do you think?"

Words clogged in Mae's throat. "I'm speechless."

"Alert the media," Libby teased. "Suzanne wanted to help, too, but we were a tad afraid of her rhinestone obsession. In the end we let her make up the bed."

Mae took note of the butterfly and ladybug accent pillows and grinned.

Libby continued. "Bob asked me to let you know he's *willing* to let you bake him a devil's food cake while he naps on the couch, if it would make you feel more at home. In fact, he suggested Sean add a *Feed Bob* button to the intercom system in case you needed him to come over in a hurry to test a batch of cookies."

"Very sweet of him to offer," Mae giggled, knowing well the intercom system designed for her safety was Dr.Rashan's suggestion. In place of a name or number, the electrician labeled each call button with a photo. Libby, Dom, Kevin, and Sean were at her fingertips should she require assistance. *But that's a long way off,* Mae thought to herself. "Before I accommodate your husband's sweet tooth, I should unpack. Where are my suitcases?"

"By the front door. Kevin had to drop and run. Sara has a check-up and he wanted to go with Suzanne."

"He's a good husband."

"That he is."

The women returned to the living room and found Stump asleep atop the largest piece of luggage.

"Stump," Libby scolded. "Get off Gram's bag."

"That's okay," Mae laughed. "Will packed a homemade doggie biscuit for him from a bakery that caters to pets. Stump probably can smell it through the bag."

"You do realize once you give him one he's going to come over mooching for snacks all the time?"

"That's fine. I'll stock the cupboard with little treats."

Hearing the word "treat," Stump perked up and

jumped off the bag in anticipation. Fidgeting from paw to paw, strings of drool formed at the corners of his mouth.

Mae said, "Okay, big guy, hang on a second. Don't make a puddle. Let Gram unzip and give you what you're begging for." She dug into the bag and pulled out a femur-sized biscuit.

"Holy crap!" Libby shouted. "That's not a little treat, that's canine Nirvana. What possessed Will to buy something that enormous?"

"Wait until you see the gifts he sent for the rest of you. I had to buy another suitcase to carry them all."

"Yeah! I love Will gifts! They're always so much fun."

"You didn't have to lug them through the airport."

For the better part of the afternoon, Libby helped Mae unpack and settle in. Clothes tucked into their rightful spots and suitcases stowed in the walk-in closet, Libby switched on the propane fireplace in the living room. They snuggled into the couch with cups of tea. Stump, refusing to accept the treat-train had left the station, slept at Mae's feet.

"Myrna is picking me up for yoga in the morning," Mae said. "I told her I'd take the senior shuttle but she insisted. It is times like this I wish I still drove. Daddy was right though, cataracts and traffic don't mix."

"Agreed," Libby said with a chuckle. One of the hurdles still left to jump in Mae's new arrangement was transportation. Her condominium offered complimentary shuttle service for shopping and appointments, however the new situation had bugs to work out. "Remember, Dom goes to the senior center all the time and he's more than happy to take you.

Maybe you can give him some dating pointers on the way. I swear the man has the romance of a cucumber. Last week he took Dolores to the movies, guess what they saw?"

Mae shrugged.

"*Bloodmate*. Can you believe that? What made him think an educated woman in her sixties would want to see a teen vampire battle is beyond me. Honestly, I wanted to smack him in the head with one of his tomato shovels."

"I'm sure his intentions were good, if not the choice in film. How did Dolores react?"

"She made a valiant effort to find something positive to say. The best she could muster was 'the popcorn wasn't over-salted.' Next time, she picks the film."

Mae yawned.

Libby noticed the bags under mother's eyes and said, "Why don't you take a nap before dinner and we can catch up more later? The kids won't be home for a couple of hours and Bob is bringing home take-out."

"I think I will. Travel makes me sleepy. A good nap and a bath in my beautiful tub will set me back to full strength in no time. I'll come by around five with Will's gifts." She grinned. "Charlie will be exceptionally pleased."

Libby groaned. "Do I want to know what Will bought for him?"

"No," Mae laughed. "But it may be wise to soundproof his room. This particular instrument has an ear-bleeding quality like no other."

"Dear Lord, I can't wait." Libby walked to the door. She clapped for Stump. "Come on boy, time to go. Gram needs a rest and you're a bed hog." The dog raised his head, debated, and thumped back down.

"Let him stay." Mae said. "As long as he doesn't snore too loud, he's welcome."

"I can't guarantee anything."

"If I've learned anything the past six months, Libby, it's that life does not come with guarantees. All we can do is live each day like it's our last and take what comes our way with an open mind and an ounce of patience.

A warm smile crossed Mae's face as she continued. "I've got a lot to be grateful for—a family who loves me enough to change their entire lifestyles to accommodate an old lady's not-so-golden years, a stunning home full of tender memories and new possibilities. Heck, I'm even grateful for a snoring dog's affection." Stump rolled over and groaned on cue.

She scratched his pink belly and said, "The point is, the road ahead will have its share of potholes. Lord knows I've bumped over a few already. But I'm less afraid now than I was when we first met with Dr. Rashan, and that is thanks to you and your brothers. You've made this time of my life a blessing rather than a curse."

"We wouldn't have it any other way, Mom," Libby said with a sniffle. She knew her mother's battle was just beginning and there was no way of telling how long the war would rage. But one thing was for certain, McGinns never went down without a fight.

"Get some rest, Mom. I'll send Charlie out to get you for dinner when Bob gets home." She closed the door and left woman and dog alone to snooze away the afternoon.

Stump followed Mae into the bedroom. Pulling back the crocheted bedspread, she slid between the soft cotton sheets and patted the bed beside her. "Come on, you old lump, I know you're not going to sleep on the rug when there's half a queen with your name on it."

Stump leapt on command. "Good boy," she said as he circled into place and plopped down against her. "Try to keep the snores to a minimum, I'm a light sleeper." He blinked. "I'll take that as a yes."

Before drifting off, she reached overhead and traced the carved Celtic cross in the headboard. "Bernie," she whispered. "I need your help. I'm in a good place and doing all the right things, but I'm worried. There's still so many unknowns, so many things that can happen in the blink of an eye. This disease crept up on my mother like a thief in the night and stole her memories, dignity, and everything she held dear. I need to know I won't suffer the same fate. Can you give me a sign, anything at all to let me know you're with me, looking out like an angel on my shoulder?"

A canine snore fit to break the sound barrier shattered the silence. Mae erupted in uncontrollable laughter. "Not a lightning bolt, but I'll take it."

A word about the author...

Kathryn Elliott is a lifetime journalist with awards in political satire, human interest, and commentary. A Connecticut native, she is a happily married mother of two sons with high hopes one of them will pay for a delightful rest home.

A true believer in laughter's healing power, Kathryn writes characters whose flaws resonate with readers long after "The End."

Adding Lib is her debut novel, and the first in The McGinn Series.

Visit Kathryn at:
http://candidkathryn.com/

Thank you for purchasing
this publication of The Wild Rose Press, Inc.

If you enjoyed the story, we would appreciate your
letting others know by leaving a review.

For other wonderful stories,
please visit our on-line bookstore at
www.thewildrosepress.com.

For questions or more information
contact us at
info@thewildrosepress.com.

The Wild Rose Press, Inc.
www.thewildrosepress.com

Stay current with The Wild Rose Press, Inc.

Like us on Facebook

https://www.facebook.com/TheWildRosePress

And Follow us on Twitter
https://twitter.com/WildRosePress